THE **Opposite**

OF **Dark**

Debra Purdy Kong

Debra Purdy Kong

TouchWood
Editions

TouchWood Editions
www.touchwoodeditions.com

Library and Archives Canada Cataloguing in Publication
Kong, Debra Purdy, 1955–
The Opposite of dark / Debra Purdy Kong.

Print formats: ISBN 978-1-926741-20-8 (bound).—ISBN 978-1-926741-21-5 (pbk.)
Electronic monograph in PDF format: ISBN 978-1-926741-38-3
Electronic monograph in HTML format: ISBN 978-1-926741-39-0

I. Title.

PS8571.O694O66 2011   C813'.54   C2010-906343-0

Editor: Frances Thorsen
Proofreader: Lenore Hietkamp
Cover image: Bus sign: Daniel Wildman, stck.xchng
Texture overlay: Dimitris Kritsotakis, stck.xchng
Design: Pete Kohut
Author photo: Jerald Walliser

BRITISH COLUMBIA ARTS COUNCIL   Canada Council for the Arts   Conseil des Arts du Canada   Canadian Heritage   Patrimoine canadien

We gratefully acknowledge the financial support for our publishing activities from the Government of Canada through the Canada Book Fund, Canada Council for the Arts, and the province of British Columbia through the British Columbia Arts Council and the Book Publishing Tax Credit.

MIX
FSC FSC™ C016245

The interior pages of this book have been printed on 100% post-consumer recycled paper, processed chlorine free, and printed with vegetable-based inks.

1 2 3 4 5 14 13 12 11

PRINTED IN CANADA

For my mother, Vivian, who waited a long time for this.

One

WHEN BENNY LEE hit the M3 bus's brakes for the third time in a minute, tension rippled through Casey's lower back. Usually relaxed and patient, old Benny was slipping. Maybe she would, too, if this was her first day back driving a bus in tedious, noon-hour congestion after six months on nights. Vancouver might be beautiful, but the traffic would always be horrible. With any luck, she'd nail the pervert sharing her seat before Benny put her in traction.

Casey unfastened the buttons on her tight leather jacket and took a deep breath. She exhaled slowly through her nose, like the yoga video had instructed. The exercise was supposed to release tension. Fat chance.

The suspect pressed his thigh against hers. His gray suit, crewcut, and square glasses portrayed respectability, yet his flushed, middle-aged face and wandering hand suggested something else.

His hand crept closer to her thigh. He always chose the right side of the bus, always picked an aisle seat near the exit, and always made his move as the bus approached its next stop. Lately, he'd grown reckless by staying on the M3 instead of switching routes like he used to.

Fingers spidered closer to her leg. Casey watched Benny drive. As arranged, she would speed dial Benny's cell number just before she was ready to nab the guy. Victims had reported that the suspect didn't carry a weapon, so Benny would keep the doors shut until she'd cuffed him. The problem with this plan was the passenger distracting Benny with loud complaints about dirty seats and rude passengers.

The M3 approached Commercial and Broadway, and the suspect's thigh nudged Casey's a little harder. She removed her cell phone from her pocket. Adrenalin raced through her as she watched pedestrians head for the SkyTrain entrance at the intersection's southeast corner. The light turned green and the bus eased forward. Sweet, overripe aftershave nauseated her. Oh crap, the jerk was panting. Fingertips crept toward the garter peeking below her miniskirt. Casey hit speed dial, then shoved the phone in her pocket. The suspect moaned. Benny eased the bus to the stop as the pervert squeezed her left thigh.

"Right!" Casey grabbed his wrist and flashed her ID badge. "MPT security. Your party's over, dude."

The man jerked his arm free. A moment later, he was out and running. Benny had missed the signal.

"Benny, make the call!" Casey rushed down metal-riveted steps and onto the sidewalk crowded with people waiting to enter the bus.

Running north on Commercial Drive, the suspect smacked into pedestrians. Even in stilettos, Casey gained on him. She'd spent too much time practising to let criminals get away. The sidewalk became an overpass and chances for escape diminished. Below them, rail tracks ran along a steep ravine. Casey heard the whirl of an approaching SkyTrain.

The suspect tried to barge through a group of teens, allowing Casey to close the gap. She leapt and tackled him. They hit the ground and rolled into a chain-link fence. Straddling his back, she clamped the cuffs on him and said, "I'm making a citizen's arrest for sexual assault."

"You can't do that!"

"Section 494 of the Criminal Code says I can." Casey caught her breath as she removed a card tucked behind her security license. "Under the Charter of Rights and Freedoms, it's my duty to inform you that you have the right to retain counsel without delay."

By the time she'd finished reading everything on the card, people had started to gather.

"Do you understand?" Casey asked him. "Do you want to call a lawyer?"

"I want you to get my wallet and get the hell off me, bitch!"

Casey spotted an open wallet near the suspect's face. Wary of accusations of theft, she said, "I'll watch it till the police arrive."

"I'll sue you, you whore."

"Wrong profession. As I said, I'm with Mainland Public Transport security."

Maybe she should sue him for a new pair of stockings. Reasonably priced fishnet was almost impossible to find. Casey glanced at the gaping hole on her shin and then popped a stick of gum in her mouth. Chewing always slowed the adrenalin.

"You'd better find my glasses too," the suspect said.

They were wedged among weeds and grimy candy wrappers at the fence, but Casey opted to stay where she was. She noticed the family photo in the guy's wallet: three young kids, the suspect, and a plump brunette. Casey shook her head. What kind of family man spent his lunch hours squeezing women's thighs on buses? How pathetic was that?

Benny hurried up to her. "Sorry, Casey. You okay?"

"Yeah, fine."

"I called the cops and Stan wants you back at the office. Some detective's on his way to see you. Looks like your week's off to a hell of a start."

Casey popped a bubble. She'd handed the authorities a fair number of delinquents over recent weeks, so police chats were becoming routine.

The Vancouver police arrived at Commercial Drive later than expected. Forty-five minutes passed before she bounded up Mainland's two flights of stairs and into the security department. It'd take at least another half hour to write her report.

As she greeted the security department's admin assistant, Amy, Casey spotted a new chair next to Stan's door.

"Does Stan know it's pink?" Casey asked.

"It's not pink, it's dusty rose, or so the catalogue says." Amy lifted the bifocals from the chain around her neck and took a closer look while she tried not to smile.

Casey grinned. "I'd emphasize the dusty part."

"I thought I heard your voice," Stan said, emerging from his office.

Oh lord, her supervisor was having yet another fashion disaster day. Hard as Casey tried, she couldn't convince Stan that checkered sports jackets and striped shirts didn't work for most human beings. She and his wife had nearly given up trying.

"So you caught the pervert single-handedly," he said.

Based on Stan's disapproving tone and the way he crossed his arms over his chest, Casey knew what was coming.

"What happened to observe and report? Since when do my officers put themselves in danger?"

"But he wasn't armed and I experienced the crime firsthand, excuse the pun." She flashed a smile, but Stan didn't look amused.

"Tackling someone is hardly non-violent intervention, Casey. I thought I told you that use of force isn't part of the game plan anymore."

Casey sighed. It was hard to keep up with, let alone apply, all the changes and restrictions Mainland had imposed since she first trained in security. And why was Stan being such a hard-ass when she'd caught the guy?

He lowered his arms. "Write up your report after you see our guests." He nodded toward the door.

"Guests? Benny said a detective wanted to see me."

"There are two of them."

She noticed the way Stan's lips pressed together until they almost disappeared between his gray beard and moustache. His lips always vanished when he was tense. "What's up?"

His gaze didn't quite meet hers. "You'll see."

Hmm. The last time Stan avoided eye contact and tensed up like that was two years ago, when she'd told him she was divorcing Greg. He never had coped with crying women too well.

"Tomorrow you can start on the purse snatchings you've been bugging me for," he said. "Drop by for details whenever. I'm going to grab some lunch."

Leaning close to the door, Casey heard male voices. She strutted inside. It took three seconds to realize that her black leather miniskirt, torn stockings, and stilettos were making a bad impression.

The older man, stiff and solemn in his brown suit, stared at her spiky hair while the younger guy glanced at her D cups. Understandable. The girls were barely contained in the tank top under her jacket.

On the other side of the door, Stan yelled, "I ain't sitting in a friggin' pink chair!"

Casey smiled as she nodded to the officers. "I'm Casey Holland."

"Detective Lalonde with the West Vancouver Police Department," the older man said, displaying his shield. "This is Corporal Krueger."

West Van police? What were they doing out of their jurisdiction? As Krueger shook Casey's hand, his long thick moustache twitched.

"While we waited for you, Mr. Cordaseto told us a bit about MPT," Lalonde said. "I'd forgotten that the government's pilot project became privately funded. I thought it was still at least partly subsidized."

"Funding ran out, but the government insists on fewer cars on the road, so investors bought it twelve years ago, for a good tax break, apparently. Mainland fills the void in the suburbs and shares the load with TransLink buses on busier routes."

"I understand you've worked here ten years?"

Why were they interested in her background? "Yes—five as a driver and five in security."

"And you're a civilian doing police work?" Krueger asked.

Casey didn't appreciate the disdain in his voice. "It's not much different than loss prevention work in retail, except we're mobile, and, as you guys know, it's too expensive to have police riding buses all day nabbing vandals and creeps. Most of the people we catch commit petty crimes and end up with fines, probation, or community service."

"The suspect you pursued today sounded dangerous."

"Not really. He squeezes thighs and runs away," she replied. "If he was armed or more aggressive, the police would be involved."

"Do you like this work?" Krueger asked.

"It's more interesting than being a driver, unless you count the time a guy pulled a knife on me. After that, I went into security to learn how to protect myself and others."

She was proud of the gutsy reputation she'd earned among Mainland's staff, even from old-fashioned farts who thought women didn't belong in security.

Lalonde said, "Few people would choose security work after an experience like that."

Casey shrugged. "Had to face my fears."

"You work alone?" Krueger asked.

"Pretty much. We have only one other full-time person, plus Stan. There are three more part-timers who work other jobs."

"There's that much of a demand?" Lalonde asked.

"On and off. It usually starts with passenger complaints." She watched Krueger remove a notepad and pen from his pocket. "So, how can I help you guys?"

Lalonde glanced at his partner. "A fifty-five-year-old Caucasian male, whom we believe is Marcus Adam Holland, was killed between 8:00 and 10:00 PM yesterday evening." He paused. "Are you his daughter?"

"What?" She frowned. "I don't understand."

"Are you related to Marcus Adam Holland?"

"I'm his daughter, yes."

"When did you last see him, Miss Holland?"

"Three years ago, on March eleventh, in a casket. He's buried at Cedar Ridge Cemetery, Detective."

Lalonde and Krueger exchanged unreadable looks until Krueger scribbled something down.

"How did the man you buried die?" Lalonde asked.

"My *father* died from botulism."

"This body hasn't been dead three years," he replied. "His wallet contained a valid driver's license and credit cards, several to jewelry stores."

Eeriness crept up Casey's spine. Dad had given her a piece of jewelry every birthday.

"I never did get his wallet and passport back. Assumed they were stolen. But I have a death certificate. Maybe someone at Vital Statistics screwed up."

Casey didn't like the way these guys looked at her. What was it? Pity? Skepticism? Ambivalence? She sauntered behind Stan's old mahogany desk. "Can you give me a clearer description of the victim?"

Lalonde turned to Krueger who flipped through his notepad. "Green eyes, blond hair, graying at the temples, one point eight meters tall." Krueger looked up. "Five feet eleven inches."

Casey wasn't aware she'd been gripping Stan's chair until her fingers began to ache. A wallet and similar appearance didn't prove Dad had been alive these past three years.

"Did you see the body?" she asked.

Lalonde nodded.

"Did you notice a small white scar by his left eyebrow?" She didn't like this second exchange of looks between Lalonde and Krueger. Why weren't they answering? "How, exactly, was the man killed?" As Lalonde glanced out the window overlooking the yard, Casey's patience withered. "If it's him, then I'm family, so don't I have a right to know?" Still no response. "Come on, guys, I'm used to working with the police; this conversation doesn't go beyond this room if you don't want it to."

Lalonde finally said, "The victim was struck repeatedly about the head with a sharp heavy object."

She pushed the grisly image from her mind. "Where did it happen?"

"In his house on Marine Drive in West Vancouver."

The eerie sensation wound around her neck and began to squeeze. "Dad didn't own a place there."

He'd dreamed of it, though; an ocean view house on pricey real estate. But he hadn't had the bucks. So, what was dream and what was reality? Casey slumped into Stan's old Naugahyde chair.

"An anonymous caller tipped us off about the body around midnight," Lalonde said.

"Male or female?"

"Male. Could you provide a list of your father's relatives, friends, business associates, and other acquaintances?"

"It'd be three years old." Casey rested her elbows on the desk. "If he was alive, don't you think I'd know?"

"Some people deliberately disappear to start over," Lalonde replied.

"Do these people stay in the same city and provide a body for burial?" Predictably, all she got was more silence. Was she annoying them as much as they were annoying her? Too bad. She wasn't the one with the identity problem.

"Miss Holland, we'd like you to come to the morgue," Lalonde said. "The coroner can't start the autopsy until you've identi—"

"I know." She met Lalonde's gaze. "I want to see the body up close. Not on some monitor or in a snapshot or whatever they do down there. Face-to-face, okay?"

Lalonde watched her. "The wounds to his head are extensive."

"All right." She could take it. Had to. Wimping out in front of these guys would be humiliating.

"Mr. Cordaseto told us you could take the afternoon off, so I'd like to do this now."

"Fine." It took some effort to get to her feet. "Dad and I were close, Detective. He was a proud and honest man. He wouldn't have deceived me like that." She couldn't think. "Any idea why the man was killed?"

"There was cash in his wallet, but the hard drive's missing from his PC. No storage devices of any kind anywhere, and he might have had a laptop too." Lalonde slipped his hands in his coat pockets. "There's a photograph of you in the master bedroom."

No, couldn't be. "As far as I'm concerned, Dad's been gone three years. If you think otherwise, then show me proof."

"Do you remember the name of his dentist?" Krueger asked, pen poised over his notepad.

"No. I take it fingerprints haven't helped identify him yet?"

Krueger shook his head.

Casey headed for the door. "Let me change first and wash the grunge off my face."

"That's unnecessary," Lalonde replied. "The sooner we go to the morgue, the quicker we'll have answers."

"This is a costume to attract trash, Detective." She turned to Krueger. "Go figure, huh?"

Casey tried to move fast to the women's locker room downstairs but Lalonde's news had a paralyzing effect. The same thing had happened three years ago when that doctor called from Paris. She was at work then, too, eating a cheeseburger. In a heavy French accent, the man explained how botulism had killed Dad. Her first response had been anger. No one had even bothered to let her know he'd been sick. After the call, she threw up. Greg was driving the M9 at the time, so Lou had taken her home.

Casey reappeared twenty minutes later to find the detectives looking curiously at her, trying not to seem surprised. Casey attempted a smile. She'd replaced the gelled spikes with her usual light brown curls, the heavy makeup for a trace of lipstick, and the skimpy clothes with plum trousers and a silk blouse.

"Did you need to perform an entire makeover?"

"Why do a half-assed job?"

"For expediency?"

Following him to the exit, Casey rolled her eyes and waved at a worried-looking Amy. Lalonde chose the back seat of the Sebring, while Casey sat in front with Krueger.

"Tell me about the food poisoning in Paris," Lalonde said.

"Dad died nine days after eating at a burger joint called Alvin's All-Canadian Café. The bacterium was in a mayonnaise-based salad dressing."

"How many others were ill?"

"No one, according to my lawyers."

"Lawyers?"

"I'd heard that adults stood a fairly good chance of surviving the toxin. I wanted to know if the hospital had been negligent. The lawyers didn't think so. Apparently, botulism's not easy to diagnose when only one person's been infected, and it took too long to find the source. By the time the doctors knew what was wrong, Dad was too far gone."

"Bit odd that only one person was infected, isn't it?"

"I thought so. It turned out that some fool used the remains of a jar of mayonnaise that hadn't been refrigerated. The restaurant was busy at the time and no one would take responsibility for it."

The drive to the airport to collect his body had been surreal and, in some ways, offensive. She'd had to pick up Dad from the cargo area, not that she would have wanted him swooping down the chute at the luggage carousel. But still . . . cargo.

Losing someone she loved and trusted had depressed her for a long time. Her adult relationships had never been as strong or trusting.

"I guess a blood analysis hasn't been done yet," Casey said. No one answered. "You guys really don't want to tell me much, do you?"

Lalonde kept his gaze on the window.

Casey rubbed her arms and shivered. The morgue was colder than she thought it would be, or was she shivering because of the possibility that all her grief had been wasted on a lie? An attendant accompanied Lalonde to a labeled, oversized drawer and Casey's heartbeat quickened. Lalonde produced a key and unlocked the compartment. The attendant slid a shrouded body toward them.

Someone touched Casey's arm and she jumped. Krueger. Sympathy flashed across his face as he guided her nearer the body. She'd tried to mentally prepare for the sight of mutilated flesh and a close resemblance to Dad. One of last year's criminology classes had discussed body decomposition. Nasty stuff. She vowed to stay cool and calm.

Lalonde turned to her. "Ready?"

Feet apart, arms crossed, and standing strong, she said, "Go ahead."

One glimpse of the victim's face and her stomach somersaulted. Gashes crisscrossed his scalp and descended to what remained of the left side of his face. Dried blood and bits of gray stuff matted his hair. Dozens of cuts mangled the upper half of his left arm and shoulder.

"Is this man Marcus Holland?" Lalonde asked.

Memories of Dad raced through her mind, images so vivid it was as if no time had passed and grief was just beginning.

"Is he your father, Miss Holland?"

"Just a sec." Her legs grew shaky. Casey looked at the attendant. "Is there an appendectomy scar?"

She'd only glimpsed the scar once, by accident, after Dad's operation twenty years ago.

Lalonde nodded to the attendant who lifted the sheet. Casey looked at the floor.

"There is," the attendant said.

"Well, Miss Holland?" Lalonde asked.

Casey swayed toward the body, then recoiled, terrified of touching it. She tilted to one side. Hands gripped her arm and shoulder. Perspiration dampened her upper lip.

Lalonde said, "Get her some water."

How could this man be Dad? It didn't make sense. "No bloody way!"

"Are you saying this man isn't your father?"

Pulling free of Krueger's grasp, she charged out of the room.

Two

NORMALLY, CASEY LIKED Mondays. If the day went well, it set the tone for the week. If today's events had set the tone, she'd stay in bed tomorrow. Sitting here beside a grave marked "Marcus Adam Holland," she wondered who the hell she'd been visiting for three years. Casey picked blades of grass. How many times had she come here to think things through? The silence had always offered answers. Now there were only questions. The peace Cedar Ridge Cemetery had brought her was gone.

She studied the marble marker Lou helped her choose. Greg hadn't wanted any part in funeral arrangements, so Lou volunteered. He always had been more supportive than her husband. Lou had met Dad lots of times. Three hundred people strolled past the open casket that day, and no one had said a thing about mourning the wrong guy. His deception had been perfect.

Why had Dad abandoned the people he loved? She thought he'd been happy with his life. Busy with work and a parade of bimbos until he outgrew the silliness and hooked up with Rhonda. While Casey hadn't seen much of him those last two years, they'd still shared problems and secrets. They'd been so much alike that she often knew his thoughts before he told her. Soulmates. Of course, she'd once thought the same about Greg.

How had Dad managed to fake his death? Casey smacked the black marble. Behind her, someone's knee cracked. She turned to find Detective Lalonde picking a quarter out of the grass.

"Did you drop this?"

"Doubt it."

He pocketed the coin. "With six kids to support, even the loose change counts."

"Are all six yours, or is it a blended family?"

"Blended about as well as oil and water, but that stays between us."

"My theme of the day," Casey sighed, "Dads with secrets."

"Did you hit the headstone out of frustration or anger?"

She ran her hand over the clipped grass. "The funeral was a scam."

"Then the man in the morgue is your father?"

"Looks that way." She stood up. "Sorry about running off. I needed time alone."

"No problem. You were never out of sight."

She met Lalonde's gaze. "You said you found him in a house on Marine Drive?"

"On the main floor, in front of a chair in his den. It appears the killer came up from behind while your father was still seated."

Casey pictured the cuts on his left side. "He must have raised his arm to ward off the blows."

Not an image she wanted to dwell on. She focused instead on pansies surrounding a nearby tree trunk. A large, deep blue and black Steller's jay squawked from a branch.

"What did your father do for a living, Miss Holland?"

"He was an architect with his own firm. His associate and friend Vincent Wilkes inherited the business."

Lalonde removed a notepad and silver-framed glasses from his pockets. "Address?"

After providing the information, Casey added, "It's a renovated house on Tenth Avenue, just off Granville, but I don't know if Vincent's still around. We haven't kept in touch."

She saw Lalonde's attention turn to a man standing in front of a grave about fifty feet away. The man's hands were clasped together, his head lowered.

Lalonde turned back to her. "Your father spent a great deal of time in Europe."

"Dad loved to travel. He worked for a lot of Europeans who'd bought property here and he usually vacationed overseas. He was always bringing back exotic piece of art: masks, carvings, glass sculptures."

"He must have been quite successful. But even though Mr. Holland wore expensive suits and owned a Jaguar, he hadn't filed a tax return in three years and his checking account was almost depleted. Do you know if he had assets in foreign banks?"

Maybe loyalty was a habit, but Casey didn't want Lalonde to know about Dad's money problems. How on earth could he have afforded a Jaguar and a house in one of the country's most expensive areas?

"He never mentioned foreign banks."

"We found a one-way ticket to Amsterdam in his den. He was scheduled to leave this week. His passport shows that this was a frequent destination."

"I don't know anyone living there." Casey gazed at the Fraser River on the other side of the cemetery. "Dad was a social guy. Couldn't stand being alone." She turned back to his grave. "I still have trouble believing he cut himself off this way."

"Maybe he thought he had no choice."

She knew what he was thinking. Dad had broken the law and faked his death to escape, but then why stay in Vancouver? "Whose name is the house in? Who pays the taxes?"

"We're looking into that."

"It should be simple to find out, or are there complications?"

"Let's just say that nothing about this case appears to be straightforward," he replied. "Your father could have been in serious trouble, Miss Holland. Something so dangerous that someone felt compelled to kill him with a heavy knife or meat cleaver."

"A cleaver?"

"Possibly—there was a collection of them in the kitchen. And bits of onion on the countertop. Dirty dishes by the sink. Looked like he hadn't cleaned up from dinner."

"Had he eaten alone?"

"It appears so."

"I've never known Dad to use a cleaver." She shook her head. "From the depth of some of those cuts, it seems someone was really pissed at him."

"Someone close to him, perhaps?"

Crap. She should have realized she was a suspect. "In case you were wondering, I was at a baby shower for one of Mainland's clerical staff last night from seven till eleven. A dozen people can vouch for me."

"They have. Since you took so long getting back to the office, I had time to chat with your colleagues. They think highly of you, by the way."

"Good to know." But the gossip would be flying now. "I guess you'll want to exhume this body?"

"Not until I hear from the coroner."

"When you know who this man is, let me know, okay? And I'd still like forensic proof that the man in the morgue is my father." Lalonde said nothing, and she had nothing else to tell him. "I'd better make some calls."

"You do know you're unqualified to investigate this matter, Miss Holland."

She kept her irritation in check. "You don't mind if I share the news with a few friends, do you?"

"You can talk to anyone you like as long as it's commiserating, not interrogating."

She started to leave when Lalonde said, "Do you know where I can reach your mother?"

A chill ran through Casey. "I haven't talked to my mother since Dad booted her out of the house seventeen years ago."

"She was the one who told us you were next of kin and where you live and work."

Casey could almost feel the blood leaving her face. How long had Mother known? Why would she even care?

"How'd you find her?"

"Her name and number were in an address book at the house. It took several hours to reach her, which is why we didn't contact you earlier."

Why would Dad have kept that info? "I bet Mother thought it was funny that he'd died twice."

"Shocked, I'd say. I've tried to reach her again, but her assistant said she's left for the day. I gather you wouldn't know where she is?"

"I don't know a thing about my mother's life." Didn't want to either.

"She runs her own clerical service agency in Vancouver, Holland Personnel."

Casey shrugged, uncomfortable with Lalonde's scrutiny.

"I'd still like you to compile a list of old friends, family, and acquaintances along with contact info," he added.

"Okay, but I'd like to know if any names on my list show up in his current address book."

Again, she started to leave.

"Did you know you're being followed?"

Casey saw him nod toward the man she saw earlier. As the man started toward the cemetery's south exit, Casey made a note of his height, clothes, and the black ponytail dangling down his back.

"Is he familiar?" Lalonde asked.

"No."

"Krueger noticed a black Saab when we left your office, and again when you left the morgue. Every time you changed buses the car pulled over and waited."

"When are you going to question him?"

"Shortly. Krueger's running a license check. Meanwhile, here's my card. Call me when your list's ready."

"I want to talk to that guy."

"No, we'll handle this, Miss Holland."

She ignored him and marched toward the man, vaguely aware that her thoughts were frazzled and this was a dumb move, but the day's events had mangled the sensible approach to mystery solving.

"Miss Holland, come back here right now."

"Shut up," she mumbled, and began to run.

The man must have heard them. He turned to her and then began racing toward his vehicle. Before Casey could reach him, he roared away in the Saab.

Three

FOR AS LONG as Casey could remember, Rhonda Stubbs had played a major role in her life. Lord knows she'd been a more involved and empathic caregiver than Mother. She'd been the only female friend Mother had had, until Mother destroyed it all by sleeping with Rhonda's husband. By the time Rhonda was engaged to Dad years later, Casey had learned to appreciate her as a trusted confidante and source of comfort when things were tough.

So, why hadn't she told Rhonda about today? Was it because of what happened when she broke the news about Dad three years ago? Rhonda had responded by pouring a large pot of beef stew into the sink. "It was for Marcus," she'd said. "No point now." She'd then collapsed. Tonight, Casey had tiptoed upstairs and into her apartment unnoticed. She'd told herself she wanted scientific evidence before saying anything about Dad. Truth was, she didn't know how to tell Rhonda without traumatizing her again.

Casey paced around the living room. She had to find a way. Rhonda needed to be told and she deserved to hear it from someone she thought of as family. After all, Rhonda had evicted a tenant in this big old house so Casey could move in after she walked out on Greg. Casey loved the large rooms and hardwood floors in this third-floor suite. She especially loved the comfy, cushioned seat in the bay window. It was a great refuge when she needed to make plans or to relax. But relaxing was impossible right now.

Casey bumped into her in-line skates propped against a stationary bike. She'd hardly used the bike since Rhonda bought her a yoga video. Tonight's workout would require something more strenuous than the mountain pose, so she climbed on and started pedaling fast so her muscles would soon burn.

To cope with the day's shocks, she'd kept busy by calling Dad's friends, but no one claimed to know anything about his resurrection.

One guy called her a pathetic practical joker. Two more implied she was nuts and cut the conversation short while others were so patronizing she'd wanted to smack them. The most infuriating call had been to Vincent Wilkes.

Casey wasn't surprised that Lalonde had already contacted him or that Vincent was still an architect. The shock came when he told her that Dad had built a house in West Vancouver just before he died.

"Marcus planned to tell you about it when the final touches were done, which they pretty much were just before his death," Vincent had said. "So, I assumed you knew." And then the infuriating part, "Your mother didn't mention the house?"

She'd wanted to know how Mother knew about the place. All Vincent would say was, "About two weeks after the funeral, Lillian came by to pick up those photos of you that Marcus kept on his desk. She said she wasn't interested in either of his houses."

Casey peddled harder. Mother hadn't been at the funeral, hadn't been invited. And Casey hadn't noticed the missing photos. Vincent had packed Dad's personal belongings and delivered them to the house. Eighteen months passed before she could bring herself to open the box.

Casey didn't expect to hear from Mother. The last time they'd spoken was seventeen years ago, on Casey's thirteenth birthday, about ten months after her parents split up. Casey had been stunned to find Mother waiting outside the school. Maybe it was wrong to refuse the gift Mother had brought with her, but she couldn't let Mother think she'd been forgiven for wrecking so many marriages.

Casey's muscles ached, but she kept going until she heard familiar taps on the door. "Come on in, Summer." God, how would *she* handle the news? Summer was only eight when Dad died. She'd cried all through the funeral and wouldn't go to school for a week.

Summer stepped inside, carrying a plate of half-finished chocolate cake and wearing her favorite night shirt and moose slippers with the floppy felt antlers. She really was growing fast. Every time Casey saw her, she looked a little more like Rhonda, thank god. The dark eyes and thick black hair made it easy for Rhonda to convince the world she'd given birth to her, a lie she intended to carry to her grave.

Grabbing a clean towel from the laundry pile she hadn't got around to folding, Casey dabbed her brow. "Need a towel? Your hair still looks wet."

"I'm fine."

"How was your swim practice?"

"Good. Coach says I'll do great at the meet, but I don't know." Summer prodded the cake with her fork. "Like, I don't feel ready."

"You said that last year, and you won a medal."

"Only third place. Want some cake?"

"I wish, but chocolate brings on a crappy mood, remember?"

"I thought that was only chocolate bars." She sat in Casey's rocking chair. "How come you didn't have supper with us?"

"Lousy day," Casey rubbed the back of her neck and slumped onto the sofa. "I wouldn't have been good company."

"Sometimes I wish *I* could cook what I wanted. It'd be cool."

"Sometimes it is, but your mom's spoiled me too much. I need to do more on my own."

Rhonda didn't agree. Thought the new microwave was a waste of money.

"Can I borrow your bike for school tomorrow? Mine blew a tire."

"Sure, and I'll get you a new tire. A mechanic at work owes me a favor."

Two quick knocks on the door told Casey who her visitor was. Trepidation quickened her heartbeat.

"Come on in, Rhonda."

Oh lord, she had on her hideous, pea-green sweat pants and red flannel shirt again. Rhonda was a worse fashion disaster than Stan, but where Stan didn't know any better, Rhonda simply didn't care. Not in the last three years anyway. Her thick hair was pulled away from her face with plastic ladybug clips.

"Almost bedtime," Rhonda said to Summer. "Finish up. And have you seen my pastry cutter?"

"You left it in the bag of flour again." Summer shook her head as if the burden of having a forgetful mother was too much.

Rhonda turned to Casey. "You look exhausted."

"I am." She dabbed her face, hoping to hide the stress.

"Mom talked to some guy about renting the room." Summer raised a forkful of cake to her mouth. "He lasted, like, two minutes before she got rid of him, which is good 'cause he smelled like stinky fish."

"And I didn't like the nasty grin on his face when I told him the vacant suite's under your bedroom," Rhonda added. "I won't have him chasing you all over the house when I'm still hoping that you and Lou—"

"Rhonda, don't go there. Not tonight."

Rhonda watched her a moment, then turned to Summer. "Finish your cake in the kitchen, hon, and then brush your teeth. I'll come say goodnight in a few minutes."

Casey hugged Summer. "Sweet dreams."

When she left, Rhonda said, "Lou would treat you a thousand times better than Greg did."

"Until our last year together, Greg was one of the good guys, remember?"

The night he proposed, Greg had surprised her with a bottle of champagne and a rowboat ride, both handled awkwardly. In the middle of the lake, he'd given her a diamond chip on a thin gold band now abandoned in a safe-deposit box.

"Anyhow, I wasn't completely blameless."

Rhonda's mouth fell open. "How is his adultery your fault?"

Casey couldn't make Rhonda understand that she'd worked harder at her job than she had at her marriage. The depression after Dad's funeral hadn't helped. If she hadn't been so self-absorbed she would have realized how far she and Greg had grown apart.

"What's wrong?" Rhonda asked. "Did Greg say something nasty?"

"No, I didn't even mention Greg. You did."

Rhonda strolled to the kitchen table. "I see you've been trying health food again."

"Just rice and beans."

"You've been going through albums." Rhonda turned a page. "Feeling nostalgic?"

"Sort of."

"I remember when most of these were taken." Rhonda closed the album. "So, when are you going to kick Greg and his bimbo out of your house? You need to sell the place, Casey. Invest in RRSPs and stuff."

"I have an RRSP." Casey took her dirty plate to the sink.

Rhonda had never approved of her renting Dad's old house to Greg, the same place she and Greg had shared after Dad died. But Greg paid the rent on time and took good care of the yard, or so she assumed. It had been a long time since she'd driven by. She could have rented the house to someone else; could have quit her job so she wouldn't have to see Greg at work, but she'd needed to show people that a broken marriage hadn't destroyed her.

"I'll sell it when I find something I want to buy."

"Mutual funds are good."

Every time Rhonda went on about money, it meant she was having financial problems. No surprise there. The studio suite had been empty for three months. Only university students would put up with a hot plate and teensy shower, and most of them, including Rhonda's other tenant, had gone home for the summer.

"Rhonda, if you need cash, I can help."

"I don't want your money."

She never did. Dad had left Rhonda only a few personal mementoes in his will. Casey still felt guilty for benefiting from a hundred-thousand-dollar insurance policy. After paying his debts, funeral expenses, and taxes, she'd offered half of what was left to Rhonda. Rhonda's stubborn streak, however, was unparalleled in this universe.

"How about going camping with Summer and me on the Victoria Day long weekend next month?" Rhonda said. "We could clean that grubby sleeping bag in your car."

Casey sat at the table. Three days without the frequent knocks on her door was too appealing to give up. "It's still four weeks away."

"That's okay." Rhonda sat beside her. "Whatever's bothering you should have passed by then and you won't look so sad."

Damn, should have done a better job of hiding it. Rhonda was a pit bull when she wanted to know something.

Casey took a deep breath. "There's something I have to tell you about Dad. It's bizarre and kind of horrible."

"Out with it then."

"I saw him today," she said with a dry feeling in her mouth, "at the morgue."

"What?" Rhonda didn't blink. "What are you talking about?"

While Casey told her about Detective Lalonde's visit, Rhonda's face grew pale. "I don't believe this." By the time Casey finished describing her trip to the morgue, Rhonda was rubbing her temples and dragging her fingernails down her face. Mention of the Marine Drive place brought her to her feet.

"I take it Dad never said anything about it to you?"

"He'd talked about building us a house once." Rhonda's voice trembled as she wandered around the room. "I thought it was one of his pipe dreams." She picked up two teddy bears from the collection on the shelves and hugged them tight. Tears spilled down her cheeks. "Are you sure it was him?"

"Forensic evidence isn't in but, yeah, I think it's Dad."

Bears squished between them, as Casey embraced Rhonda, who clutched her for long, anguished seconds.

"I could have identified the body." She put the bears back and sniffled. "You should have been spared that." She wiped her eyes with her shirttail. "Why didn't Marcus contact us?" Her voice broke. "We were his family."

"Don't know." She'd been asking herself that question for hours. "We didn't see him much those last months. Now there are three years to piece together. I want answers and Lalonde won't share much. I've already phoned Dad's old friends, but no one knows anything. Tomorrow, I'm going to Marine Drive."

"I'll go with you."

Casey had hoped to see the place alone. "I'm leaving before six."

"Then we'd better get some sleep." Rhonda's hand shook as she opened the door. "Guess it's my turn to arrange the burial." She grimaced. "Can't wait to tell the funeral people we're doing it again because the first try didn't last."

"Thanks for offering, but I'll do it. What'll you tell Summer?"

"No clue. But she'll know something's up the moment I say good-night." More tears slipped down Rhonda's cheeks. "You okay?"

"Yeah. You?"

"I will be."

After more hugging and sobbing, Rhonda left. She'd taken the news better than expected. Still, Casey's heart ached for her. She would probably spend the night wondering why the man she'd adored had faked his death.

Casey tried neck and shoulder rolls to ease the strain. She attempted a full bend, but felt light-headed from too much stress and coffee, too many questions darting through her mind.

She retreated to the window seat. Gazing at the enormous weeping willow in Rhonda's front yard, she took slow deep breaths. Not exactly meditation, but close. Under tonight's bright moon, the leaves almost glowed, and the darker recesses of Rhonda's weedy corner lot were gently lit. Through the trees, Casey could see part of Napier where it crossed Violet, and a glimpse of a black Saab parked in front of the house. She leapt up.

Somewhere in the back of her mind, Casey had known the stranger would reappear. She darted out the door, hoping the guy wouldn't anticipate her behavior as well as she did his.

Four

CASEY MADE IT as far as the sidewalk before the Saab's engine started up. She was three steps away from the vehicle when the driver sped off toward Victoria Drive. Damn, she should have gotten into her car this time, instead of trying to run after him again. Stan sometimes lectured her about her impatience, but the habit was hard to break. After all, she was her father's daughter. That's what everyone had told her . . . that's what she'd always believed.

Casey rubbed her arms in the cool night air. Streetlights illuminated fences and empty sidewalks. Usually, at least one person would be out walking a dog. Not tonight. She inhaled the scent of freshly mowed grass and then headed inside.

Crawling out of bed in the morning had been tougher than usual. After leaving a message for Lalonde last night about her stalker, she hadn't slept. She'd been tempted to watch TV and tidy up a bit, but Summer and Rhonda's bedrooms were below her living and dining areas, and this old house wasn't soundproof. She'd finally dozed off some time after three. The alarm rang at five-fifteen.

Casey picked a thread off her navy pinstriped jacket, tucked her clutch bag under her arm and inspected her appearance in the mirror. Skirts weren't her idea of comfort, but the business outfit might attract the purse thief on today's agenda. While she pulled a brush through limp, old-perm curls, Rhonda's knock broke the silence. Casey tossed the brush on her bed. She'd hoped Rhonda would still be asleep when she left. She opened the door and found Rhonda holding a pan of blueberry muffins. The ladybug hair clips still drooped over her ears, and she had on yesterday's sweats and flannel shirt.

Rhonda looked her over. "My, my, how conservative. Who are you after today?"

"A teenager who steals purses and the occasional wallet. Apparently, he's a cash-only guy."

She looked at Casey's running shoes. "Are you expecting a chase?"

"It's possible."

"Then you'll need breakfast." Rhonda offered her the pan. "Thought we could eat on the way to West Vancouver."

Casey's stomach growled. "Thanks. Let me fix your hair." She retrieved the brush. "Did you sleep at all?"

"A couple of hours."

Rhonda's pale complexion was a sharp contrast to the dark, puffy sacs under her eyes. Last night, she'd been doing laundry in the basement when Casey ran outside. Thank god she hadn't heard a thing. Rhonda looked too vulnerable to know that a stranger had been watching the house.

"I reread Marcus's postcards," Rhonda said. "He left no clue about going underground. I could go over the stuff he sent you, if you want."

"I did. There's nothing in them."

Rhonda used to read Dad's postcards out loud. To spare her feelings, Casey had never told Rhonda that she'd received a couple of long letters inside birthday cards.

"Wish I'd gone the hi-tech route," Rhonda said. "He and I would have kept in touch better."

Rhonda refused to spend money on a cell phone and hated computers. Wouldn't even try out Casey's PC.

"Rhonda, are you sure you want to see the house?" Casey slowly brushed Rhonda's thick dark hair. "And what about Summer?"

"I told her about Marcus last night and that I'd be going to his place this morning."

"How'd she take the news?"

"More confused than anything."

Who wasn't? "I've got to be at work by eight, so you'll be back before she leaves for school."

"What if the cops aren't finished looking around?" Rhonda asked. "How will we get in without a key, especially if there's an alarm system?"

"As closest relative, I could inherit this place, and there's nothing illegal about dismantling any alarm system and using lock picks on my own house." She didn't add there was plenty wrong with trespassing on a crime scene, but Dad's secret life would torment her until she had some answers.

"I wonder if he left this place to you in a new will?"

Casey put the brush down. "I'll call his lawyer later."

"What about the lock picks? Aren't you out of practice?"

She smiled. "I still play with them now and then."

When she was twelve, an uncle gave her a nine-piece set for Christmas. Her parents' disapproval had sparked a heated argument during dinner that night, but Casey had begged to keep the tools. Dad only agreed when she promised not to use them for anything illegal. By age seventeen, she'd become skilled enough to impress friends at parties. After moving here, she taught Rhonda, who'd become fed up with tenants changing their locks then losing their keys. Learning to pick locks was much cheaper than calling a locksmith.

"We'd better go," Casey said.

The trek downstairs and along the narrow hallway toward the back felt longer than usual. She didn't look forward to this excursion to West Vancouver. Much as she wanted to see the house, she worried about what she'd find and how Rhonda would cope. She entered Rhonda's kitchen and opened the back door.

"I'll leave some muffins and a note for Summer," Rhonda said, trailing behind.

"Okay."

Casey flipped on the porch light, then took her time down the rickety wooden steps. Heading out before daybreak was depressing, but it'd be lighter within the hour. She trudged through the overgrown grass, climbed into her Tercel, and tossed fast food wrappers onto the sleeping bag in back. She hadn't had to stake out troublesome bus stops for months. One of these days, she should do a little spring cleaning.

"Too bad you don't drive something nice," Rhonda said as she clambered inside. "The wealthy folks of West Van are going to sneer at this rust-ravaged garbage can."

Casey had once thought about buying something newer and then decided to keep her money until she drove this one into the ground. Besides, she rode buses for free. Unfortunately, Mainland Public Transport didn't have West Vancouver routes.

"Would you like to take your old beater instead?"

"No." Rhonda removed a muffin from a plastic bag as Casey cruised down the back lane.

"Detective Lalonde asked about Mother yesterday," Casey said.

"Really?"

"He found her name and number in an address book." Casey made a right turn onto Commercial Drive. "It makes me wonder if she knows more than she told Lalonde. I mean, she knew about me, and Mother always did attract trouble."

"Lillian didn't attract trouble, she sought it out. That's partly what made her so interesting."

"She came from a corrupt family, Rhonda. Wasn't Mother's policy to run away before anyone asked questions?"

"Not always." Rhonda picked at a blueberry. "Danger fascinated Lillian. In tenth grade, a classmate had a seizure in the science lab after school, and only Lillian and I were there." Rhonda popped the berry in her mouth. "I went to get help, but Lillian wanted to watch."

Casey turned left onto Venables. "Watching people suffer evolved into making them suffer. How many marriages did her affairs destroy? Six? Seven?"

"Five, but things worked out for some of us. Your dad and I fell in love."

What about all the other families? "You sound awfully forgiving."

"The older I get, the more I understand Lillian's instability." She turned to Casey. "She needed men to feel alive. She couldn't control it. My lousy ex, on the other hand, could have controlled his lust if he'd wanted to."

"Semantics."

"I've known your mother since we were seven years old, sweetie. I knew her better than her folks and Marcus did. She's to be pitied, not hated."

Maybe, maybe not. Minutes later, she drove across the Lions Gate Bridge, grateful for not having to use this aging three-lane structure often. Beautiful as West Van was, with its executive homes and panoramic views of ferries gliding back and forth, she preferred living among the wider variety of incomes, lifestyles, and ethnic backgrounds in East Vancouver.

By the time she reached Marine Drive, Casey found herself brooding over Dad again. Had he lived alone? Given his charm and looks, he should have found a lover. She glanced at Rhonda, who was trying to see beyond all the locked gates and tall hedges. The sky had lightened up enough to provide glimpses of elaborate, multi-level houses. Some were built closer down to the water, so only roofs and skylights were visible from the road.

"How could Marcus have afforded this area?" Rhonda murmured.

"Do we want to know?" Casey scanned house numbers posted on gates. "There it is, on the left."

She pulled over and studied a two-story structure partially concealed by bushes bordering the property. Two police cruisers and a familiar Sebring were parked in front. Crap, what was Lalonde doing here so early?

"We'll never get inside now," Rhonda said.

"This is waterfront property. There's probably beach access somewhere."

Casey drove on until she spotted a footpath between two homes. She parked on the shoulder, four houses down from Dad's place.

When they reached the beach, Rhonda said, "Oh god, Marcus brought me here once. Showed me where he wanted to build his dream home." She walked on.

While Casey picked her way along the narrow rocky beach, she remembered Dad saying that Rhonda made him feel good about himself, that he felt easy and relaxed around her. Why had everything changed?

"When did Dad bring you here?"

"A month after we got engaged. Then he got busy with work and we never came back."

Five years ago. They'd never set a wedding date. Surely Dad

wouldn't have faked his own death to avoid marriage. He'd ended relationships before, maturely and face-to-face. He wouldn't have run from Rhonda, would he?

Dad's trademark rectangular design was easy to spot. Homes on either side were varying levels and angles, but Dad had preferred straight, simple lines that critics had called boring. Truth was, he hadn't cared as much about exteriors as he had interiors. Casey studied the thirty-foot high cliff. Rocks and boulders provided a gradual incline. She hitched up her narrow skirt and began to climb.

"You can't be serious," Rhonda said.

"I want a closer look at the house."

The cold rocks were sprinkled with damp sand, pebbles, twigs, and the occasional beer can. By the time Casey reached the police tape along the perimeter, her hands were gritty.

Open, vertical blinds covered first-floor windows that ran the length of the house. Second-floor windows were exposed. The left half of the sloping roof was mostly skylight.

"Pull your skirt down," Rhonda called from behind. "We're attracting attention."

Casey spotted a guy leaning over the second-floor balcony of the house on their left. Brown, shoulder-length hair shielded most of his face. A moment later, she saw Lalonde strolling toward her. Damn.

"What are you doing here, Miss Holland?"

"Satisfying my curiosity." She ducked under the tape and rubbed grit from her hands. "Do you always start this early?"

"There's been a break-in, and I got your message about the Saab." He watched Rhonda climb up. "You should have called before you went after him."

"There wasn't time," she mumbled, so Rhonda couldn't hear.

"What if he hadn't driven away, Miss Holland? What would you have done?"

"Casey, help." Clinging to a boulder, Rhonda struggled to climb onto the property.

After Casey hauled her up, Rhonda extended her hand to Lalonde. "I'm Rhonda Stubbs, Casey's friend."

"Lalonde."

She lowered her hand. "You're the one who made her go to the morgue."

Lalonde stared at her.

"Have you been able to tell if anything was stolen?" Casey asked.

"So far, everything looks exactly as we left it. The neighbor next door woke early and heard a loud noise about an hour ago, so he called us." Lalonde nodded toward the guy on the deck. "It looks like someone took a hammer to the window pane in the door on the neighbor's side."

"There's no alarm system?" Casey asked.

"It's been sabotaged." He watched her. "Is this a return visit, by any chance?"

"First time. Okay if we look inside?"

"No, the crime lab technicians are still working."

"Are they using portable lasers to look for fingerprints and threads?"

She'd never seen Lalonde smile before and wished he hadn't. His teeth were yellow and slightly crooked. "You a wannabe cop?"

"I'm working toward a criminology degree, and forensics interests me." Dad had hoped she'd earn a degree, but Greg hadn't wanted a wife with more education than he had.

Lalonde looked at Rhonda. "Did you know the deceased?"

"Marcus was my fiancé, at least he was three years ago." She shook her head. "We didn't know he was alive, Detective, I swear. I don't understand any of this." Rhonda turned and wandered toward the house.

Lalonde signalled to an officer to go after her.

"Did your license check on the Saab turn up anything?" Casey asked.

"The car's been rented by a man named Theodore Ziegler from San Francisco. Your father's address book also shows a Geneva address for Mr. Ziegler as well as an email address." Lalonde looked at her closely. "Is the name familiar?"

"No. Have you questioned him?"

"Ziegler's proving difficult to find. He hasn't checked into the hotel listed on the rental agreement or any others we've contacted so far, nor is he answering messages sent to the email address we found for him. If you see him again, call us immediately." Lalonde watched Rhonda argue with the cop who was ushering her back to them.

"I just want a quick look through the window," Rhonda said.

"I checked into your botulism story." Lalonde retrieved his glasses and notepad. "I understand the alleged Mr. Holland didn't enter a hospital until his vision was already impaired. Also, he couldn't swallow and was partially paralyzed." He peered at her over his glasses. "Any idea why he waited so long to get help?"

"No." But she'd wondered the same thing.

"Marcus hated hospitals," Rhonda said, rejoining them.

Lalonde consulted his notes. "A woman named Simone Archambault was also affected, although her symptoms weren't as severe. She went to a hospital outside Paris, which could be why your lawyers didn't know about her, Miss Holland."

Casey noticed Rhonda's frown. Another woman in Dad's life wouldn't be welcome news.

"Does that name mean anything to either of you?"

"Not at all," Casey replied.

Rhonda shook her head. "Did she survive?"

"Yes, it seems she told the medical staff what was wrong with her. After her recovery, Miss Archambault left France, then vanished. Relatives haven't heard from her in two years, though they did say she used to live in Victoria." Lalonde flipped a page. "They gave us a landline number, but we haven't been able to reach her. It seems she doesn't have a computer or a cell phone. Relatives said she's an eccentric who's been living off the grid. Local authorities are trying to track her down."

"Dad had no friends or family in Victoria that I recall. He did have friends living in other areas of Vancouver Island, though; Ladysmith and Qualicum Beach, I think. Maybe she was a client."

"Did you mention Marcus to the Archambault woman's relatives?" Rhonda asked Lalonde. "Do they know him?"

"They knew that she and a man in his fifties had shared the same table at Alvin's All-Canadian Café, but they claim to know nothing about him." Lalonde looked at Krueger, who came to join them. "Also, the restaurant has new owners, and we haven't been able to locate any staff who worked there back then."

"If I knew the family's address," Casey said, "it might trigger a memory." No point in adding that Simone Archambault's relatives might tell her more than they'd tell a cop.

"How old is this Simone woman?" Rhonda asked. "What'd she look like?"

Lalonde stared at her a moment, then flipped another page. "Seventy-five and petite."

Casey and Rhonda exchanged perplexed looks.

"Ask Vincent Wilkes about her. He would have known Dad's clients and many of his contacts," Casey said. "So, when will you guys be finished with the house?"

"My advice, Miss Holland, is to stay away until the killer's caught." He turned to Krueger. "Escort these ladies off the premises."

Casey fumed as she and Rhonda headed for the front yard. Hell, she hadn't asked for any of this to happen and she didn't deserve to be treated like gum on the bottom of his shoe. Krueger stayed with them until they reached the road.

As they started toward her car, Casey said, "Let's talk to the neighbor."

The properties were divided by a high wooden fence. Casey had to ring the bell twice before the guy who'd been watching them from the deck opened the door. Up close, he was just a pimply teenager. While he gaped at Casey, he pulled up cotton gym shorts which promptly slumped back down onto narrow hips.

After introducing herself, Casey said, "The man who lived next door was my dad."

"Oh." He blushed. "Sorry about what happened."

"Thanks, and this is my friend, Rhonda."

He nodded. "I'm Gil."

"Nice to meet you." Casey watched his gaze slip to her breasts. "Listen, the cops won't tell me much and I was wondering if you heard anything the night my dad was killed. I was told it happened on Sunday between 8:00 and 10:00 PM."

"I—I, uh." He tried for her face again, "I told them I heard a car pull into his driveway a little before eight."

Interesting. "Did you see the car?"

"No." He wiped his hand on his shirt. "Just a lady in the house."

"What lady?" Rhonda asked.

"And where in the house?" Casey added.

"In a room with a lot of books," Gil replied. "It's on the ground floor, next to our fence."

"So, you can see into the room?" Casey asked.

"A little bit of it, when I'm in the garden, like I was then." Gil lowered his voice. "Saw her through the knothole. It's opposite a door with a window in the upper half."

Must be a good-sized knothole, Casey thought. How much time had he spent looking through it? "Do you often garden at night, Gil?"

"No, but my parents will be back from Arizona soon. I'm supposed to have all the gardens ready for planting and the lawn mowed by then, and I've kind of put it off." He shrugged.

Gil zeroed in on her boobs again, but Casey didn't mind. It was a small price to pay for crucial information. If he'd witnessed the murder, she'd toss him her bra and throw in a belly dance.

"Gil, did the woman look in her seventies?" Rhonda asked.

"I only saw the back of her, but she didn't dress old. She was in some sort of blue sparkly outfit with a matching hat."

Rhonda's eyes narrowed. "What was the woman doing? Did you see her hair color?"

"She was standing and talking, and her hair was either really short or pushed up under the hat 'cause I didn't see it."

Casey knew what Rhonda was thinking: the woman could have been a lover. She wanted to ask Gil if he'd seen them embrace, but Rhonda was developing a pout.

"Too bad you didn't see the woman's car," Casey said.

"I can only see his driveway from my bedroom upstairs. Anyway, I gave up on the stupid garden pretty quick, then went inside and cranked up the music. Crashed about eleven-thirty." He glanced at Casey's breasts again. "I did look out the window once, but the car was gone. Must've left while I had the music on. Didn't hear an engine start."

"Can you see into the room with the books from your bedroom window?" Casey asked.

"Angle's too sharp, but when I closed my drapes I saw that the lights were out. Didn't think in a million years anyone was dead in there." He tucked strands of hair behind his ears.

Rhonda fidgeted. "Had you seen the woman before?"

"Nah. Didn't see him around much either. No parties, loud music, not even a barbecue."

"Did you tell the police about the woman?"

"Uh-huh. They came in and looked out the window, tracked freakin' dirt all over the carpets."

Casey sighed. What else had Lalonde not bothered to tell her?

Five

CASEY STEPPED OUT of her Tercel and glanced at the back of Mainland Public Transport's admin building. The drab gray paint and two floors of narrow, paned windows always reminded her of a warehouse rather than an office building.

On her way to the entrance, she heard three-hundred horsepower engines starting up in the yard behind her. Most people couldn't bear the smell of diesel fuel, but to Casey it meant paychecks, friendships, and busy-ness. In summer, when the windows were open, the yard was noisy, but she didn't mind. The atmosphere was more informal than downtown's tinted-glass towers with talking elevators. Here, people used the stairs and talked to one another.

She'd barely entered the building when a man's loud curses caught her attention. They came from the ladies' locker room farther down the corridor. Casey pushed the door open and nearly stepped on scattered makeup, magazines, and clothing. Sickly sweet perfume from a broken bottle seeped into a pair of socks. Hands on hips, Stan stood in front of a group of open lockers.

"It looks like some moron used bolt cutters on five padlocks, including yours," he said. "See if anything's missing. The cops will be here, eventually."

"Any idea when it happened?"

"Between two and five this morning. Janitors found the mess when they showed up. They might have scared the freak off. The men's room wasn't touched."

Casey picked up the black garter belt and stockings she wore yesterday.

"Aside from this, how are you doin', kiddo? Any leads on your dad's killer?"

"Not that I know of."

"Did they get hold of that woman?"

Casey shoved the lingerie in her locker. "How did you know about her?"

"I overheard the detectives yakking about some lady who saw your dad the night he died."

"Did they happen to mention a name or description?"

"Not that I heard."

Casey dumped her bag on top of the stockings. "Everything's here and none of it's valuable, so I'd better get going."

"I'll have new locks put on today."

"Thanks."

She was jogging toward the M15 when she heard a familiar voice calling her. She turned and saw Lou running to catch up.

"Hey, gorgeous," he said, slowing to a stop. "You running to catch a bus or preparing to leap over one?" Lou's gray eyes shone over a pair of dimples and a sweet smile.

"I'm trying to be on time."

He gazed at her outfit. "Let me guess, high-powered executive, right?"

"And purse thief target." She stopped to tuck in her blouse.

"I heard you left early yesterday."

"I did, but came back around quarter to five to read up on this assignment. You were gone by then. Anyway, I have news that only a horror fan like you can appreciate."

"Oh?"

Casey put her arm around Lou, something she'd caught herself doing a lot lately. Lou returned the gesture. Rhonda thought Lou was in love with her, but Casey didn't think so. She and Lou had been friends for years and he'd never even hit on her. Sure, they'd gone to pubs, shared tons of pizzas, and seen the occasional movie together, but he'd never asked her on a real date. Lou had had his share of girlfriends, but she'd noticed that he looked more intensely at her lately. Did it really matter, though? She wasn't good relationship material, but neither was Mother, and if there was a person Casey didn't want to emulate, it was her mother.

"You want to talk about it at my place tonight?" Lou asked. "I've restocked the Coors."

"Casey, hurry up!" A wall of hairy, freckled flesh shouted from the M15 bus. "We're late."

She started for the bus. "How about I give you a lift to bowling tomorrow? We can talk on the way down, because tonight I've got to see a house, which is part of my news."

"That doesn't sound so terrible."

"It is, trust me."

"Can you give me a hint?"

Casey thought about it. "Resurrection."

"Good word, but I have no idea what you mean." He rubbed his chin. "Before I forget, I've got two sets of tickets, one for a new blues singer and the other for the Canucks, nosebleed section. Which would you rather see?"

"You're joking, right? It's the playoffs!"

He laughed. "Just checking."

"So, who will you take to the blues thing?"

"Mom. The tickets are another birthday present from her anyhow."

Casey always had liked Lou's eclectic tastes and an energy for life as strong as Dad's had been. When her marriage ended, Lou was one of the few people who hadn't said, "I never liked Greg." In fact, he and Greg had been buddies until they got into a fight after Casey ended the marriage. She'd been too busy feeling sorry for herself to ask Lou why he'd sided with her. Now, it didn't seem important. She was just grateful for his friendship.

"Move it, Casey!" Wesley shouted.

"All right, all right. Geez." They didn't call him Rude Wesley Axelson for nothing. She started to jog. "Later, Lou."

"I'm looking forward to it."

She hurried up the steps.

"About bloody time." Wesley started the bus.

"Would you relax. The day's barely started and you're already grumpy."

Wesley pulled away fast, forcing Casey to grab the pole behind his chair. She tapped his head with her clutch bag. "Try not to injure the team, Wes."

→   →   →

When Casey returned to her apartment around lunchtime, she collapsed on the sofa. No one had tried to grab her clutch bag all morning, damn it. She would ride again from three to six. Afterward, she'd visit more of Dad's West Van neighbors and see if anyone had known him.

She looked up the funeral home's number and then dialed. "I'd like to speak to the director, please."

"He's not available at the moment," a woman replied. "May I help you?"

"My name's Casey Holland. Your funeral home handled arrangements for my father's burial at Cedar Ridge Cemetery on March eleventh, three years ago. Only, his body showed up at the morgue yesterday."

Her response took a few seconds. "Let me see if I can reach Mr. Nay."

Mr. Nay came on the line and tried to sound like he had no food in his mouth. After highlighting events, Casey asked if an exhumation had been ordered. Nay reported that he hadn't been contacted by anyone, and as far as he knew Marcus Holland was still in plot 352.

"Then what should I do with the second Marcus Holland when his body's released?"

"Uh . . . well, let me consult with the morgue and our head office, and I'll get back to you."

Casey gave him her cell phone and landline numbers. She covered her face with her hands. It was all too weird. Twenty-four hours had passed since this ordeal began. In some ways she felt worse than she had yesterday. The thought of a second funeral made her cringe. The first one was bad enough, especially after some freak trashed Dad's house, forcing the reception to move to Rhonda's place. This time, no announcements would be made in the paper.

Casey felt a headache coming on. Before it got worse, she made a quick call to find out when Dad's remains could be claimed. After a long wait and a couple of transfers, she learned that Mother, of all people, had asked to claim the body. Since Mother wasn't next of kin, Casey refused to give consent.

She wasn't too surprised that Mother hadn't tried to contact her about Dad. After all, Casey had made it clear that she didn't want any contact between them, and Mother hadn't come to the funeral three years ago. Why did she want his body now? What made her think she had any right to him?

Casey grabbed a teddy bear from her shelf and threw it across the room. Rhonda used to say it was better to lash out at stuffed animals than people. Soon all the bears were bouncing off the sofa, thumping against walls, or skidding along the floor. Adrenalin pumped with the ferocity that only criminals and her mother could bring on.

Casey's vision blurred and the throbbing in her head escalated. Damn. A migraine was coming. She didn't get them often, but the symptoms could be harsh. Casey closed her eyes a moment. The only remedy for it was to take a painkiller and sleep.

Casey shuffled to the bathroom, popped a couple of pills, and then slid under her comforter. The last thought she had before dozing off was that she'd have to pick up all those bears.

Six

BY THE TIME Casey had finished another uneventful shift, grabbed some food, then talked to Dad's Marine Drive neighbors, it was dark. No one admitted to having known Dad. Few had even seen him, and most didn't want to discuss the night of the murder because the police had already asked enough questions.

"Marine Drive's a busy street," an elderly neighbor said, "with cars speeding along all the time. Some passenger in a vehicle could have spotted a car in your dad's driveway, or saw someone entering the house. I did see a couple of people walking their dogs that night. One of them is a tall lady with short red hair who lives down the street. Didn't recognize the other young fella."

Casey had spoken with a woman who'd been walking her dog, but the lady had been back home by seven-thirty and hadn't noticed anything. Casey had also tried to reach Dad's lawyer, but the guy's number was out of service, nor was he listed anywhere. The only good news was that her migraine had gone away and her nap had dredged up a useful memory: an easier way to enter the house than lock picks would be.

On the chance that Lalonde's people hadn't finished with the crime scene, Casey put on the gloves from her first aid kit. She removed a flashlight from the glove box and then a tire iron from the trunk, should a weapon be needed.

Standing by her car, she studied the house. Crime scene tape still stretched along the property, but there were no signs of police anywhere. Despite Lalonde's warning to stay away, the temptation to unravel Dad's secrets had drawn her here like an enormous magnet. She needed to walk through those rooms, needed to try to make sense out of everything she'd learned.

She'd seen enough this morning to know that floodlights were everywhere. Motion sensors would probably light up the yard the second she stepped onto the property, which was why she'd told the neighbors, including Gil, that she'd be here tonight, so they wouldn't worry about activity at the house.

Casey checked to ensure her cell phone and lock picks were tucked inside her jacket pockets. Taking a deep breath, she ducked under the tape and stepped in front of a tall bush. Two narrow windows flanked each side of the double doors. As expected, no lights were on in the house. Her flashlight scanned each side of the door in search of a potted plant. At their old place, Dad had kept a spare key buried in the pot. She'd often badgered him to buy a fake plant with sand so she wouldn't have to stick her hand in dirt to pull out the little bag with the key. Dad had refused. Said she'd learn not to forget her key this way. He'd been right. But there were no potted plants here, not even a hanging basket.

The second Casey stepped forward, the floodlights and porch lights came on. She stopped and looked around. Okay, fine. Nothing to worry about. Glancing at the damaged alarm system by the front door, she marched across the yard and down the right side of the property, noting the fence between this and Gil's place. She reached the only door along the exterior, the one Gil would have seen from his garden. The broken window looked boarded up tight, and more crime scene tape was fastened across the door.

The floodlights allowed Casey to see the single lock without the flashlight. Studying the deadbolt lock, she smiled. Dad never had liked big fancy locks. Still, it took Casey some time before the tools did their job. Pinpricks of sweat dampened the back of her shirt. She recalled Lalonde's warning and feared what she might find, but she couldn't walk away. There'd be no peace until she understood what had motivated Dad to create a new life. Face the fear, she told herself. It's what he'd taught her. Casey opened the door.

Inside, her flashlight exposed a computer monitor, banker's lamp, and phone on a teak desk. She checked the phone. Still in service. Her flashlight beam swept past a pair of French doors opening onto the living room. Left of the doors, bookshelves built into the wall stretched to more French doors at the far end of the room. Those doors appeared to lead to the foyer. To Casey's left, three tall windows overlooked the front yard.

Aside from a few office supplies, the partially open drawers were empty. In the credenza behind the desk were a half-dozen liquor bottles and glasses. A printer sat on top of the credenza, the CPU, minus the hard drive, beside it.

Casey stepped farther into the room, stopping at the edge of a rug. Dad's body had been found here. She saw what looked like light-colored dirt on the navy rug and possibly darker splotches, though it was hard to tell the color. A pale blue and coral upholstered chair, however, revealed a few blood spatters. She swept her flashlight to the right and spotted four indentations where another chair must have sat, the chair Dad had been using when attacked. Probably taken by the forensics team. Beyond the rug, a trail of dry blood droplets led to the foyer. As far as she knew, Lalonde hadn't yet found the murder weapon. Maybe the killer took the cleaver with him.

Casey stepped back and leaned against the desk. The room's smell was a strange combination of metal, chemicals, sweat, and possibly blood. She could almost picture Dad sitting with his legs outstretched and eyes closed like he always did, unaware that someone was creeping toward him with the cleaver raised.

Casey stood straight to banish the image. Who was capable of such brutality? Not anyone she knew, surely. Why dwell on suspects anyway? Lalonde could deal with that. She entered the living room, where an elaborate entertainment center filled the wall to her right. A smoked-glass coffee table and more chairs were placed before a long sofa facing the full-length windows. Moonlight exposed a rippling, silver-laced ocean.

As Casey tiptoed down the room and into a small nook off the main living area, the yard's motion sensor lights switched off, darkening the interior too. She found her way into a dining room where a crystal chandelier glistened in moonlight from the windows.

In the foyer, a suit of armor stood by the staircase. Dad had always wanted one, who knew why. Her flashlight zeroed in on another door just beyond the armor. This had to be the kitchen. To build one in the center of a house was so like Dad.

Casey reached for the door handle, then spotted traces of blood and hesitated. If this was Dad's blood, how had it gotten this far? She'd never thought about who cleaned up after the police were done with a crime scene. Was it up to the victim's family?

Opening the door slowly, Casey stepped inside. A rectangular island dominated the room. She thought she smelled onions. More blood splotched the floor and cupboard below the sink. She stared at the stains. Had the killer come in here to wash up before leaving? With that many strikes to the scalp, a fair amount of blood must have splattered him or her. There was no sign of a dishcloth, soap, or towel, or even dirty dishes. Placing the tire iron on the island, she knelt to examine a slightly squiggly pattern. Made by coarse material? A corduroy trouser leg maybe?

Casey strolled around the kitchen. Had Dad left clues about his life somewhere? She walked around the room twice until she remembered the shelf paper. When Mother still lived with them, Dad used to hide money and his itinerary from her under the lining paper at the back of the cutlery drawer. He'd wanted Casey to know where he'd be, told her that Mother had enjoyed too many wild shopping sprees to be trusted. Casey later learned the real reason for Mother's desperate need to keep tabs on his itinerary was so she could plan her trysts. Casey had lost count of the times Mother had tried to trick or bully information from her.

She never did learn when Dad had first suspected Mother's infidelity. But when he caught her in the act with Rhonda's husband, he wasted no time ending things. "Acknowledge the problem and act quickly," that was his motto. Having been on the receiving end of this method in her teens, Casey had learned to use the strategy well.

Dad wouldn't have needed that sort of hiding spot in this house unless he'd planned for her to be here at some point. On the other hand, he had lived with plenty of secrets and maybe hiding notes beneath lining paper was merely the habit of a paranoid man. Casey started on the drawers nearest her. When she reached the cutlery drawer, a tiny bit of one corner felt slightly loose. She removed the plastic cutlery tray, pried the corner up with her fingernail and then peeled it back. She hadn't gone far when she felt a slip of paper.

Casey slid the paper out and found herself looking at a grocery receipt. The receipt wasn't large: eight items bought, nothing unusual, but Dad had bought these items about a month before his death in France. On the back, the name "Simone Archambault" had been written in Dad's familiar scrawl, along with a telephone number. So, they had known each other before that night at Alvin's All-Canadian Café. Vincent said Dad had intended to tell her about the house. Why had he wanted her to find Simone's name this way? She stuffed the receipt in her pocket and put the shelf paper and tray back in place. Picking up her tire iron, Casey left the room and climbed the spiral staircase.

At the top of the stairs, the darkness dissipated slightly and she caught a whiff of damp soil. Casey pointed the flashlight on a small atrium in the center of the floor. Six trees dominated the area, two of which nearly reached the glass ceiling. Entwined branches created a collage of leaves. Smaller plants sat on tabletops.

Casey started forward when something struck her shoulder. A second strike on her back forced her to her knees. With the third strike Casey's forehead smacked the tiled floor. She dropped the tire iron. Someone kicked it away.

With both hands on the flashlight, she swung it against her attacker's leg so hard the batteries rattled and the light died. A deep voice grunted. She thought of the ponytailed guy. The light blinked back on and she struck again. Her attacker yelled. Casey tried to scramble away but a kick to her ribs made her collapse. She rolled onto her back, dropping the flashlight.

The man lunged for the light, but she grabbed it and scuttled backward along the tiles. All she could see was a dark sweatshirt with a hood pulled so low that it covered most of the face.

He tried to stomp her foot and missed. Casey kept moving but couldn't gain any ground. He grabbed her ankles, pulled her toward him and knelt down, straddling her hips. The flashlight darted over his jeans, the floor, table legs. His thighs squeezed her body. Hot, bony fingers gripped her neck until Casey rammed the flashlight into his crotch. He groaned in agony and collapsed onto his side.

Casey bolted for the staircase. She took the steps two at a time, leaping over the last three. Gasping for air, she turned the deadbolt, yanked the door open, and raced outside.

Seven

THE WELT ON Casey's left shoulder throbbed the next morning and her arm felt heavy, as if encased in iron. Her bruised lower back was stiff and sore, but it could have been worse. If the man had had a gun, if he'd followed her home . . . She was fairly certain he hadn't. She'd checked the rearview mirror a thousand times. On the other hand, if her attacker had been the ponytailed guy, Theodore Ziegler, he knew where she lived anyway. She wished she'd had the presence of mind to aim her flashlight on her assailant's face instead of acting like a bloody amateur.

When she had returned home last night, she'd called Simone Archambault first, then Stan to update him on events and ask for today off to go to Victoria.

"You know you can call anytime and I'll do what I can do help you out," he'd replied, "but it sounds like you're getting in over your head, Casey. Are you sure Victoria's a good idea?"

"I don't have much choice. Simone Archambault is the best lead I have to Dad's past, and she won't tell me anything until I prove who I am. Apparently, Dad showed her a photo of me once, so she insists on meeting in person."

Stan didn't say much after that, except to say that they still hadn't found the individual who'd vandalized the lockers.

Casey left her apartment and headed downstairs into Rhonda's kitchen.

"You're early again," Rhonda said, nibbling on a piece of toast. "Going back to the house?"

"No, I have another assignment," one involving a forty-minute drive to the Tsawwassen terminal, a ninety-minute ferry ride to Swartz Bay, and another half-hour drive to Victoria. Hardly a quick jaunt, but it had to be done. She felt guilty for not telling Rhonda about Simone, but if Rhonda found out she'd want to tag along, and Casey wanted to talk to the woman alone.

"Tell Summer her bike tire will be fixed tomorrow." Casey headed for the back door.

"Sure." Rhonda took another small bite of toast. "Want to have supper with us tonight?"

"Actually, it could be a long day, so don't worry about me."

"Then you don't know when you'll be back?"

"Gee, *Mom*, I'm not sure."

"Okay, backing off." Rhonda put the toast down and raised her hands. "But just one more question, totally off topic. What did Detective Lalonde come to see you about last night?"

Uh-oh. "You knew?"

"I was in the tub when I heard voices outside. Thought it might have been Lou, but when I got out a bit later and heard it again, I peeked out the window and saw Lalonde walking away."

Rhonda's en suite bathroom and bedroom windows were at the front of the house above the porch. Casey had been on the phone with Stan when her buzzer rang, and she brought Lalonde up to her apartment so they could talk privately. Afraid to lose what little cooperation the detective had given her, Casey hadn't told him about her visit to the house. Hiding the pain to her shoulder had been tough.

"He wanted to know, among other things, how long you'd been engaged to Dad."

Rhonda plugged in the kettle. "Why? And why wouldn't he ask me?"

"The great detective wouldn't say."

She didn't want to tell her that Mother had called Lalonde from Geneva, Switzerland, of all places, to ask if she could claim Dad's body. It seemed she felt it only right to remove the "burden" of funeral arrangements off her "poor daughter" and make them herself. *Poor daughter*. The words burned like bile in Casey's throat. Lalonde also said that Mother hadn't approved of Rhonda's engagement to Dad, but he didn't give a reason. He had made a point of saying that he'd found Mother candid and cooperative. At that point Casey realized Mother had totally conned him.

Mother came from a family of con artists who associated with criminals, and the whole clan disliked cops. She hadn't introduced

Casey to many of her relatives, but she had talked about working in an uncle's pharmacy when she was sixteen. Her job was to change the expiry dates on pill bottles and packaging to sell as new meds. Casey figured the family had a lot of heart attacks and unwanted pregnancies to answer for, among other things.

Even if she knew who the killer was, Casey doubted Mother would tell the authorities if it compromised her interests. That Mother was in Geneva, the same city where Theodore Ziegler had another address, had made her wonder exactly what Mother's interest was in all this. She'd asked Lalonde about it, but his response was to remind her that this was a police investigation.

"The great detective can't locate Dad's dental records. Do you know who his dentist was? Because I don't remember."

"I don't either." Rhonda removed a jar of instant coffee from the cupboard.

"Lalonde might have a DNA test performed on the body, but results could take time."

"What for? You identified your father."

"It sure looked like him, yeah. But now that there are two deceased Marcus Hollands, DNA testing could be necessary for at least one of them, if not both. I think they'll want to compare their analysis with DNA they know is Dad's."

"What's wrong with fingerprints?"

"That's also why he was here," Casey answered. "I gave him the birthday cards I got from Dad, and do you still have his comb? They'll need hair samples for testing."

Rhonda nodded. "I never cleaned them or his razor and toothbrush."

After the funeral, Rhonda had asked for all of Dad's personal items, including his clothes. As far as Casey knew, she'd kept everything.

"Whatever Marcus was up to," Rhonda said, "he kept it secret to protect us. You know that, don't you?"

"I don't know anything right now."

"He loved you, Casey. He would have done anything to keep you from harm. After Marcus kicked Lillian out, he hired a private detective to watch over you in case Lillian's family tried to kidnap you."

"He never told me that." But then Dad apparently hadn't told her lots of things. "Gran and Gramps wouldn't have taken me."

"Your aunts and uncles would have, if Lillian told them to. Those people had connections. Could have had you out of the country in two hours."

Casey believed her. "I should go."

"Have you started funeral arrangements?" Rhonda asked.

"Yep." She hesitated. "It seems that Mother wants to claim his body."

Rhonda snorted. "I always knew Lillian wanted him back, but his corpse? That's sick."

"Yeah, well, she's not getting it, and I'll tell her so myself if I have to."

Last night, Lalonde handed her a message from Mother, asking Casey to call her collect at the Geneva number. Undecided about what to do, she'd shoved the message in her jeans pocket, the same jeans she was wearing now.

Rhonda poured a teaspoon of sugar into a mug. "You said Lalonde called Lillian when he found Marcus's body."

"Yeah."

"Has he been in touch with her since?"

Oh, great. "Yes."

Rhonda glanced at her as she took milk out of the fridge. "Did Lalonde bring up Lillian's name last night?"

"Why do you ask?"

Rhonda sloshed milk over the sugar. "Just wondering if Lillian discussed me with him—if that's why he asked about my engagement."

"He did, and it's been bugging me because Mother was long gone before you and Dad got together, so how'd she know about you two?"

Rhonda rubbed sleep-starved eyes. "I didn't want you to know this—thought it'd upset you—but Lillian's been keeping in touch with me for some time."

Casey's cheeks grew warm. "You've got to be kidding."

"Kidding about your mother's impossible." Rhonda's smile was bleak. "She called what felt like a hundred times to apologize for ruining my marriage. Claimed she wanted to be friends again, and to see you again. She still asks about you."

Casey couldn't believe it. "What do you tell her?"

"Just the basics," Rhonda's teaspoon clanged against the mug. "She said she was so sorry for hurting you and me. She said, 'I swear I'll never hurt you again, Rhonda; just tell me how I can make it up to you, Rhonda; we know each other too well to stay apart.'" Rhonda dropped the teaspoon in the sink. "As if she could scam me. The second I told her that Marcus and I were engaged, I knew she hadn't changed."

"Why?"

"She said, 'He'll never need you as much as I do. He'll never understand you as well as I do, Rhonda.' Every time she called she went on about how he and I were wrong for each other." Rhonda removed a green bucket, brush, and Pine Sol from the cupboard below the sink. "I would bet Lillian said the same thing to Marcus. She hinted that they'd stayed in touch. When you said her name was in his address book I wasn't surprised."

"Why would Dad have done that?"

"No clue." Rhonda filled the bucket with water. "Lillian kept calling me after Marcus's funeral, supposedly to see how I was doing. I wonder if she knew he was alive."

"If you didn't want Mother's friendship, why say anything at all? Why not just hang up on her?"

"You won't believe this, but I felt sorry for Lillian." Rhonda picked up her scrub brush and rubber gloves. "She was so desperate for news about you. I'm a mom, Casey. I can't imagine being estranged from my daughter, not watching her grow up."

"Did you and Dad ever discuss Mother?"

"I told Marcus about the calls, but he wouldn't talk about it. Thought he was still bitter. Now, I'm not so sure." Rhonda lifted the bucket out of the sink. "Somehow, I don't think Lillian's finished with us."

"What do you mean?"

She plunked the sudsy bucket onto the floor. "Sooner or later, she might appear on our doorstep to try and make peace with you."

"After all of these years?"

"I think she hates that you and I are close." Rhonda put the gloves on. "She wants to be part of your life again, probably to try and come between us."

An unsettling thought. Was that why Mother wanted her to phone?

Rhonda began scrubbing the floor. Rhonda always cleaned floors when she was under stress, which was why Casey was glad she hadn't mentioned the phone message. Her friend had to be far more stressed than she was letting on. Why else would she abandon partially eaten toast and a fresh mug of coffee to wash a floor she'd just washed yesterday?

Eight

SIMONE ARCHAMBAULT LIVED on a muddy lane bordered by sulphuric-smelling ditches and prickly weeds. Her cottage was a gray, clapboard shack about as appealing as a war bunker. The venetian blinds covering both windows were closed.

Casey walked along two planks laid across the marshy front lawn until she reached the door. She'd barely started knocking when the ominous barks of a large dog started inside. Simone poked out from behind the curtain. Casey heard, "Stop it, Georgie!"

The door opened and Casey found herself looking at a tiny woman with hunched shoulders and deep lines across her forehead and around her mouth.

"I'm Casey Holland."

Simone studied her through bifocals. "Yes, you are." She looked so malnourished that Casey was caught off guard when Simone grabbed her wrist and hauled her inside. "Not followed, were you?"

"No." She'd been diligent about checking her surroundings. "Why do you ask?"

"I want privacy."

The Doberman pinscher growled.

"It's okay, Georgie." Simone led him into a room and shut the door.

Casey followed her to a plywood table under a window at the back of the cottage. The fridge and stove looked forty years old. Above the sink, two plates, four cans of vegetable soup, and two cans of dog food sat on a shelf. Charcoal sketches of barren landscapes and soaring eagles were the only decoration on dingy, beige walls.

"Did you draw these?" Casey asked. "They're really good."

"My nephew." She eased into a chair. "Sit down, please."

Her French accent wasn't strong, but Casey doubted she'd be hearing much of it. Simone didn't strike her as the chatty type.

"Thank you for seeing me." Casey watched Simone's curt nod. "As I mentioned on the phone, after what happened Sunday night, I'm trying to learn more about my father's past. Did you know about the murder?"

Simone watched her a long time. "No, and that person is not Marcus."

"Evidence suggests otherwise." As Casey described her trip to the morgue and the revelation about his West Vancouver home, Simone's stoic expression didn't change. "Your family in France told the police they didn't know Dad."

Her eyes widened. "The police talked to them?"

"Yes." Why did Simone look so worried? "The detective's name is Lalonde. I'm sure he'd like to talk to you."

"Botulism killed Marcus. If you had seen him, you'd know."

"I wish I had, but I didn't know he was sick until some doctor called and said he'd died."

"Marcus gave me your home number." Simone looked down at her gnarled, arthritic hands. "I called your house three times, but no answer. I didn't know where you worked. Marcus only said you were in security. Your profession troubled him."

Something Casey had known.

"And then I became too ill to continue calling."

"It's lucky you recovered."

"I had only a small taste of his potato salad." She shrugged and looked at her tiny patch of yard through the window.

"As I also mentioned on the phone, I only learned about you yesterday." Casey waited for a response, but none came. "How did you and Dad meet?"

"An acquaintance referred him. Said Marcus was an excellent importer."

Casey sat back in the chair. "There must be some mistake. My dad was an architect. Are you sure we're talking about the same Marcus Holland?"

Simone watched her. "I have a picture. Stay here."

She left the room, returning a moment later with a snapshot of Simone and Dad at a birthday party. Dad was wearing his silk tie with the penguins on it, the one she'd bought him for Christmas six or seven years ago. One day, he got ink on the tie. Casey thought he'd thrown it out. After his funeral, while she was packing his clothes for Rhonda, she found the tie neatly folded and wrapped in tissue at the back of a drawer.

"When was this picture taken?" Casey asked.

"Five years ago, on my seventieth birthday."

"How long had you known each other?"

"Ten years."

"And he was an importer back then?"

"Yes."

Casey wasn't sure which irritated her more: that Dad's other life had gone on for so long or that strangers knew more about him than she did.

"I had no idea," she murmured. "Why didn't he tell me?"

"Marcus didn't want you to know that his architectural practice was failing. Architecture was wrong for him."

"He was a good architect. Ran his own firm for years and he was always busy."

"He was disillusioned and poor," Simone replied. "Imports and exports brought in money to keep his architectural firm alive."

"So, it was a side business." Casey knew about the disillusioned and poor part, so why the big secret out a second income? Unless . . .

"Simone, what did Dad import for you?"

"Rare decks of tarot cards; all kinds. Celtic, Egyptian, I Ching."

"Really?"

Simone blinked at her. "Through those cards, I helped people with problems. Clients still look for me, which is why I need privacy."

What on god's earth would Dad have had in common with a fortune teller? He'd never believed in that stuff. "Judging from this photo, I gather you two were also friends?"

"Yes."

Casey handed the photo back to Simone. "Do you know if he imported anything else besides your cards?"

"Furniture, art."

"Anything else?"

"I don't know." She gazed off into space. "He had an assistant at his architectural firm. Vincent, I think his name was. He might know."

Vincent Wilkes knew about the importing business? She'd have to have another chat with him. Aware that Simone was watching her rather intensely, Casey tried not to squirm.

"Marcus often mentioned you," Simone said. "He had hopes for a grandchild."

Another thing she hadn't known, and why was this old woman refusing to believe that Dad had faked his death?

"Simone, were you with Dad when he died?"

"No."

Casey thought she saw a glimmer of fear. "Then can you be sure it really happened?"

"Marcus died in the hospital, no mistake."

"The man you ate with might have been an impostor."

"If he were alive, he would have come for his book."

"What book?"

"A notebook. He said to give it to you if he died. It's the other reason I needed you to come here."

Simone walked to a large wooden trunk under the window at the front of the cottage. Following, Casey watched her retrieve a key from a chain hidden under her shirt. Simone knelt and unlocked the trunk. The lid creaked open.

Casey stepped closer as the woman removed decks of tarot cards and small wooden boxes. Simone lifted out a cassette tape labeled "Mozart: The Last Four String Quartets" and a folded sheet of paper smudged with charcoal. Simone hesitated over these items then quickly exchanged them for a zippered, blue book. The book was a little larger than a paperback. Simone shoved it into Casey's hands, as if she couldn't bear to touch it.

"When I came home two years ago, I called you again," Simone said. "A woman said you'd moved away and wouldn't give any information."

"My ex-husband's girlfriend; she moved in right after I moved out."

Simone pointed at the book. "It's yours now. Take it."

Casey opened the zipper. "What's inside?"

"All I know is that it was valuable to Marcus." Simone returned her things to the trunk. "You must leave now."

A house key fell from the pages and Casey smiled. "Have you ever been to Dad's home on Marine Drive?"

"No." She shut the lid. "Don't tell anyone you saw me or where I live, promise?"

"As I said, the police might want to talk to you. Frankly, I'm a little surprised they haven't found you yet."

"Only Marcus and one other friend knew this phone number and address. This was my hidden retreat. I moved here permanently after I left Paris. I don't want people to know where I live."

Was this more than a privacy issue? Was something troubling this woman? "Simone, do you know anything about a Marcus Holland look-alike? As far as I know, Dad never had a long lost twin."

Simone locked the trunk. "I know nothing about the person in the morgue."

Casey flipped through dozens of pages containing names, phone numbers, email and street addresses. "Do you know who these people are?"

"I haven't looked in the book. You should go now."

Casey turned to the last page and stared at the name "Theo Ziegler." Dad had written down two addresses, one for San Francisco, the other in Geneva, plus two phone numbers and an email address.

"Simone, did Dad ever mention someone named Theo Ziegler?"

Simone glared, as if offended by the question. "I don't know those people."

Was this true? Casey zipped up the book. "Thanks for seeing me."

"I pray I've done the right thing. There are too many decisions to make. Difficult."

"I don't quite know what you mean."

"Go now."

Casey removed a pen and pad from her purse. "If you want to talk or need anything, please call me." She jotted down her home number on the back of her business card.

Simone struggled to her feet. "You will keep this visit secret? I swear on the lives of my family that I know nothing about that man in the morgue."

"Why do you want to keep my visit a secret?"

"I don't want to be involved in a murder investigation. I just want peace and quiet."

"Okay, I won't tell a soul." Unless her promise turned out to be undeserved.

Simone opened the door. She scarcely gave Casey time to step outside and say goodbye before shutting it.

In her car, Casey studied a slip of paper tucked into the back of the book. Dad had written the address of the house on Marine Drive. Below, he'd drawn two vertical rows of x's and o's and a bunch of squiggly lines. Had he been doodling, or was there a point to the squiggles? She thumbed through the book. Most of the addresses were European, a few were American. Simone was one of two Canadians who'd lived close to Dad, the other was Vincent Wilkes whose old address was listed. Both of them had stars beside their names. Casey turned to Ziegler's name. No star there.

It'd be impossible for her to meet all the people in the notebook, but she could try emails and phone numbers. Several other names had stars beside them, and Casey didn't recognize any. Had they been Dad's friends? It was possible, since Mother's name, street and email addresses, plus a cell phone number were also listed, yet she had no star by her name. For the second time this week, she wondered why Dad had listed Mother at all.

Casey sighed. Everywhere she went Mother's name cropped up; with Detective Lalonde, her father's address books, Rhonda. Now the woman was passing messages to her through the authorities.

Casey pulled the crumpled phone slip from her pocket. As she looked at the brief note Lalonde had written, she couldn't help feeling that Mother was moving closer, preparing to make contact as Rhonda had predicted. Was that such a bad idea, though? If Mother and Dad had kept in touch all those years, how much did she know about this importing business? Had she known Dad was alive? Casey shoved the number back in her pocket.

Nine

CASEY CHEWED THE warm, misshapen ball of falafel for three seconds before her taste buds couldn't take any more. She spit out the ochre-colored mess in the sink. So much for a nutritious supper; grainy garbanzo beans saturated with spices and parsley flakes wasn't for her, with or without the yogurt and cucumber dip. Good thing the bowling alley made a decent burger.

As Casey fetched the last Coors from the fridge, she heard Rhonda's knock. When she opened the door she was surprised to find Rhonda standing beside a tall, thin man sporting blue-tinted glasses and tight, blond curls.

"Hi, Casey, I'd like you to meet my new tenant, Darcy Churcott."

"Hi," he said in a raspy voice. "Good to meet you."

"You too." She turned to Rhonda. "I didn't know you'd interviewed anyone."

"That's because you've been gone all day."

True, she'd only got home from Victoria forty-five minutes ago and had just finished sending a carefully worded email to Mother. Casey had thought about calling her, but she wasn't ready to hear Mother's voice again.

"Since Darcy now has the Summer seal of approval, he'll be moving in tomorrow," Rhonda said.

"Great." Rhonda never rented a room unless Summer approved of the applicant.

"Darcy's an electrician," Rhonda said, "but he had knee surgery a few weeks ago."

"The doc says I can go back to work in a few days."

"I think you'll like it here," Rhonda smiled at him.

"Thanks, Mrs. Stubbs."

"Whoa." Casey laughed. "If you don't want to be evicted before you move in, call her Rhonda."

"Yeah, sure." He smiled. "I'd better go pack." Leaning on the rail, Darcy started down the steps. "If I ever get on skis again, shoot me. It's not as much fun as everyone says."

"Don't talk to me about fun." Rhonda snorted. "My last date's idea of fun was to let his parakeet hang upside down in his hair and peck the mole on his cheek."

Darcy called over his shoulder. "I hate birds."

"Something else in common." Rhonda stepped inside Casey's apartment and shut the door. "He'll make a fun foursome."

"Foursome?"

"You and Lou, Darcy and me."

"Aren't you moving a little fast? You don't even know if he's attached."

"He isn't, I asked."

"Anyway, Lou and I are not a couple." She sipped the Coors.

"But you hang out together. So why don't the four of us go to the neighborhood pub this weekend."

"How do you know Darcy doesn't have other plans?"

Rhonda spotted the blue notebook Casey had left on the coffee table and changed the subject. "That looks familiar." She unzipped the book and flipped through the pages. "Oh my god, it's Marcus's address book." She looked at Casey. "He used to keep this with him all the time. Where did you get it?" Casey had hoped a brief answer would work, but one question led to another, and before long Rhonda knew about the meeting with Simone Archambault and Dad's import business.

"I didn't know about any import sideline," Rhonda said, scanning the book. "Almost none of these names are familiar."

"What about Theo Ziegler on the last page?" When she and Lalonde were talking about him at Dad's house, Rhonda had wandered off and hadn't heard his name mentioned.

"No idea," Rhonda replied, staring at the name.

"While I was on the ferry, I tried calling the handful of Canadian and American phone numbers in the book, but the numbers were either out of service or the person I wanted had changed companies.

I'll try emailing people later." She'd also see if Ziegler's name popped up on the Internet.

"The notebook's old and could be a gigantic waste of time. Besides, isn't fact finding Lalonde's job?"

"This is family history research, not a murder investigation."

Rhonda sat on the sofa. "If Marcus had wanted us to know about his other life, don't you think he would have told us?"

"Not if circumstances forced him underground."

"Circumstances that could have got him killed."

Watching Rhonda turn the pages, Casey wondered if that book was the reason someone had broken into the house on Marine Drive. Was it possible that the locker break-ins at work were also connected? Probably not. After all, several were opened and cash was stolen. Or was that what the perp wanted people to think? Was the key to an expensive home the reason for the book's value, or the names in that book?

"Vincent Wilkes and Lillian are in here." Rhonda put the book down. "How much do you think she knows about Marcus's other life?"

"No clue." But she hoped to find out soon.

"You should give the book to Lalonde."

"I will when I'm done with it." Casey put her beer down to pick up the bowling shoes she'd left by her stationary bike. "At the moment, he's probably busy contacting names in the current book."

"Casey, there might not be any difference between investigating a crime and researching Marcus's life."

"If there isn't, I'll back off."

Rhonda put the book down and sighed. "No matter what you discover, Marcus is still gone. Maybe the secrets should stay buried."

Wrong. He'd bloody lied about his life and he died violently. Secrets had to be exposed.

As Casey swallowed the last of her hamburger, Lou said, "Think you'll be able to toss a bowling ball after all that food?"

"Totally, and I bet my score will be higher than yours." She looked around. "Marie should be here by now."

"Actually, she's not coming. Her babysitter canceled at the last minute."

"Too bad," although not entirely. She welcomed the break from her coworker's competitive streak, one that covered everything from bowling scores to landing assignments and grabbing Lou's attention. Casey used to chalk it up to insecurity, but she later realized that Marie had a thing for Lou and had decided Casey was a rival.

"By the way, that purse thief struck again and Marie nearly caught him."

"Crap, the count's up to four purses and one wallet now. What happened?"

"She was eastbound on the M8 around lunchtime when the guy struck at the Broadway and Renfrew stop. Marie saw it happen, but the kid took off fast. She got a good look at him, though."

"Really?" A twinge of jealousy rippled through Casey, though she wasn't sure if this was because Marie had made a point of telling Lou about it or that she could ID the guy. "Did she say what he looked like?"

"Acne on his face, full lips, tall and thin with a ball cap and black and yellow backpack."

"Hmm, the backpack doesn't match earlier descriptions."

"Maybe he bought a new one. They found the wallet, and the victim said she had eighty bucks in it. Credit cards were still there."

"As usual," Casey said, and rubbed her aching shoulder. She needed to catch that kid soon.

"You okay?" Lou asked.

"Yeah, fine."

On the way here, she'd shown him her wounds and told him everything that had happened. Typically, Lou hadn't said much. He'd never been one for spouting opinions. Still, the surprise and worry on his face had been easy to read. When she described what she saw at the morgue, Lou had actually cringed.

"By the way, Rhonda has a new tenant," Casey remarked. "He's an electrician."

Lou slid closer to her on the bench, "Thought hers was a girls-only house."

"She needs the bucks and probably hopes he'll do a little free rewiring."

"Think he'll fit in?"

"He and Rhonda seem to have hit it off; innuendo has been flashing all day." Casey looked around for their teammates, who were still at the food counter.

"Rhonda's seeing romance, huh?"

"Rhonda's seeing a heart-shaped, vibrating bed with mirrors on the ceiling." When he didn't crack a smile, she asked, "What's wrong?"

Lou watched people throw practice balls. "I know you can take care of yourself, but you're getting into some potentially dangerous, heavy-duty family stuff, Casey."

"I can handle it."

He watched her. "You sounded sad when you filled me in."

The bells and whistles of pinball machines rang on the other side of a partition.

"You mean depressed again?"

He paused. "It was hard to see you go through it after Marcus's funeral."

Hard to experience, too; mercifully, a good therapist and the right medication had shortened the ordeal. She touched his arm. "I'm not depressed, just angry and shocked. I mean, Dad's secrets go back a lot of years, and I need to know why."

"Why don't you wait until the cops solve the murder, then take your time researching the past. They may find out things you couldn't."

Casey stared at the rows of pins. "Would you like to see Dad's fancy West Van home tomorrow?"

"It's too risky."

"Not with two people in the middle of the afternoon. Even in the dark, my assailant wore a hood pulled over his forehead. My guess is he won't go near the place in daylight, but if it'll make you feel better, we could bring friends."

He shrugged.

"No one's going to stop me from going through those rooms, Lou. I need to know."

"Could be that the truth isn't worth knowing."

Meaning secrets should stay buried, like Rhonda said? Absolutely not. "Remember the night I was driving the M4 bus and that drunk pulled a knife on me?"

"I'll never forget it."

Lou was the first to see her stumble out of the bus back at Mainland. He'd put his arms around her until she stopped shaking. Greg had arrived later and told her she should get a secretarial job.

"I went back to work the next night because if I didn't, I was afraid I'd never drive again." Casey paused. "I have to face the past right now or the fear will get worse. I can't spend the rest of my life wondering where my courage went."

"Yeah." Lou watched their approaching teammates. "I was afraid you'd say that."

Ten

CASEY WINKED AT Lou as she unlocked Dad's front door with the key from the blue notebook. She pushed the door open and raised the pipe wrench, should her hunch about the thug's absence be wrong. The wrench wasn't much of a weapon, but it was better than nothing. She'd look for the tire iron she'd lost Tuesday night.

Standing on the threshold, Casey listened for sounds and peered around the door.

"Crap, look at this," she said, pulling Lou inside.

A dozen wooden crates, each packed with items wrapped in newspaper, sat in the foyer.

"These weren't here two days ago." Casey looked at the staircase and again listened to the quiet.

"Want to leave?" Lou whispered.

"No, but let's see if a red Jaguar's in the garage."

A minute later, they were staring at an empty garage.

"I'll show you the den," she said.

In the den, the bloodstained chair and carpet were still here, but everything else was gone except the phone. Was her attacker a professional thief who'd found an unoccupied home, or somebody listed in one of Dad's address books?

In the living room, she and Lou strolled between more sealed crates before venturing into the empty dining room. Back in the foyer, Casey smacked the wrench against a crate.

"All this packing in a day and a half?" Again, she looked at the staircase. "Someone's worked fast, or he had help."

"Any ideas who?" Lou asked.

"Theo Ziegler comes to mind. I called Lalonde, but he still hasn't been able to find him. Ziegler hasn't been following me that I could see, so I'm thinking he's been busy here."

"A thief and a killer?"

"Possibly. Lalonde wouldn't tell me what, if anything, they've dug up on him, so I did a little research on the net and found a website for a TZ Incorporated, based in Geneva. It's just a little one-page site, but it states that Ziegler's owner of a company that specializes in unique imports and exports. His is the only name on the site, along with a contact number."

"Which I assume you called?"

Casey smiled. "I talked to a woman who said he's out of town indefinitely. She wouldn't give me any info about the company and asked me to call back in a couple of weeks. Ziegler's either warned her to shut up or the police have already scared her off." She began rummaging through a crate. "When I left my name and number and asked that he call me, her voice went all squeaky, so I'm wondering if she knows the name Holland. It'll be interesting to see if Ziegler returns my call."

"Let's go upstairs." Lou looked at the staircase. "Want me to lead?"

"Since I dragged you here, that wouldn't be fair."

Casey took her time with each step, alert to the silence. At the top of the stairs, she looked over her shoulder and then scanned the area for intruders. She hadn't noticed the five doors in the dark the other night, or the wood paneling on the far wall. In daylight, the atrium was bright and cheerful. Lou wandered past a row of vibrantly colored plants.

"I knew your dad loved gardening," he said, "but why bring the whole yard inside?"

"It's not the whole yard; the grass is still out there."

Lou touched several flower petals. "Silk." He gazed at a half-dozen trees, most of them more than six feet high. "The trees are real. Red maple, purple leaf plum." He studied the tree at the far end of the room. "Japanese maple."

"Impressive."

"Remember the tree doctor I went out with?"

Casey remembered all of Lou's girlfriends. "She really liked you," although she'd been totally wrong for him.

"She dragged me through tons of parks and forests, very educational."

Casey spotted the tire iron in a corner, picked it up, and gave the weapon to Lou, "For your protection."

"Thanks," he said, as he looked around, "but I don't think I'll need it."

She searched three rooms where more crates were sealed shut, closets emptied, and mattresses upended.

"Hey," Lou called from the room behind the stairs, "I found a pool table."

Casey stepped inside and watched him stroke the table's surface. "Must have been a new hobby." She gazed at the diagonal violet, mauve, and pink stripes on one wall. Not Dad's taste at all. "I'm not letting anyone take anything. I'll hire a security service and talk to the cops before we head back."

"Do you want to empty the crates?"

"No, I should be back on the M8 by lunch hour."

"I thought he doesn't normally strike at noon."

"I know, but a time pattern's emerging and it fits a high school student's schedule. I'm thinking our guy's a student and not a street kid like Stan thinks. So, I want to check out the schools on or near the M8's route." She headed out the door. "Let's take a peek at this last room."

In the northwest corner, above the living room, an enormous master bedroom—not yet packed—was flooded by natural light from the large skylight. On the king-sized bed lay half a dozen paintings and one pen-and-ink drawing, each partially covered with brown wrapping paper and a bill of sale.

"Simone told me that Dad's dealt in art, among other things." She studied the bills from Oregon and California. All were made out to TZ Inc. "They can't be stolen or the police would have confiscated them."

While Lou studied the artwork, she wandered to the French doors and out onto a balcony. From this height, she could see the shoreline and a strip of beach. She turned and stepped back inside.

The room would be packed up soon. One empty crate had been placed in front of the closet filled with casual wear and suits. When had Dad started wearing Armani? There was no sign of women's clothing, no trace of makeup or other female toiletries in the en suite bathroom.

Lou sat on the edge of the bed while Casey spotted two pewter-framed photographs on the night tables. She scowled at a familiar snapshot of Mother taken years ago; light blond hair curling onto her shoulders, sapphire necklace, royal-blue strapless gown. Mother was laughing, her head tilted, conveying coyness.

Hadn't Dad thrown the picture out the window after their final fight? From the dining room below her parents' bedroom, Casey had heard the whole thing. She'd learned about Mother's promiscuity only a few days before the final showdown and had come home from school to find them already shouting at each other. She'd watched Mother's possessions fall onto the patio, heard the picture's glass shatter. She'd seen Dad drag Mother downstairs and shove her outside. Casey never saw the photograph again. Why had he kept it? Dad always believed that once hurt, there was no going back for more.

"Is that your mom?"

Lou's voice jolted her to the present. "Biologically speaking; people used to say she was a cross between Marilyn Monroe and Grace Kelly." Casey watched him pick up the picture. "Who do you think she looks like?"

"She looks like you."

"No way."

"Same smile, same violet eyes, and I know you color your hair brown."

"Doesn't matter; we have totally different body types."

"Maybe your mother doesn't share your love of cheeseburgers."

"Funny, Lou."

"Did you hear back from her yet?"

"Yeah, she emailed and said Dad's importing business was a long story and that I should phone her. She didn't even bother to answer my question about why she wanted to claim Dad's body."

"How about the other names? Any luck with them?"

"I got a few emails from people who claim not to have heard from him in over three years. I'll try more numbers and emails later today."

Casey picked up the second photo, this one of a pretty woman with short dark blond hair and dark eyes. She appeared to be in her mid twenties. Casey removed the picture from the frame and flipped it over. No name or date.

She opened a drawer in the night table. Among the antacid tablets and nail clippers was another photo, face down. Casey picked it up and found herself looking at her own wedding portrait. Dad must have heard about the divorce. She dumped the picture back into the drawer.

"What was that?" Lou asked.

"Nothing."

She focused on the letter-sized pen-and-ink drawing Lou was holding. The artist had created an incredibly detailed picture of a cove occupied by sailboats and motor boats. On the bottom right corner, a delicate hand had written "F.H.T. Mason, October 1982."

"Your mom collects pen-and-inks," Casey said. "Think she'd like it?"

"Hell, yeah."

"Then take it."

He looked at her. "No, it's too valuable."

"Lou, none of this has any value for me. All of this stuff belonged to a part of Dad's life that I was excluded from, so please give it to Barb on her next birthday or for Christmas or whatever."

Lou shook his head.

"Look, someone's stealing everything anyway, and while this stuff doesn't hold any value for me, it doesn't seem right that someone else is taking it either."

"Okay, well, then thanks, I appreciate it," though he still looked uncertain. "Are you sure you don't want anything? There's a cool glass statue on the bureau."

Casey gazed at the gorgeous sculpture of a leaping dolphin. Exquisite as it was, she sure as hell didn't like what the piece represented, nor was she interested in profiting from Dad's other life.

"Got any plans after work?" Lou asked.

"Actually, I've arranged to see Dad's friend and colleague, Vincent Wilkes. It should be interesting."

Eleven

CASEY STARED AT the bungalow that had once been Dad's office. The patch of soft green lawn she used to play on was now a rock garden. The picket fence was still here, though no longer green but cobalt blue to match the door. The cedar-shingle siding on the upper two-thirds of the cottage was a darker gray than she remembered; the river rock on the lower third also looked darker. Curtains had been exchanged for shutters.

Casey had thought about asking to meet Vincent at a neutral spot, and then decided she wanted to see this place again. Vincent had worked with Dad for as long as she could remember, yet Casey hadn't known him well. The guy had kept to himself and preferred to work at night.

Casey swung open the gate and strolled to the door. The Please Walk In sign had been exchanged for an alarm system. Beneath the alarm was an intercom. Seconds passed before a pensive voice answered the buzzer. "Hello?"

"Hi, Vincent, it's Casey."

"Come in."

As she stepped inside, hot dry air filled her lungs. Why did Vincent have the heat up on such a warm spring day? She slipped off her jacket and glanced at what she remembered as Vincent's office door to her left. Dad's larger work area was across the hall. In the early days, Mother would bring her here when Rhonda couldn't babysit. In a corner of Dad's room, she'd had her own red table and chair, crayons and toys.

The door to Dad's old room opened and Vincent stepped out. "Good to see you again, Casey."

"You too." She tried not to look shocked at how much he had aged in three years. His hair was white and his eyes were enveloped in creases, and his hand felt frail and scratchy when she shook it, like crinkled paper that had been flattened out. "Thanks for seeing me this late on a Friday afternoon."

"No problem. I'm always here."

Casey followed Vincent into the room where the somber sound of a Gregorian chant played. They sat in a couple of easy chairs at the far end of the room.

"So, you moved into the big room," she said. "Good plan."

"I use both."

She sat next to a large, glass tank containing sand, rocks, and thick, leafless branches. A reptile crawled out from behind a branch and she jumped up. "What the hell is that?"

"A Western skink."

"Skink?"

"It's a lizard. He's known for his slender body and bright blue tail."

Casey studied the creature. At the top of its tank, a heat lamp was attached to a wire mesh cover. She glanced at the terrariums beside the skink's home, afraid to look too closely. All of them had heat lamps.

"So, Vincent, this decor is new." Casey hoped she sounded more relaxed than she felt. "How many lizards to do you have?"

"Two dozen; reptiles are less complex than people, and easier to live with. I use the office across the hall for clients who aren't comfortable near them."

Good lord, weren't there laws about this? She pushed up her sleeves, realizing why it was so warm. "What made you keep them here?"

"This is my home now. I had to give up my condo to keep the business going."

"I take it things haven't been easy?"

"No."

Given Vincent's pets, musical taste, and this god-awful heat, Casey wasn't surprised.

"There's a little profit coming in now." He glanced at his clasped hands. "I work six and a half days a week, when I can manage it. Even have a part-time employee. And I like working with this menagerie close by." Vincent smiled. "If I don't like someone, I can bring out Sydney."

"Sydney?"

"My papa iguana; he's a beauty. Just don't wear a hat when you're around him. Sydney hates hats."

Casey glanced at the closed door while another Gregorian chant began to play, this one even more somber than the last.

"Aside from the bizarre news about Marcus," he said, "how's life been treating you?"

Casey briefly described her breakup with Greg and her residency at Rhonda's place. When she switched to the subject of Dad, Vincent's gaze shifted to the terrariums.

"I don't know what to say about all this. It's unbelievable." Vincent adjusted a strap on the sandals Casey had always seen him wearing. "You want some coffee? The pot should be ready."

"That'd be great, thanks." On second thought, she wasn't sure she wanted to be left alone in lizard-land.

Vincent pushed himself up from the chair, as if the gesture required effort. Dad once told her that Vincent had health problems, but she couldn't recall the details. As he left the room, Casey listened to a depressing music for ten long seconds before she sought a distraction. Cautiously, she approached the terrarium next to the skink and peered through the glass.

The creature inside looked like a tiny dinosaur. About twenty-five inches long, its squat body was covered in spines. Horns projected back from a fringe behind its head. The beast's brownish yellow body blended fairly well with the sand.

Casey strolled toward Vincent's desk, where small terrariums sat on shelves behind his chair. Terrain inside the tanks varied from rocky deserts to miniature forests and jungles. All of the cages had water dishes, boxes, and makeshift hiding spots. Many had bowls of fresh vegetables. She looked tentatively through the nearest glass and spotted five bright green baby iguanas. Okay, these creatures weren't so bad. The lizards with brownish bands on their backs in the next tank were even smaller.

Casey started toward the cages under the window at the front of the house when she noticed a cane propped against a chair. Then she remembered. Vincent had multiple sclerosis, though he'd been in remission back then.

When he entered the room carrying a tray with the coffee things, she offered to help, but he turned her down.

"Who's the skink's neighbor?" she asked.

"A short-horned lizard that a friend and I caught with a pole and noose in Alberta." He placed the tray on a table between the chairs. "When Charlie's threatened, he ruptures a blood vessel in his eye and squirts blood as far as a six feet."

"Neat trick," and totally disgusting.

Vincent poured the coffee. "How's Rhonda? Still the world's greatest cook?"

"She's fine, and how do you know about her cooking skills?"

"She used to bring us picnic baskets filled with chicken and salads and wonderful strudels."

"I didn't know that." She accepted the mug he handed her.

"Rhonda hung around a lot waiting for Marcus that last year. A couple of times she showed up, thinking he'd returned from one of his business trips when he hadn't. She seemed lonely."

"Yeah, well, Dad was around less and less. Rhonda said he'd been on lots of business trips. In fact, the last time I saw him was that Christmas. Less than three months later I was arranging his funeral." She watched Vincent pour a packet of sugar in his coffee. "I know about his import/export business, Vincent. A woman named Simone Archambault told me. Do you know her?"

"The name's vaguely familiar."

"Simone implied you knew something about this business," she said, watching his mouth clamp shut, "and I need to know more."

"All I did was help Marcus with the bookkeeping now and then. You know how little patience he had for accounting."

"Was the business called TZ Incorporated?"

"Yes."

"Simone said his architectural practice wasn't doing well and that importing was helping him bring in extra cash."

"It did that." He sipped his coffee.

"How long had he had this sideline?"

"About fifteen years. By the end it wasn't a sideline, it was his whole life."

The stifling room was making her sweat. "Fifteen years? Are you kidding me?"

"Afraid not. The more money Marcus made through importing the less interested he was in acquiring new architecture clients or in even designing. He was always taking off somewhere, living the high life."

"I don't frigging believe this." Casey's thoughts were reeling. All that time without saying one bloody word to her. "What did he import?"

Vincent shrugged. "Nothing terribly exotic or illegal, that I know of. Mostly art, rare carpeting, artwork, unusual pieces of furniture, some of it antique."

"Then why did he keep it from me?"

"Truthfully, I think Marcus was embarrassed that his firm was failing; you know how proud he was. Also, for most of those years he was only a courier, a delivery person for someone else."

"Theo Ziegler?"

Vincent nodded. "How did you know?"

"A little research. The guy's been following me since the murder and the police want to talk to him." She watched his gaze drift to the terrariums again. "Do you know the man?"

"We've never met, but we spoke on the phone occasionally, which is also what I told the police."

"What do you know about him?"

"Just that he was Marcus's employer and later his partner. They were also good friends, though one day I overheard Marcus arguing on the phone with him about money. I knew it was Ziegler because Marcus called him by name."

"When was this?"

"About six months before he died, maybe longer." Vincent gazed into his mug. "I tried to convince Marcus to give up importing and return to architecture, but he brushed me off, said he'd sort things out."

Casey squirmed in the chair. She didn't like what she was hearing. "Vincent, how is my mother involved in all this?"

Vincent blinked at her a couple of times. "Have you been in touch with Lillian?"

"I emailed her and then she phoned me back. To hear Mother's voice after all these years was surreal and awkward. When I told her about Ziegler she kind of freaked out and said I should leave town immediately. She asked me to meet her in Paris and she'd explain everything. She also said she knew about the import business, but wouldn't say how until I saw her in person." Casey watched him. "What I'm looking for, Vincent, is a heads-up about what's really going on."

Vincent sipped his coffee slowly. "Why Paris?"

"Probably because it's one of two places Dad apparently went to most, at least that's where the postcards and occasional phone call came from. Anyway, I want to talk to medical staff who'd tried to help him, and Mother's already planned a visit with friends there."

"When are you leaving?"

"As soon as the travel agent can book a flight to England, which is my first stop. That reminds me, do you know a man named Daphne Reid?"

"He was one of Marcus's regular clients."

"I spoke with him last night. He knew about the murder because the police had contacted him, but he played dumb with them because he didn't want to get involved, or so he said. Reid claims to have a pretty good idea about who killed Dad, but he said he wouldn't tell me more until he got something in exchange."

Vincent nodded. "Marcus had said more than once that Reid was a bit of a weasel."

"Dad was supposed to have delivered a pen-and-ink drawing to Reid this week, and now Reid's pissed because he has a buyer willing to pay double what TZ Inc. paid. I found the drawing in the West Van house, so I'm taking it to him in exchange for information."

She'd been embarrassed to ask Lou for the drawing back, but if he was really as relieved as he'd sounded, he was fine with it. Happily, he hadn't told his mother about the drawing.

"I asked Mother if she knew Reid, and she said only by his greedy reputation." Casey added, "But based on everything she's heard, he's not violent, just stupid."

She didn't mention that Mother had suggested accompanying her to meet Reid, but Casey wasn't ready to deal with both of them at once. She still wasn't sure she wanted to see Mother after all this time, especially when Mother had been so evasive about her reason for being in Geneva and about what she knew about TZ Inc.

"So, Vincent, what's the deal with Mother? Is she somehow involved in the import business? After all, she knows Ziegler."

Vincent's expression was about as cheerful as the Gregorian chant. "Wouldn't it be better if she told you herself?"

"Mother exceled at leaving out key bits of info, and obviously, she's still at it. But she's family, Vincent. If Dad was murdered because of the import/export thing and Mother's involved, couldn't she be in danger too? Maybe that's why she left town right after the murder. So, please tell me everything you know."

Vincent stared off into space. "When you were little, Lillian was our record keeper. The firm was struggling, so she brought in extra money by helping clients furnish the homes Marcus designed." A flicker of blue drew his eye to the tank beside her. "Lillian had a talent for interior design and for finding the right art and fabrics, and for networking, which was how she met Theo Ziegler. Ziegler put Lillian in touch with people who could supply whatever she needed. He also helped eliminate red tape."

"When did she meet him?"

Vincent shifted in his chair. "About twenty years ago."

Casey put her coffee down and sat forward. "Twenty years?"

Vincent nodded. "When Ziegler's business grew, he hired your mother to deliver goods, pick up checks, that sort of thing. Ziegler's business kept growing while Marcus's firm went further into debt, so Lillian got him some courier work. It was supposed to be temporary, but the more Marcus learned about the business, the more fascinated he became. Then five years ago, Ziegler offered him a partnership."

"So you ran the firm while Dad played importer? And was Mother a courier all that time?" Casey shook her head.

"Yes, but she also established her own personnel business. After the divorce your parents rarely saw each other."

"I tried calling Dad's lawyer to see who legally owns the West Vancouver house and contents now, but he's not listed in the phone book."

"The man was this firm's lawyer, too, and he died months ago." Vincent watched the skink. "Marcus's will was drawn up five years before the botulism tragedy. Maybe he never had it changed, which means you'll inherit everything." He shook his head and stood, wincing slightly. "I didn't know Marcus had left the business to me until the lawyer called."

"Dad wouldn't have given the firm to someone he didn't trust." Casey followed him to the other end of the room and watched him ease into a chair behind the desk. She wandered past the desk toward the cages beneath the picture window. "Aside from Paris and Geneva, it seems that Dad also spent a fair amount of time in Amsterdam. Does the name Gislinde Van Akker mean anything to you? I have an address for this person, but no other information."

"It could be a client, but I don't really recall."

It took a moment before Casey realized she was gazing at a boa constrictor coiled against the glass. She jumped back.

"None of them are venomous," Vincent said, and smiled.

"Good," but hardly comforting. She sought refuge in the chair in front of his desk. "Did you ever hear the name Gustaf Osterman?"

"Lillian mentioned him a couple of times. I remember her referring to him as the chameleon, though I don't know why."

"What else did she say about him?"

"Nothing, really. But her eyes shone whenever she mentioned him, like she was in love."

Casey doubted it. Mother hadn't loved any of her conquests. Casey had told Mother that she'd hoped to find Osterman in Paris, but all Mother said was that they'd talk later.

"Did the police ask you for a list of Dad's contacts and clients?"

"They came and took Marcus's Rolodex and all the old ledgers we kept on TZ Inc."

"I imagine they would." Casey stood and retrieved her jacket. "If I learn anything useful, I'll let you know."

"All I really want to know is why Marcus faked his death and went underground," Vincent said.

"You and me both." She stopped at the door, "If Dad had come back to reclaim his old life, what would have happened?"

"I don't know." Vincent looked at her. "But I'm too busy and too tired to lose sleep over it."

Maybe it was the creepy reptiles. Maybe it was the disturbing chants or simply the lighting, but she thought Vincent's eyes had adopted a cold-blooded stare and his complexion turned a pale shade of green. Casey hurried out of the room.

Twelve

CASEY STUDIED THE half-filled suitcase on her bed. She was thinking about what else to bring when a knock on the door broke her concentration. Before she could move, Rhonda was marching toward her bedroom. Lately, she'd been entering Casey's suite uninvited, as if Dad's murder had somehow granted her the right. Casey wanted to remind her that, technically, she was a tenant, not family, but that line had been crossed long ago. Even family members had a right to privacy, though.

"Summer's upset about your trip," Rhonda said.

"Why? She knows I'll only be gone two weeks."

"Marcus went to Europe and didn't come back. Summer sees it as a place where bad things can happen."

Hard to argue the point, since Casey had her own doubts about leaving. Dad's life had been all about secrets. If he'd died because of those secrets, her questions could cause big trouble. And as for trepidation about seeing Mother again after all these years, lord, she didn't even know how to express it. She hadn't told Rhonda they'd be meeting and she hadn't discussed Rhonda with Mother; didn't want to go there when there were more urgent questions on her mind.

"I still don't understand why you have to trek all over Europe looking for answers," Rhonda said.

"It's just three or four places over a two-week period. I'll be home before you know it."

"Hasn't your passport expired? You've had it a while, right?"

"Only three and a half years, from when I planned to join Dad in Amsterdam the Christmas before he die—disappeared, remember?"

Rhonda nodded. "What does your supervisor say about all this?"

"He's okay with it because Marie can cover for me. Besides, I did a little investigating and figured out what high school the purse thief probably attends, so Stan's happy."

"Are you sure the thief's a student?"

"Yep. I compiled a chart that showed the times he strikes, and the pattern definitely fits someone who has to be in class by eight thirty-five, takes lunch between twelve and one, and is out by three."

The kid was becoming more predictable all the time. As much as Casey wanted to bust the kid herself, Marie hadn't made many arrests lately and deserved a chance. Of course, if she succeeded, everyone at Mainland would hear about it for weeks. Still, it couldn't be helped. When it came to family history research, no one was going to do this for Casey, and the sooner she pursued leads before they vanished, the sooner she'd have answers.

"Do you want me to talk to Summer?" Casey asked.

"That would be good. And have you returned Lalonde's call yet? Does he know you're going away?"

"No on both counts, but I'll contact him once I'm there," especially if Daphne Reid had useful information about the killer's identity.

"Mom?" Summer called from the doorway. "Someone's on the phone for you."

"Be right there." She turned to Casey. "Call every two or three days or I won't be able to sleep, okay?"

"I'll try, I promise."

Rhonda left as Summer entered the room.

"How's the new bicycle tire?"

"Great, Darcy and I went riding yesterday. It was fun."

"Oh? I didn't see you guys go out."

"It was after supper. You and Lou had already left for the hockey game."

In the few days he'd been living here, Darcy had hovered around Summer and Rhonda a lot. He'd also come up here uninvited to chat a few times, which had gotten irritating so she'd cut their conversations short.

Casey shoved her underwear in the suitcase. "I gather his knee's healed?"

"Uh-huh. He's coming to swim practice with us tonight."

Man, didn't this guy have a life?

"What's wrong?" Summer asked. "You look kind of weird."

"I'm just a bit nervous about my trip. Which reminds me, your mom says you're upset that I'm going."

"No, I'm not, she is. I mean, it's not like you'll be gone a long time." Summer picked up a folded T-shirt. "You wanna go?"

"Yes and no. I'll miss you guys."

She gave Summer a hug, then fetched the blue notebook, tossing the loose slip of paper containing the doodles and Marine Drive address in a drawer. She'd already given Rhonda a copy of contact info for the few people she'd managed to get in touch with.

"Hello? Anyone home?" Darcy's raspy voice called out.

Too bad Rhonda had become more adept at opening doors than closing them.

"We're in here," Summer called back.

As Darcy entered the bedroom, he winked at Summer then turned to Casey. "Sorry to interrupt, but I just wanted to say bye before you left."

Rhonda thought his raspy voice sounded seductive. Casey couldn't stand it. "Thanks."

"I'll pack some peanut-butter cookies for you," Summer said.

"That'd be awesome. And if I don't get a chance to say this later, look after your mom, okay? I know you'll do a good job."

Summer grinned. "Three more months till I get a puppy."

When Rhonda came down with the flu last December, Summer did a lot of cooking and cleaning. Rhonda had said if she was still acting responsibly by her birthday, she could have a dog.

After Summer left, Darcy said, "Rhonda really depends on you, doesn't she?"

"We've known each other a long time."

"I think all this family stuff you've been going through is getting to her. She talks about your mother a lot, claims the lady came from a family of greedy criminals."

Crap, why had Rhonda brought that up? Casey stuffed socks into corners of the suitcase.

"Glad to hear of no criminal streak in you," he added. "Know what I'm saying?"

"Not really." What was his point? "If you'll excuse me, I need to finish packing." She shoved her red pumps in a plastic bag.

"I hope you find what you're looking for in Europe."

Had Rhonda told him about the murder too?

"I never knew my dad," Darcy went on. "He took off when I was little."

Question answered. Damn.

"Casey?" Summer called from the stairwell. "Lou's pulling up."

"Okay, I'll be right down."

"But then, I guess no one really knows anybody," Darcy went on.

"Not true." Casey looked at him. "Some people can see right through others."

His unblinking eyes gazed at her through blue-tinted lenses. "Yeah, sure," he said, chuckling on his way out the door.

Five minutes later, Casey carried her luggage downstairs and heard Summer chatting in the living room. She poked her head inside to find Lou listening to Summer complain about one of her swim practices. Casey gazed at the appliquéd picture above the fire place. Dad had bought the piece for Rhonda at a craft show. The variety of stitching, thread, fabric, and wool had produced an astounding portrait of what Rhonda called her "Glamor Ladies." In the scene, two well-dressed women stood at a bar. Both had their backs to the viewer, but one of them was looking at a man standing at the end of the bar. Casey wasn't sure whether it was the color and texture or the image that was so provocative, but the picture always captured her attention.

When Summer finished talking, Lou noticed Casey and stood, "Ready to go?"

"As soon as I get the cookies Summer promised."

"Oh, yeah." Summer hurried out of the room.

Lou's expression grew serious. "So, this is really happening?"

"Yes."

He nodded. "Europe can be pretty lonely if you're on your own."

He would know. Right after she and Greg got married, Lou back-packed around Europe for six months.

"Wish I could go with you," he added, "but I used all my holidays."

Casey squeezed his arm. "You're a good friend."

"Ditto, so you'll understand when I say that going alone is a bad idea."

"Yeah, I understand." She studied him a few moments. "Remember the part in *The African Queen*, when Bogart had to get into the water to move his boat? And when he climbed out, there were leeches all over him?"

"Are you saying you want me here in the swamp?"

"I'm saying I might need your help getting the leeches off me when I come home."

He attempted a smile. "I can do that."

"And I have another favor to ask."

"Anything."

Casey gripped his hand. In all the years she'd known this man, Lou had never let her down. Maybe Rhonda was right. Maybe she should give romance another chance, but with her best friend? She couldn't stand the thought of losing him if things didn't work out.

"Could you look in on Rhonda and Summer while I'm gone? Hang out with them maybe?"

"Are you worried about them?"

"Kind of. The new tenant's been hovering around them since he's been here," she whispered, "ingratiating himself in their lives, and I'm getting a bad vibe. Darcy needs to know that someone else watches out for them besides me."

Lou's jaw tightened. "I want to meet this guy."

"Not now, okay? I've got to be at the airport in thirty minutes. But could you stay at my place some nights and make your presence known?" She picked up her luggage and ushered Lou toward the kitchen. "Rhonda would love to cook for you."

"No problem, I'll be in the guy's face."

As they entered the kitchen, Summer handed Casey the cookie bag and Rhonda hung up the phone.

"Summer, how about you help Lou take my things to the truck? I need to talk to your mom a second."

"Sure."

When they were out of earshot, Casey said, "Lou's going to stay at my place some nights—thought you might like the extra company."

"Sure." She picked up a dishcloth. "You know, I've been thinking that Marcus might have been planning on coming back to us."

Good god. Where had that come from?

"That's why he stayed in Vancouver," Rhonda added. "He was waiting for his chance, only somebody didn't want him returning to his old life so he, or she, killed him."

Interesting theory, but Casey didn't buy it.

"I can read your face," Rhonda said. "You think I'm wrong."

"I'd rather deal in facts."

"You think Marcus didn't love me enough to want to come back, don't you?"

"I don't think that at all."

But given that Dad had been away so much during that last year, Casey had wondered if his love for Rhonda was as strong as Rhonda believed. They'd been friends since before Casey was born and grew closer after Dad threw Mother out. Rhonda had been the one to ask Dad out on an official date, and she was the one who'd proposed. Rhonda had described how they'd been having the time of their lives at a restaurant, eating lobster, drinking champagne, and before she knew it she'd popped the question. She didn't have a ring, so she gave Dad her copper bracelet, but Casey hadn't seen Dad wear it often.

"Rhonda, I should get go—"

"God, sometimes you're so much like Lillian."

What the hell was bringing all this on? Rhonda knew comparisons to Mother infuriated her because they were partly true. Hard as Casey tried, certain traits couldn't be banished. There was a big difference, though, between manipulating situations to expose truths and manipulating situations to hide them.

"Come outside." Casey stepped onto the back porch and glanced at the kitchen to make sure Darcy wasn't nearby. "Darcy sure seems attracted to you."

Rhonda grinned. "I don't know why a young stud would waste time on a pudgy middle-aged divorcée, but I'm enjoying the attention."

"He seems to spend a fair amount of time with Summer too." Casey glanced over her shoulder. "Doesn't the guy have anything better to do?"

"Not that I know of, but I went through his stuff yesterday, just to make sure there's nothing kinky or weird about him."

Casey's mouth fell open.

"Don't look so shocked. You know I'd do anything to protect my daughter, and his references could have been bogus. Anyhow, I didn't find any porn magazines, and he doesn't own a computer." She glanced over Casey's shoulder and then lowered her voice further. "I know none of this proves he's the picture of innocence, but I'm watching him as closely as he watches me."

"Do you think he's up to something?"

"Maybe cheap rent and sex," she shrugged. "He's on his cell phone a lot, but I have no idea who he talks to. Darcy never mentions family or friends."

Rhonda had been known to eavesdrop from time to time. Casey suspected this was why she had no long-term tenants. How many other tenants had had their suites searched?

"Don't worry, Casey, I'll keep an eye on him. Maybe learn more through some pillow talk, and let me tell you, I'm looking forward to the research."

"Not a great plan, Rhonda."

"I know what I'm doing, sweetie. I'm not a total fool."

"True." But she had her gullible moments. "I should go."

Rhonda reached for her arm. "Stay safe, and don't forget to call."

Casey gave her a big hug. "I will."

She hurried down the steps and into Lou's pickup. As Lou pulled away, she looked back at the house. Darcy had joined Rhonda and Summer on the porch. As mother and daughter waved, Darcy stood between them, arms around their waists, and a smile on his face.

Thirteen

TO KILL TIME on the airplane, Casey had read about the barren, open spaces of England's North Yorkshire County. Much had been written about the crimson and purple foliage of the moors in autumn, but the brilliant spring greens she saw in and around the village of Goathland were breathtaking.

At the tiny train station, one of the locals told Casey she could arrange for a taxi at the pub up the road. She'd found the village cabby starting his lunch and had agreed to meet him in a half hour.

As she strolled through the village, past open fields and toward the moor, the afternoon sunlight made the fields almost glow. It was a sharp contrast to the stone fences and brown stone houses. Casey had never been in a village where there were more sheep than human beings, and these animals acted like they owned the place. Two strutted down the road. Some grazed in cottage yards while others rested in the fields. Still, this was a beautiful spot, evidently known for its hiking trails.

Once sitting inside the taxi, Casey grew more apprehensive about meeting people from Dad's other life. Her anxiety grew as they approached an H-shaped hotel in a shallow valley. The building was protected on two sides by enormous oak and beech trees. The walls were streaked with soot. Blinds covered most of the windows as if to indicate that neither light or visitors were welcome.

"This is a rather isolated site for a hotel, isn't it?"

"It's full up in summer with ramblers," the driver answered. "There are also the permanent lodgers."

He parked in front of double wooden doors at the center of the building, then retrieved Casey's luggage. A bald, pale man looked at her through a window pane near the door. A moment later he was gone.

The hotel lobby displayed a scruffy collection of wing chairs, gouged tabletops, and faded paintings of fox hunts. Casey told the young desk clerk she was here to meet Daphne Reid and asked for directions to the gift shop he managed.

"Go out the main doors and down the side of the building," she said.

"Thanks."

Ten minutes later, Casey had dumped her things in her drab and chilly, second-floor room and was heading outside. She strolled around the side of the building and walked past a giant checkerboard embedded in the spacious lawn. Wet leaves were scattered over the squares, a soggy paper bag marooned in a puddle. It must have rained heavily last night.

The gift shop was locked, a Closed sign propped between a collection of dolls and music boxes in the form of tiny, thatched-roof cottages. Peeking through the window, she saw a room that looked more like an art gallery than a gift shop. Unframed canvases filled the walls. More were stacked against shelves.

Casey turned and spotted a man kneeling in front of a flower bed. The gardener pulled out a weed, wiped his hands, and then repeated the process. Stepping closer, she recognized the same bald head she'd seen in the window.

"Excuse me," Casey said. "Sorry to bother you, but could you tell me where Daphne Reid is? The gift shop's closed."

He looked around and then pointed at a man and woman approaching a tall thick hedge on the far side of the lawn. "That's him, heading into the maze."

Casey jogged across the yard and caught up to Reid as he was kissing the woman. "Sorry to interrupt," she said as the couple turned to her, "but I'm Casey Holland and we spoke on the phone about my dad, Marcus."

"Right." He gave the woman a tap on her rear. "Off you go."

The woman, who looked about seventeen, glared at Casey as she marched back toward the hotel.

"So, where's my drawing, luv?"

"In my hotel room."

He smirked. "Let's have a look then, shall we?"

"Can't we talk first?"

"Not until I make sure you brought the right drawing. Let's go to your room."

Casey sighed. The jerk was already trying her patience. "You'll get your picture, Mr. Reid, provided I get the information I need."

His smirk turned to a sneer as he removed a pen knife from pants pocket. "You think you can order me about?"

Casey backed up. "Hey, I'm not looking for trouble."

As Reid looked past her shoulder his sneer vanished. A moment later he was running into the maze, chased by a man with a black ponytail who ran past Casey. Holy crap, what in hell was Theo Ziegler doing here? She'd come too far to let Reid disappear, and since she wanted answers from Ziegler too, Casey started after both them. She hadn't gone far before she saw Reid slip on the mud and fall. The knife disappeared in the hedge.

It took only three seconds before Ziegler had him pinned to the ground. Reid grunted and tried to scramble away, but the mud was too slippery. Twisting his upper body, Reid took a swipe at his opponent and missed. Ziegler forced Reid face down in the mud, but let him turn his head as Ziegler sat on Reid's back, holding his wrists together.

"What do you want to do with him?" Ziegler asked.

His long, black eyes under neatly shaped brows reminded Casey of characters from ancient Egyptian art.

"Get some answers." Casey came closer. "Why did you take off when you saw this man, Mr. Reid?"

Reid gasped for air. "He's a mate of yours, isn't he? That's why he came after me."

"Then you've never seen him before?" She glanced at Ziegler who returned an amused expression.

"No."

Strange. Dad and Ziegler had either kept their client lists quite separate or Reid was lying.

Reid squirmed under Ziegler's weight. "Tell your mate to bugger off."

Ziegler yanked his arms upward. "You're not the one in charge, so why don't you tell the lady if you killed her father." He looked at Casey. "It's what she came to find out, isn't—?"

"What? No! I didn't kill Marcus. W-who said I did?" Reid stammered. When he tried to throw Ziegler off, Ziegler pushed his face into the mud once again and yanked Reid's head back by his hair.

"Can you prove you weren't in Vancouver on Sunday, April twenty-fifth?" Casey asked.

"I was in London that night, at a gallery opening in Chelsea." He gave her the name.

"You said you have an idea about who killed my father," she said. "Let's hear it."

"Marcus's partner, Theodore Ziegler."

Casey watched Ziegler's amusement fade. "Why do you think that?"

"There have been rumors about big money problems between them for years. Latest one is that Marcus stashed three million American dollars that was supposed to go to TZ Inc. It wouldn't surprise me if Ziegler ended things for good."

"Are there any facts to back up these stories?"

"If you don't believe me, talk to his fiancée. She'll know."

"Fiancée?" What did Rhonda have to do with this?

"Lives in Amsterdam; name's Gislinde."

Oh, no. "You've met her?"

"No, but Marcus and I had a few drinks last time he was here, and he told me what a fancy bit she is. There were problems between them, mind you; something about his past with other women. Maybe she killed him."

Casey looked at Ziegler. "Let him up."

Ziegler took his time doing so.

"I still want my drawing," he said, as he tried to wipe the mud from his face.

"I'll get it after you open the gift shop. I want to buy a souvenir."

"Bloody tourist." He stomped off, cursing and muttering to himself.

Not wanting to be left alone with a possible killer, Casey followed close behind. She walked fast, her muscles tense and her body ready to bolt. Ziegler stayed close behind, but said nothing. As they crossed the lawn, Casey noticed that the gardener was still working and other people were wandering around in the afternoon sunshine. At least there was safety in numbers.

At the gift shop, Daphne unlocked the door and went inside, but Casey stayed near the cluster of people window shopping. She studied Ziegler, who, apparently oblivious to the mud on his clothes, looked at her chest, then up at her face. The black jumpsuit with gold zippers across his chest, thighs, and arms was a bit flashy and kind of weird for a businessman.

"You took a big risk confronting Reid," he said.

"I didn't see the knife until he flashed it at me, and I've had run-ins with bigger guys. Bigger knives, too." Casey crossed her arms. "Why have you been following me?"

"I needed to know if you were being watched by some nasty clients of Marcus's, which you were. I'm here now, as I was in Vancouver, to protect you."

Not the answer she'd expected. "If the clients are that bad, why didn't you tell the police? They've been trying to talk to you about Dad's murder from day one."

"They would have probed into my affairs, so I thought it'd be better to approach you over here, away from prying eyes."

Casey stepped back, "Pretty convenient, Mr. .Ziegler."

"Call me Theo. And for the record, I didn't kill Marcus."

"Can you prove that?"

"I expected you to ask, so I brought these." Ziegler reached in a pocket and pulled out an airplane boarding pass and ticket, which he handed to her. "I was flying to Vancouver that night. We didn't touch down until ten-fifteen."

The pass and ticket looked legitimate. Still, she'd have Lalonde check it out. "Why did you take off so fast from my house that Monday night? You must have seen me approach your car."

"Yes, but I spotted the clients up ahead and went after them."

Another convenience. "Who are they?"

"A couple of Mexican businessmen only known as Carlos and

Joseph, and no, I don't have proof of their existence, although I've been trying to find it."

Casey noticed that the window shoppers were wandering into the gift shop. "Is Reid's story about the stolen money true?"

"No. The truth is that a little over three years ago, one of Marcus's more complicated deals with these Mexicans fell through and they wanted their fee back, but Marcus said he'd fulfilled his part of the bargain. The clients threatened to kill him, so he went underground."

"How much was the fee?"

"Three million in cash."

God, what type of importing had Dad been into? "What was the bargain?"

"I don't know; the clients demanded secrecy."

"But if it was complicated and worth that much money, wouldn't he have told you?"

Theo scanned the grounds, glancing at the gardener. "We had separate client lists and most of them insisted on privacy, so we only shared information when necessary. Marcus thought it'd be better if I didn't know about the arrangement, which proved to be a good plan because Carlos and Joseph came after me at one point. It took a hell of a lot of convincing to get them off my back."

Casey wondered, again, what else TZ Inc. imported and exported besides art, furniture, and unique tarot cards.

"Marcus would have had a detailed record of the transaction somewhere," Theo said, "and he kept contact information on everyone, but my staff and I couldn't find anything at the Geneva office he shared with us." Theo watched her. "You wouldn't have come across these names, by any chance? They could be on a memory stick or a computer printout or a Rolodex, or in an agenda book. He always carried one."

"No, I haven't." If Dad had wanted Theo to have the book, he would have left it with him and not Simone Archambault.

"Casey, my sources tell me that Joseph and Carlos discovered Marcus was still alive a few weeks ago. Since you're his heir, I'm afraid they'll come after you for the money."

"What makes them think it's still around, especially when Dad owned an expensive home and car?"

"For reasons I never understood, Marcus kept the cash from this business arrangement hidden away."

That sounded a bit strange. "Where did the money for the house and car come from?"

"We had some profitable years." Theo's large brown eyes softened. "Marcus once told me that he wasn't around for you as much as he thought he should have been. I think he built that house as a gift for you. I believe he planned to move to Amsterdam permanently."

Casey shook her head. Damn it, the house should have been for Rhonda.

Theo said, "Can you think of any place Marcus might have hidden a couple of suitcases or duffel bags full of cash? Some place only you'd know?"

"Not offhand." Even if she could, she wouldn't tell him. Maybe Theo wasn't a killer, but she sure as hell didn't trust him. "Wouldn't the money be in a bank?"

"From what I heard about the Mexicans' connections, they would have tracked it down by now. These guys are ruthless, Casey. That's why Marcus couldn't contact you. He was afraid Joseph and Carlos would use you to get to him, but I can protect you."

"Why would you care? Wasn't your partnership with Dad ending?"

"Reid got that wrong too."

Casey wandered toward the gift shop entrance. "Did this Gislinde woman and Dad have problems like Reid implied?"

"I have no idea, I rarely saw either of them."

"Maybe Dad left the money with her."

"She told me that they'd paid her a visit, which is why she now has a bodyguard."

"What's she like?"

"Young, naïve, and quite self-absorbed with her own little fantasy world."

"Does she know about the murder?"

"Don't know; I haven't told her."

"I will."

Theo looked at her. "You're not leaving for Amsterdam right away, are you?"

"No, I've had enough traveling for one day."

"Can I buy you dinner tonight? I know a sensational Italian restaurant not far from here."

"Thanks, but I don't think so." She thought of Mother's warning to stay away from him. Besides, she'd planned some sightseeing in the seaside town of Whitby. "And thanks for your help with Reid, but, if you'll excuse me, I have some souvenirs to buy." And phone calls to make. With that, she disappeared inside the shop.

As the bus ambled along the road to Whitby beneath a sky dotted with clouds, Casey watched shadows spill over the moor. The shapes looked like people hovering in the distance, but after a second look they disappeared, only to reappear farther along the road like ghostly hitchhikers slipping in and out of the earth.

Because of the time difference, she hadn't been able to get hold of Detective Lalonde, so she left a message with the West Vancouver Police Department about Ziegler's presence here and his alleged alibi. Since she hadn't brought her cell phone on this trip, she left the hotel's number.

A second phone call to Mother in Geneva had eased her mind a little. It seemed that Mother had done her own research and confirmed that Theo had been on that flight and therefore couldn't have killed Dad, which was why she hadn't freaked out when Casey told her he was here in England. Even if he wasn't a killer, there were still trust issues. "Don't spend too much time with him," she'd warned. "The man's a chronic liar and a manipulator." Mother would know, having mastered those skills herself.

When the bus stopped at the harbor, Casey stepped down. She'd walked two blocks before Ziegler approached her, this time in a sport jacket and white shirt. Oh, hell.

"Please have dinner with me. I promise I'm not up to anything sordid," he said. "I hate eating alone and I know a great Italian restaurant only a block from here. It's a busy, very public place, and I'll even pay a taxi to take you back to the hotel, so you won't have to be alone with me, okay?"

Well, she was hungry, and she doubted the guy would take no for an answer, anyway. "All right, but you don't have to pay, and how do you know there's a good Italian restaurant down the road?"

"I spent several summers in Yorkshire. My father's parents are from these parts."

As they walked, she said, "Where's your mother's family from?"

"Everywhere. My heritage encompasses three continents and half a dozen cultures."

He did all right by them. "Are you married, Theo?" Not that she cared, but acting casual and friendly might get him to open up about a few things.

"Part of me still likes to think so. I'm a widower. So, what are your plans after Amsterdam?"

"A trip to Paris. I want to see some people there, including a man named Gustaf Osterman who might have been a client of Dad's. Do you know the name, by any chance?"

The lashes on those long dark eyes flickered a moment. "He's a former employee, but we didn't part on the best of terms and I haven't seen him in years." Theo pointed the ruins of a building high on a cliff overlooking the North Sea. "There's Whitby Abbey. I'll take you to see it tomorrow, if you like."

"Sorry, but I'm leaving town early." No reason to tell him she'd be heading for London first to meet with a couple of Dad's clients she'd tracked down. "I've been wondering why Dad stayed in touch with his fiancée after he went underground? If these Mexicans were after him, wouldn't she have been in danger too?"

"Exactly. I told Marcus that if he wanted to make his death real, he'd need to break contact with his European friends, which he did, except for her. Gislinde's an interior designer who moves around with her work, so she hasn't had a fixed address in some time. Marcus thought they'd have trouble tracking her down, and I suppose he had people watching out for her as well. Anyhow, Marcus and I agreed that it'd be better if I knew as little as possible about his life, so we didn't communicate. His death had to seem genuine, particularly to his family and close friends."

Casey studied rows of buildings crammed against the lower slope of the hill on the east side of the city. "I take it you don't know the name of the man I buried?"

"No."

Theo opened a heavy oak door for Casey and ushered her into a candlelit room where a painting of a Venice canal and a golden sky covered one wall. The waiter hovered around them, his face beaming as he and Theo spoke Italian. An elderly couple emerged from the kitchen and embraced Theo. Grinning and nodding at Casey, they led her and Theo to a table with a view of the harbor. The waiter handed Casey a menu, and then draped a linen napkin over her lap.

After the couple and waiter left, Theo said, "Try the Filetto di Manzo Capricciosa. Beef medallions in brandy sauce, topped with crab meat and Edam cheese gratinée." After Theo studied the wine list, the waiter reappeared, took their orders, and left. Theo leaned forward and said, "I'd like to take you to Amsterdam."

"Thanks, but it's not necessary."

She doubted the guy was offering out of kindness. Vincent had overheard Dad argue with him about money, and Reid had confirmed the financial problems. Maybe Theo wanted the missing three million and a chance to get rid of the Mexican clients, if they really existed. She certainly hadn't noticed any Mexican men following her since the murder.

"Casey, the next stranger you approach about Marcus's murder could be carrying something more dangerous than a penknife. Why did you come to Europe in the first place? What do you hope to accomplish?"

"To learn more about a life that I knew nothing about." She paused. "To try and understand why he did what he did." Like become engaged to another woman without bothering to end things with

Rhonda. And to find out if he'd been involved in something criminal.

"I could introduce you to one or two contacts who might have kept in closer contact with Marcus than I did, though I have to say that Gustaf Osterman wouldn't be one of them. He's an anti-social man with somewhat of a mean streak, which was why I let him go." Theo nodded to the waiter who placed their appetizers in front of them. "Besides, I also speak French, Spanish, and German."

Casey slipped a mushroom cap in her mouth and clamped down. The hot food burned the roof of her mouth. Sucking in air, she reached for her water glass.

Theo grinned and sipped his wine.

"Did Dad ever mention the name Rhonda Stubbs to you?"

"Should he have?"

"She's my landlady, and she was also engaged to him."

The food about to reach Theo's lips wavered. "Is that why you want to meet Gislinde, to tell her that?"

"I'm not sure. Maybe I just need to know she's real." Casey shook her head. "Rhonda was betrayed by her first husband and best friend in a sleazy affair." No point in mentioning that the best friend was his part-time courier, Mother. "Then she lost her dad to cancer, her sister to a drug overdose, and finally Dad."

"Terrible." Theo slid the fork in his mouth. When he finished chewing, he said, "Tell me about your life."

She kept it brief. Every time Casey asked similar questions, he steered the questions back to her. By the time they were working on their entrées, she said, "Why won't you talk about Dad? There are some things I'd like to know about this importing venture of his."

"I'd rather get to know you and enjoy this meal."

After they'd finished, Theo ordered dessert for both of them: a meringue swan in a pond of chocolate with raspberry swirls.

"Sounds wonderful, but I'll have to pass," Casey said. "I'm allergic to chocolate."

"A few blemishes are worth the sweet, delicate taste of Mario's best dessert."

"It's not about my face."

She didn't want to explain the irritability that overtook her whenever she ate chocolate, though she loved the dark stuff.

"Just try the meringue and raspberry," he said. "It's fantastic."

Casey sat back. "You're almost as pushy as my ex-husband was. So, what else are you, Theo?"

"I'll help you find out over the next few days."

The waiter soon presented her with a meringue swan surrounded by loops of raspberry sauce in chocolate so dark it was almost black.

Casey lifted her fork. "You've been warned." She covered her fork in chocolate and slipped it in her mouth. Oh geez, smooth rich heaven. Casey swept up more chocolate.

"What kind of man is your ex-husband?" Theo asked.

"A superficial flake. I was twenty-eight when he dumped me for an eighteen-year-old." She plunged her fork into the swan's body, knocking it on its side. "He found himself an old-fashioned gal who thinks 'feminist' is a hygiene spray."

Theo kept his eyes on the plate and smiled.

Casey decapitated the swan. Bits of meringue flew onto the table. She'd been ironing Greg's shirts when he told her about his new love. The iron was still hot when she ran after him. Water had scalded her hand as she'd tried to press the guilt from his face. Come to think of it, she'd been eating chocolate that day, too; the last of an Easter bunny Greg had bought her. Some guys never learned.

"We were married for eight years. He always resented me for keeping my maiden name and didn't think I should be in security, mainly because I made more money than him."

She cut and stabbed the swan's body until only brown and white lumps were left.

"You've just mutilated your dessert," Theo said. "I take it you still have issues?"

"Dessert issues mainly. Some women have them. One day I found Rhonda sitting at the kitchen table with her hands covered in cherry cheesecake. She'd just mangled the thing after making it; decided it was no good."

"Sounds irrational."

"Everyone is now and then." Casey ate a forkful of meringue.

"Are you seeing anyone now?" he asked.

She hesitated. "I have a close friend."

"How close?"

Casey avoided Theo's gaze. "Lou's the most honest man I know."

"Are you sure?"

"What kind of question is that?" She ploughed her fork through the remains of her decimated swan.

"I see," Theo said. "Chocolate makes you cantankerous. Quite the opposite of most women."

She crunched the last of her swan. "I'm not most women." Besides, chocolate reactions usually didn't happen this fast. The mood swing was because of the personal questions and Greg's name coming up.

"Like it or not, I'm escorting you to Amsterdam," Theo said.

"Theo, I do not need, or want, a man to protect me, thank you very much."

He lifted his wine glass. "Maybe we should call it a night."

Casey gulped the last of her wine, both irritated and relieved that he was ending this meal. After Theo paid the bill he found her a taxi and, despite her protest, paid the driver more than enough to cover the cost. As she started to thank Theo, he planted his mouth firmly on hers. God, it felt like she was being branded. Theo's tongue tried to pry an opening between her lips. Ugly thoughts rampaged as she pulled away and cool safety came rushing back.

"That was nice," he murmured. "There's something incredibly sensuous about your anxiety."

"Thank you for dinner and the cab, but don't kiss me again."

Casey slid into the vehicle, fuming. It was bad enough that Theo was keeping things from her, but that gesture was infuriating. Just as irritating, and somewhat humiliating, though, was the horrible realization that she was a lousy dinner partner. Burning her mouth, yammering about her ex, and destroying her dessert was ridiculous behaviour.

Lou had seen her eat a thousand times. No wonder he'd never asked her out on a real date.

Fourteen

IN ONE TRAIN ride, Casey's view of Dutch tulip fields and windmills had been lost to city crowds, city noise, and zillions of particles of windswept, Amsterdam dirt. So far, the only Dutch cheese she'd eaten was the processed slice drooping out of the pricey McDonald's burger in her hand. A guy calling himself an exiled American approached her and said, "You on your own?"

"My friend will be here in about fifteen minutes."

A total lie, actually. On the way home from dinner in Whitby, Casey had decided that much of what Theo had said was bull. If he'd wanted to avoid Detective Lalonde yet protect her in Vancouver, why hadn't he called her at home? Also, if the Mexican guys were after the missing three million dollars, why hadn't they contacted her?

When Theo showed up at her hotel to buy her breakfast the next morning, she'd had to act fast. No way did she want him escorting her, or even following her to London, so she'd called Daphne Reid. Predictably, Reid was pissed to learn that Theo was the stranger who'd tackled him in the maze, so he'd agreed to help keep Theo in Goathland, provided she bought a few more souvenirs. It was worth the price. After breakfast, Theo discovered that the vehicle he'd rented in Whitby wouldn't run. Goathland was too small to have a rental agency, so Casey took off while Theo waited to have the car repaired by a local mechanic. Happily, he hadn't found her yet as she never told him about London. She'd also given him a fake hotel name in Amsterdam.

For the most part, London had been a waste of time. She'd spent two frustrating days tracking down Dad's contacts, who claimed to know nothing about the botulism death three years ago or the Vancouver murder. She had learned one interesting thing, though. The gallery opening Reid claimed to have attended on April twenty-fifth actually took place a week earlier.

Casey checked her watch. Eighty-thirty, time to leave. As she stood up, the American winked at her. "Enjoy your evening."

"I will." At least she'd try.

It had taken two and a half days to reach Gislinde Van Akker, which had given her time to sightsee and track down more names in the address book, none of them useful. Judging from the hesitancy in Gislinde's voice on the phone, Casey had sensed that the woman was stalling. She'd only agreed to see Casey at 9:00 PM tonight.

Casey stepped outside and started to walk away when a shove from behind sent her flying into a group of tourists. As she hit the ground, someone tugged on her shoulder bag. She looked up. The American. Casey gripped the strap and kicked his shin twice. A third kick sent him running into a crowd of people. She got up, but the loser wasn't worth chasing. After ensuring concerned tourists that she was okay, Casey continued on.

She walked down streets and over bridges illuminated with tiny white lights. The dirt-flinging wind had calmed down, and the warm temperature had obviously inspired hundreds of people to enjoy an evening stroll or bike ride. She scanned faces for the American, Theo, and two Mexican men, just in case. Music from street organs and chatter in different languages surrounded her. Occasionally, the amplified voice of a tour guide on a glass-roofed canal boat caused her to pause and take in the ambience. Lou would love it here. He liked boats and walking along busy streets at night. Too bad he wasn't with her. She missed his calm, practical view of the world.

Minutes later, Casey stopped in front of a row of tall narrow houses facing a canal. She'd scouted the street earlier today and had been impressed by the seventeenth- and eighteenth-century houses that looked as immaculate as they did in her guidebook. Many had been taken over by commerce, so she'd been surprised that Gislinde had given this as her address.

When Casey found the right house, she hesitated. Was she ready for this? She hadn't wanted to believe her father could betray Rhonda, not after what he'd been through with Mother. Taking a deep breath, she climbed the steps and rang a buzzer by the door. A female voice answered.

"I'm Casey Holland."

"Yes, come in."

Casey opened the door and found herself at the bottom of a narrow staircase leading up to a black door. She climbed slowly, quietly. As she reached the top, the door opened and Casey gazed at the same mid-twenties blonde in the photo on Dad's nightstand, except she now looked about seven months pregnant. Casey had been taken aback by the British accent on the phone, but that was nothing compared to Gislinde's physical condition. God, what would she tell Rhonda?

Gislinde tilted her head slightly, as if curious, or somewhat puzzled. Casey smiled, hoping she looked more genuine than she felt.

"Thank you for agreeing to see me," she said.

"You're very welcome. Please come inside."

Casey entered the room and spotted an enormous man sitting by the door. His stare was guarded, unwelcoming. He might as well have "Beware of Bodyguard" stamped on his forehead.

"That's my friend, John," Gislinde said.

Casey greeted him and received a curt nod.

"Have a seat, Miss Holland." Gislinde gestured toward the loveseat.

"Please, call me Casey."

"And I'm Gislinde. May I offer you a drink?"

"Thank you, but no. I don't want to take up much of your time."

While Gislinde stretched her legs along the sofa and adjusted her ankle-length dress, Casey glanced at the room for evidence of Dad's presence. Deep yellow walls were trimmed with black around windows and door frames. Floral tapestries covered chairs and sofa. Vases and potted plants filled spaces without making the room appear cluttered. Although candlelight illuminated the room, there were several lamps.

"This is a beautiful home, but I thought most of these houses were commercially owned."

"Some, like this one, have been restored as private residences. I'm an interior designer and I've just finished this for a client. I'm also house-sitting for him until Marcus and I move into our new home."

Her fixed smile looked unnatural. Did she know he was dead? If Gislinde had found out that he'd faked his death in Vancouver, or that he'd already had another fiancée plus three million dollars stashed away, would she have flown halfway across the world for an explanation? Would she have arrived on his doorstep in a sparkly blue hat and dress?

"Marcus mentioned you now and then," Gislinde said. "He was right, you don't look much alike."

"True." Was that supposed to be an icebreaker? "If you don't mind my asking, how long have you known Dad?"

"Four years."

Oh, god. "Dad and I didn't keep in touch in recent years. He didn't even tell me he was engaged."

"We only set the wedding date three months ago and have hardly told anyone yet. As you know, Marcus is a private person, and we've both been terribly busy."

So, why wasn't she asking why Casey was here? "Gislinde, the reason Dad and I didn't stay in touch is because three years and two months ago, I was told that he died from botulism poisoning in France. His body was shipped home, and I buried him in an open-casket service in front of three hundred people."

Gislinde frowned. "I don't understand."

"I barely understand it myself." Casey paused. "Just over three weeks ago, on Sunday, April twenty-fifth, Dad was found murdered in his West Vancouver home."

Gislinde didn't even blink as Casey described her encounters with Detective Lalonde and her trip to the morgue. When she finished speaking the room was silent. Gislinde wasn't looking at her, but at John, whose expression was undecipherable.

"Please forgive my insensitivity," Gislinde remarked, "but someone's been playing a cruel joke on you. Marcus is still alive, you see. He'll be here on Saturday."

Denial. She should have known. Hadn't she reacted the same way when Lalonde first told her?

"Really? When was the last time you talked to Dad?"

"April twenty-third."

Gislinde answered with such confidence that Casey had a feeling she wouldn't be able to convince her. "I'm sorry for bringing this news,

I know how awful it sounds, so maybe you should talk to the detective in charge. I can give you his number." She didn't know what to make of Gislinde's cold stare. "Even if I'm wrong, there are still things I'd like to know about Dad. I mean, did you notice any changes in him a little over three years ago?"

Gislinde examined a polished nail. "Marcus was as he has always been. Fun, thoughtful, passionate. Sooner or later, your stupid detective will discover the truth."

"Have you talked to Dad over the past three weeks?"

"There's been no reason to. Marcus rarely calls when he's in Vancouver. He's always been adamant about keeping his two worlds separate."

To the point where he wouldn't contact his pregnant fiancée? No way.

"Besides, he's been extremely busy completing business transactions and putting his house on the market," Gislinde went on. "Marcus wanted to rid himself of all Vancouver attachments."

"Oh, I think he did that some time ago." And she hadn't noticed a For Sale sign on the property, unless Dad had planned to sell the property.

"He will be here, Casey. Your father arrives in Geneva tomorrow to take care of some business and, honestly, if he had died, don't you think I would have heard by now?"

"Would Theo Ziegler have told you?"

She looked pensive. "You know Theo?"

"We've met, yes."

"Marcus is leaving their partnership to form his own company."

"Really? And how does Theo feel about Dad leaving?"

Gislinde adjusted her cushions. "He'll be sad to see him go, naturally, but Theo's very grateful for all the effort Marcus put into the company."

"Is he, because I heard that there were financial disputes between them in the past. I was also told that Dad has hidden three million dollars that some Mexican clients apparently think belong to them."

"Really?" Her tone was smug. "Marcus didn't steal or keep anything from anyone, but your mother wanted Theo to *think* that

Marcus stole three million dollars from the company. She framed him, you see."

Casey was aware that her mouth was hanging open, but she didn't care.

"Would you like some water?" Gislinde asked. "You've turned quite pale."

"No, I'm fine, thanks."

"I didn't mean to startle you, but I do believe that honesty cleanses the soul," Gislinde said. "You do know that she's worked for Theo Ziegler for years, don't you?"

"Yes, but why would she have framed Dad?" And why would Theo have made up the story about the Mexicans? Why the bodyguard?

A wisp of bang fell over Gislinde's pencilled brow and stayed there. "Lillian resented the fact that Marcus had been offered a partnership when she'd worked for Theo longer, so she stole from Theo and blamed Marcus for it. Of course, the situation was resolved, since Lillian still works for Theo."

Casey rubbed her forehead. To point out that her story didn't match Theo's version of events wouldn't be smart. "I assume my parents weren't on friendly terms after that?"

"They've never had much to do with each other."

What would Gislinde say if she knew about Mother's photo in Dad's bedroom, or of her history for destroying couples' lives?

"I know that Dad bought and sold art and furniture, among other things, but do you know if any of the goods TZ Inc. dealt with were controversial or even illegal?"

"Absolutely not, but the merchandise was often expensive and rare. Since clients demanded discretion, Marcus rarely talked about business."

Uh-huh, sure. Maybe former TZ staff would tell her more. "Did Dad ever mention an employee named Gustaf Osterman?"

It was Gislinde's turn to look surprised. "I remember the name, but I believe he left the company about the time I met Marcus."

"I heard that my mother was quite taken with him."

Gislinde's giggle caught Casey off guard.

"I'm sorry to say this, Casey, but it's common knowledge that Lillian is taken with most of the men she meets."

She doubted Gislinde was all that sorry. "I gather you wouldn't know if Osterman was taken with her too?"

"No, but I do know that Lillian and Theo are lovers."

Theo and Mother? It figured. "Do you know any other former employees of Theo's?"

"No. As I mentioned, Marcus rarely discussed business. You should ask Theo."

Casey felt a headache coming on. "Did Dad ever mention a woman named Simone Archambault?"

"No." Her tone became a little frosty. "Who is she?"

"A good friend."

"The name means nothing to me." Gislinde stretched her arms over her head, then slowly brought them out to the side and down onto her lap. "It's time for my meditation, so if you'll excuse me."

Casey wasn't quite ready to be dismissed. "Do you have any recent photos of Dad, and maybe one from when you first met?"

"Everything's packed away and in storage, but I have a couple of wallet-sized pictures." She got to her feet. "Oh, and that reminds me, I have something for you. Marcus was supposed to take it back to Vancouver on this last trip, but he forgot."

When Gislinde left the room Casey turned to find John glaring at her. If his eyes were lasers, she'd be smoldering from all the burn holes.

Gislinde returned a minute later and presented Casey with a long tube. "These are the blueprints for Marcus's West Vancouver house, which he'd planned to give you some time ago, but they wound up with things I'd been storing at my sister's. I suggested he take them on this trip, though I guess it doesn't really matter now that the house is being sold . . ."

"Thank you." Casey gripped the tube. "Too bad you never saw the place—it was a nice design."

"Marcus didn't want me there." There was an edge in her voice as she handed Casey two small photos. "He said the house embarrassed him."

So it should have. Casey studied a head shot of Dad. The second picture had been farther away so that his features weren't clear. "When were these taken?"

"The close-up was about a year after we met, the other was taken six months ago."

Casey handed them back. "Thank you for seeing me, Gislinde."

"You're welcome, and don't look so worried, Casey. Marcus is fine."

"Good to know." Theo hadn't exaggerated about the woman living in her own little fantasy world. She picked up the blueprints and headed out the door.

While she walked down the sidewalk she wondered how truthful Gislinde had been. Reid had implied there'd been problems between Dad and Gislinde, so how much had she known about what really had gone on with Theo, the business, and Dad's Vancouver life? And Mother framing Dad sound pretty farfetched. If Mother and Theo were lovers, though, was Mother lying for Theo, or had he fooled her too? Was the boarding pass and plane ticket Theo had shown Casey fake?

Casey stewed on this all the way to her hotel. By the time she was crossing the lobby, the trepidation she'd felt about meeting Mother began to magnify. She trudged up creaking steps and then entered her room.

Something felt different. Standing in the middle of the small, plain room, she turned full circle. Someone had been here. Her hair-brush and cosmetics bag had been moved from her bed to the night table. Casey's gaze moved around the room. There was no closet and bathroom. The only place one could hide was under the bed. Keeping her distance, she bent down and saw only dust.

She went through her luggage. Nothing was missing. The door's lock looked undamaged. Cheap hotels didn't have maid service, making it easy for intruders to break into rooms. The building's main entrance was unlocked and the senior manning the front desk was more interested in TV than the comings and goings of visitors. Or did he snoop through rooms on commercial breaks?

That the intruder hadn't returned her things to the same spot unnerved Casey. Had he wanted her to know he'd been there? Were

Mexican clients actually following her? Or maybe Theo didn't believe her story about the notebook. Had he managed to find her and follow her here? Had he, or someone else, hired the American kid to steal her purse?

Casey opened the door and stepped into the empty hall.

The hallway was still empty when she stomped back to her room five minutes later. The senior at the desk had no other available rooms, and insisted that every hotel in the city would be full at this time of year. She'd have to barricade herself in here, because she didn't want to sit in a train station all night.

Casey rubbed her temples. She should phone Lou. It'd be great to hear his voice. Rhonda would be waiting for a call too, but a migraine was blossoming, the second one this month. Not good.

After taking medication, Casey made sure the window latch was secure, then propped a chair under the doorknob. She wasn't sure if this would work, but she'd seen it on TV a hundred times, and it was better than nothing.

She removed the notebook from her handbag. Mr. Helpful-At-The-Desk didn't have a safe, nor would he keep the book for her. She slipped the notebook in the pillow case then sat on the pillow. She drew her knees up and wrapped her arms around her legs.

When she got to Paris she'd try and locate Gustaf Osterman to see what he had to say about Theo's business. Should have asked Theo what Osterman looked like. For all she knew, he'd lied about the guy quitting and Osterman was the one following her all over Amsterdam. Worse, he could have been in this room earlier tonight. Casey watched the door and waited.

Fifteen

CASEY STOOD IN a musty hotel lobby and yawned as raindrops pelted the window. It had rained most of the forty hours she'd been in Paris and she wasn't impressed with the grimy, soot-streaked buildings. Her shoes were still wet from being jostled off crowded sidewalks into overflowing gutters.

Through the window, Casey studied what she could see of this narrow road in the Latin Quarter. Although the intruder hadn't reappeared in her Amsterdam hotel room last night, she still watched for Theo and suspicious-looking strangers. She longed for the day she could stop watching, when she could fall asleep without obsessing about the past and brooding over the present, and she wanted to go home.

Enough with the quest to find contacts; the only person she'd managed to locate was Gustaf Osterman's ex-wife, who'd herself given up trying to track him over money he'd borrowed six years ago. Equally fruitless had been Casey's attempts to contact hospital staff who'd treated Dad for botulism. Unfortunately, Detective Lalonde had been right about vanished staff from Alvin's All-Canadian Café. Not one person she'd spoken with claimed to have worked there back then, no one admitted knowing anyone who had and she'd discovered that one employee had committed suicide.

To Casey's relief and frustration, Mother had canceled their meeting because Theo had shown up in Geneva and begged her to deliver several things that Dad was supposed to have handled. TZ Inc. was apparently so far behind schedule that clients were threatening to either take their business elsewhere or sue. Mother had kept repeating how deeply she regretted having to postpone their "reunion," and she'd seemed adamant that based on her research in Geneva, Theo hadn't killed Dad. So, questions about the legality of Dad's activities and whether his murder had anything to do with the import/export business or not wouldn't be answered right away. Was the cancellation

Theo's doing? Given Mother's relationship to him, Casey wondered if she would have revealed much anyway.

What with the traveling, the dreary hotel rooms, and the many dead ends, Casey longed to hear a trusted, friendly voice. She hadn't called Rhonda for five days because Rhonda would want to know how things were going, and Casey didn't know how to tell her about Gislinde Van Akker.

She approached the guest phone near the reception desk that had closed at eleven. She regretted not bringing her cell phone. Expensive as the calls would have been, it was a lot more convenient than trying to find a public phone. Casey placed the call and waited for what felt like a long time before Rhonda finally answered.

"I thought you would have phoned by now," she said. "Where the hell have you been?"

"Amsterdam and Paris. How are things?"

"Okay, under the circumstances. Darcy says hi."

"He's with you now?"

"Yep, I'm getting a fabulous rub-down. He's been fantastic through everything that's happened lately."

"Lately? What do you mean?"

She sighed. "Someone beat up Lou three nights ago."

"Oh no! Is he all right?"

"He was in the hospital but he's recovering at his mom's now. There's no broken bones, thank god, just cuts and bruises. He'll be okay, hon."

"I tried calling him yesterday." She swallowed hard. "Who would do that?"

"No clue. The cops didn't catch the guy. Lou came for dinner that night and he was hoping you'd call because he had news about the Marine Drive house. Anyway, just as he left, Lillian phoned."

"What did she want?"

"To know how I was coping with the murder. While I was telling her to mind her own business, some guy grabbed Lou and dragged him into the garage."

"Oh god." Casey pictured the old garage at the back of Rhonda's property, used for storing a cord of wood and gardening tools.

"After I hung up, I saw Lou's truck was still here, so I went outside and found the garage door open." Rhonda's voice trembled. "He was half buried in the woodpile."

Tears filled Casey's eyes. "Why Lou?"

"That's the other scary part. Lou said that the guy wanted to know who you were meeting in Europe, and he warned Lou to stay away from Marcus's place or he'd kill his family and friends."

The hair on Casey's arm and neck stood up.

"Shit, Casey, what if the psycho finds out I was at the house too?"

Casey heard Darcy say, "Don't worry. I'm here."

She wiped the tear sliding down her cheek. "Did Lou get a look at the guy?"

"No, it was dark and the maniac wore a hooded jacket."

Like the freak who'd jumped her. Casey studied the lobby's gold and turquoise carpet.

"You said he had news about the house?"

"Someone stole everything and tore up a bunch of floorboards in the living room."

"What! Where was the security I hired?"

"Apparently, the company had changed the locks but hadn't installed the new alarm system before the thief struck. They did have a guard watching the place. Seems he was beaten worse than Lou. Anyway, Lou said the alarm's being installed today."

"Did you tell Detective Lalonde what happened?"

"I did when he came by to collect some of Marcus's things for forensic testing. Jerk asked about Marcus and me, so I asked him how friendly he was with Lillian. Then he got all red-faced and changed the subject." Rhonda groaned, "Oooh, that's amazing."

"Tell Lalonde that you're worried about Summer's safety and ask if he can have an officer watch your place."

"I did. He said he'd see what he could do, like that'll help." Rhonda sighed. "I'm really worried about Summer, especially after what happened the day after Lou's attack."

Fear squeezed Casey's ribs. "What else?"

"Lillian called again, but this time Summer answered while I was doing the laundry." Rhonda's voice cracked. "Apparently, Lillian said she'd soon tell Summer all about her mother, things she wouldn't know because she was just a tiny baby."

"I don't understand. Mother was out of the picture when you adopted Summer."

"Casey, she was referring to my sister, not me. Lillian and I stayed in touch, remember? Of course she knew I'd adopted, but I never told her the circumstances surrounding Summer's birth. Well, it seems Lillian now knows not only the whole story but also that I never told Summer. She's going to tell her, Casey, I know it."

Casey leaned against the wall. "Why would Mother do that?"

"To damage my relationship with Summer."

Was Mother really malicious enough to turn a child's world upside down? "How did she find out?"

"Lillian told Summer that she'd seen my mom. Last night, I found out it's true. Mom told her everything about Summer's birth because she's mad at me for not bringing Summer around more often. God, Casey, what am I going to do?"

Casey tried to curb the feeling that Mother was dropping a net over all three of them. "I'll figure something out."

"Darcy," Rhonda said, "bring me my bathrobe, will you?"

Casey cringed.

"Listen, you won't want to hear this, but I have to say it." Rhonda cleared her throat. "I have a terrible feeling that Lillian killed Marcus. I know she didn't want their marriage to end in the first place, but to lose him to me, well . . . I just don't understand why she waited so long to do it."

Casey did, if Gislinde had told the truth. "We'll deal with this when I get back. Just make sure Summer doesn't take any more calls from her. I'll be home soon."

After their conversation ended, Casey walked down the dimly lit corridor while she tried to process the real possibility that Mother could have killed Dad. She reached her room, inserted her key in the lock and opened the door. She'd barely taken a step inside when she realized someone was right behind her. Casey turned and saw Theo.

Before she could move he'd blocked the doorway.

"You might as well let me in," he said, "because I'm not leaving until we talk."

Oh, hell. Staring at him, she decided to play it cool. Better to stay on friendly terms with him and learn as much as she could.

"You look a little damp," she said, glancing at his wet hair. "I'd offer you a towel, but this place doesn't have any." She stepped back and let him enter. "Mother must have told you where I was."

"She's worried about your safety, and she's furious with me for making her work when she really wanted to see you, but it couldn't be helped." Theo draped his wet raincoat over the room's only chair. He surveyed the pink bedspread, pink curtains, and grungy pink walls. "This is terrible."

"I know, it's like living inside a bottle of Pepto-Bismol, but it was the only thing the travel agent could book on short notice." Laughter erupted from the room above them. "The floors are pretty thin, too."

"I wish you had let me escort you to Amsterdam or wherever else you went. I know plenty of hotel managers who would have given you a reduced rate."

"Thanks, but I prefer not to rely on favors."

Theo nodded. "So, have you learned anything useful?"

"Yeah, Daphne Reid's alibi doesn't check out. I went to the gallery he claimed to have been at on April twenty-fifth, and their opening actually took place a week earlier."

"I'll look into his activities." Theo looked closer at her. "Why are your eyes so red?"

Stepping away from him, she repeated Rhonda's news about Lou, the stolen furniture, and the ruined living room floor. "I think Lou was attacked by the same guy who went after me."

"You never told me about that."

"It happened the day after I heard about the murder." Once she'd filled Theo in, he started to put his arm around her, but she moved away. Overhead, heavy footsteps crossed the room.

"I also learned that an employee who'd worked at the restaurant where Dad picked up the botulism committed suicide a few days after the poisoning. None of the staff had worked there back then and didn't know his name."

"I'll look into that as well."

"I appreciate it." So, what was all this help about, and how far would Theo take the good guy routine? "I know someone who thinks Mother might have killed Dad. A woman was seen in his house less than an hour before he died, wearing the kind of flashy clothing Mother always liked."

"What would Lillian's motive be?"

"You tell me." Casey folded her arms. "After all, she's worked for you a long time and you're lovers, aren't you?"

"That must have come from Gislinde." Theo shrugged. "Lillian and I had a brief affair three and a half years ago. She's with someone else now, and I swear neither of us killed your father."

Fine, she'd play along. "Could Gustaf Osterman have killed him? You said he left under bad terms. Since Dad was a partner, I assume Osterman's bad feelings extended to him as well?"

Theo squinted as if confused. "We haven't heard from Gustaf in ages, and I've had no threats on my life." He removed his suit jacket. "The Mexicans are still high on my suspect list."

"If they were following me in Vancouver after the murder, then they couldn't have found the money, so why kill Dad at all?"

"Perhaps they thought they'd find it in the house."

"Gislinde says that Mother took the money and framed Dad."

"She's wrong. Marcus lied to Gislinde so she wouldn't worry."

"Really." It simply didn't make sense. Why break with Vancouver friends and family to keep everyone safe, yet stay in touch with her? "Gislinde refuses to believe Dad's been killed, by the way."

"Gislinde's always believed what she needs to, whether it's true or not."

Above them, someone jumped on the bed.

"You aren't planning on getting too comfy, are you?" Casey watched him remove his tie.

"I'm not a fan of ties and jackets, but I had an all-day meeting."

"You should find out if Gislinde took any flights to Vancouver in late April. She might even have flown to Vancouver with Dad."

"Gislinde adored Marcus. She wouldn't have killed him."

"Would her adoration have turned to hatred if Mother had come between them?"

Theo's long dark eyes didn't blink. She saw the uncertainty in his face.

A thunderous crash from the ceiling and an uproar of laughter made Casey flinch. The jumper must have missed the bed. She moved to the window overlooking an alley.

"Theo, do you think the Mexicans are entitled to the money?"

"No, in fact a significant portion of Marcus's fee was supposed to go back into the partnership."

Just as she thought, Theo wanted that money. "Gislinde said Dad was planning to end your partnership."

"Yes." Theo hesitated. "Marcus wanted to form his own company. I didn't like it, but as long as he honored contract clauses, it was okay. The problem was that he reneged on a couple of clauses, so we agreed to meet and sort things out. Unfortunately, I was too late."

"How did you learn about the murder?"

"Marcus was supposed to pick me up at the airport that night. When he didn't show, I called the house and got no answer, so I took a cab and arrived shortly after eleven." Theo looked out the window. "The front door was unlocked, which seemed odd, so I walked in and found him on the floor in his den."

"The police weren't called until midnight, which gave you an hour to remove any evidence linking him to TZ Inc." Casey didn't wait for a response. "Think you swept up any murder clues?"

"I was careful."

"Are you sure? The address book Lalonde found had your name and two addresses inside, one for San Francisco, the other for Geneva." Casey watched his impassive expression. "I'm guessing you found Dad's current planner or whatever type of itinerary he kept, so why not take his address book too?"

"It wasn't in his den. I started searching the living room when I heard a dog barking out front and some guy yelling at it to shut up. I dialed the police and took off."

"Did you break in the next day to keep looking for the address book, or were you after the money?"

"Both, but first I had to find his house keys, which I never did. Do you have them?"

"I have one."

The room felt stuffy. Casey released a brass latch and pushed open the window. The odor of rotting food mingled with the damp air. She looked up and down the alley. No sign of lurkers. She turned to Theo. "Have you heard of a woman named Simone Archambault?"

Theo's eyes widened. "Do you know her?"

"We talked on the phone." No need to mention her trip to Victoria.

"How did you find her? Is she in Paris?"

"I came across her phone number in Dad's house, and I have no idea where she is right now." Dad had wanted her to find the receipt, not Theo, or he wouldn't have stashed it in their secret spot. "Simone insists Dad's been dead three years, despite the body in the morgue."

"She and Marcus were close, I gather. Maybe she knows about the Mexicans and is afraid they'll come after her."

Or she was afraid of Theo. Casey remembered Simone asking if she'd been followed.

"I need to ask her about these clients," Theo said, leaning against the wall. "May I have her number?"

"I don't remember it and the slip of paper with her number is at home." A lie, actually. "Why would Dad have told her more than he told you?"

"Possibly because hardly anyone knew Simone existed. I also know that she's elderly and slightly eccentric, so who would think she'd be privy to confidential business matters?"

Casey looked up at the sky, wishing the moon was visible. Above her, music began to play, and it sounded like people were dancing.

"Every day seems to get darker," she said. "Strange, isn't it, since we're heading into summer."

"Only if you assume that the opposite of dark is light."

"Oh?" She turned to him. "And what do you think it is?"

Theo studied her. "Truth."

Casey chuckled. "Yeah, well, I've learned a few truths on this trip and things just keep getting darker."

"May I take you out of this dark, pink misery and buy you a drink?"

"Thanks, but no, I'm exhausted."

Theo strolled to the chair and picked up his jacket. "Are you angry with me for not being more forthcoming?"

"More distrustful than angry."

He put on his coat. "What can I do to change that?"

"Answer a few more questions."

"I'll try, but I won't compromise my clients' privacy."

"What does Gustaf Osterman look like?"

He swept his hand over his hair. "Middle-aged, light brown hair, average build; but why do you want to know?"

"I'm not sure. I just have a feeling about him, that's all. Think he stayed in touch with other employees or associates of yours?"

"I doubt it." Theo put on his jacket. "Gustaf wasn't easy to get along with. Whenever you bring up his name I think of all the arguments between us."

Casey perched on the edge of the windowsill. "Is your import business legitimate?"

Overhead, more feet stomped to the beat of loud music.

"Some of the things we buy and sell are controversial, but not illegal."

"Give me an example of controversial."

"Technology."

Casey thought she heard something outside. She jumped up and scanned the alley. No sign of anyone, but she closed the window anyway.

"You're a bit edgy, aren't you?" Theo remarked.

Casey told him about the American's attempt to mug her and the invasion of her hotel room.

"I did warn you," he said.

A body crashed to the floor above her and Casey winced. Another chorus of laughter erupted. Suddenly, there was a loud bang and instant silence. A man began yelling.

"Looks like I'll have a peaceful night after all," she said.

Theo picked up his coat. "May I buy you breakfast tomorrow?"

"Sure, but I'll be checking out and heading back to England before noon." Now that he knew where she was staying it was unlikely she'd get rid of him anyway.

"Would you like to see more of the English countryside?"

"No, thanks." The last thing she needed was to be alone with this guy on a remote road.

"What more do I have to do to earn your trust, Casey?"

She thought about this. "There's one thing that would make a difference, depending on how much influence you have with my mother."

"Well, she does listen to me."

"Mother's threatened to tell Rhonda's adopted daughter the truth about her birth, to hurt Rhonda, and I'm asking you to tell her to stop."

"Why would Lillian want to hurt Rhonda?"

"There's a lot of history between them, and Rhonda's engagement to Dad didn't help things. But an eleven-year-old child doesn't deserve to be caught in the middle."

"Agreed, but I'd have more leverage if I knew the details."

Casey sighed. She didn't want Theo to know Rhonda's private business, but if it meant keeping Mother from hurting her and Summer, then it was worth the risk.

"Summer's biological mother was a heroin addict. She also happened to be Rhonda's younger sister."

"The sister you mentioned at dinner the other night—the one who overdosed?"

"Yeah, it happened two months after Summer was born. The father could have been one of several guys, none of them any good, from what I heard."

"Why doesn't Rhonda tell her daughter the truth before Lillian does?"

"She's terrified Summer will hate her for lying all these years. Rhonda made up an elaborate story about giving birth, the whole bit. Anyway, Mother recently found out the truth from Summer's grandmother. It's bad enough that Rhonda's afraid of being attacked by the same freak that went after Lou, but this too?"

"Maybe it's best if she and Summer left the area for a while, and you need protection too."

"Rhonda won't go as long as Darcy's around to protect her."

Theo's expression froze. "Darcy?"

"Her new tenant; the guy's taken quite a liking to her." As she watched him a horrible feeling coiled in her stomach. "You know him?"

"Maybe; what's he look like?"

As she described Darcy, Theo swore.

"Who is he, Theo?"

"He's an acquaintance who's after the money."

"Great, just bloody great." Despite the adrenalin rush warming her body, Casey hugged herself. "The cops are looking for a female suspect, but should they be taking a closer look at Darcy?"

"I don't know. I'd wondered about the female aspect myself, which was why I mentioned a woman when I called the police that night."

"What made you think the killer was a woman?"

"A week before I came to Vancouver, I called to give Marcus my flight time. While we spoke, I heard a woman's voice in the background. She wanted to know who was on the line, and it didn't sound like Lillian."

"Why didn't you mention this before?"

"I thought it would prejudice you against Lillian and Gislinde." Theo headed for the door. "You need to stay open to all possibilities."

"Because you think they're innocent?"

"Because a rational, intelligent person would consider all options, and you have those qualities unless you're eating chocolate," he replied. "Can you think of anyone who wouldn't have welcomed Marcus's rebirth?"

"I thought you believed the Mexican clients were behind this."

"I didn't know Joseph and Carlos were in Vancouver until after I'd tipped off police, but it seems I need to rethink things too." He opened the door. "I'll be booking a flight to Vancouver. And I promise to talk to Lillian about Rhonda."

"Thanks."

It was only after Theo had left and she'd collapsed into bed that Casey thought of the one person who'd stood to lose the most from Dad's resurrection. Vincent lizard-loving Wilkes.

Sixteen

AS THE JET touched down, Casey smiled, glad to be home. By the time her taxi reached Commercial Drive an hour later, though, apprehension had taken over. Familiar buildings looked strangely out of place, her street seemed different.

She blamed exhaustion for the illusion. Red-eye flights were a lousy way to travel and, worse, everything she'd learned in Europe was either disheartening, confusing, or maddening. Time to put this mess behind her. Once she'd spoken with Vincent Wilkes and Detective Lalonde, she was done with the past. Why bother looking for the missing three million until the killer was caught?

Part of her hoped she'd seen the last of Theo. Before she left Paris, Casey had again asked him questions about Dad and Darcy, but all Theo had said was, "The less you know the better." Then he'd had the nerve to pump her for information about Simone. He finally shut up when she told him to ask Lalonde about the lady. She'd been grateful, though, when Theo promised to check out Gislinde Van Akker's alibi and deal with Darcy the moment he arrived in Vancouver.

Casey directed the driver to the back of the house, relieved that Rhonda's and Darcy's vehicles weren't here. She didn't want conversation right now.

Stepping inside Rhonda's kitchen, she still felt alienated. It was as if she needed to move through familiar spaces and touch familiar things, so that some sort of reattachment could take place. She trudged upstairs. Where was everyone? Fear flickered through her until Casey realized this was Saturday morning. She checked her watch. Summer was usually back from swim practice by now, unless she and Rhonda had gone camping this long weekend after all, though wouldn't Rhonda have mentioned it on the phone?

Casey rummaged for her key, opened the door to her apartment, and stepped into total chaos. Cushions, books, teddy bears, and

THE OPPOSITE OF DARK   119

ornaments were scattered everywhere. Fragments of broken glass sparkled on the hardwood floor. In her bedroom, drawers had been pulled out and clothes dumped in a heap.

"God damn it!" She slumped into her rocking chair and took long deep breaths. What part of her life hadn't been tampered with, and what, or whom, would be targeted next? Casey spotted the message light blinking on her phone. She pressed the button and heard Detective Lalonde ask her to call him. The next two caught her off guard. Both were from Simone Archambault who wanted to see her as soon as possible. The last caller was Stan. Since he usually worked Saturday mornings, Casey called him first.

"Good, you're back," he said. "I need you to take over the purse snatching case. The kid stole another one last week and got a close look at Marie, so I can't use her. The cops are thinking about stepping in, for shit's sake."

Casey understood his irritation. Stan had earned the authorities' respect, which was why they let him handle riskier situations. Unsolicited police intervention would be humiliating.

"Did anyone stake out Vancouver Technical Secondary? I still think that high school's our best option."

"I've had the part-timers try a couple of times, but nothing so far."

"School's out until Tuesday, so do you want me to ride the M15 this weekend?"

"Skip tomorrow; the kid hasn't struck on a Sunday so far. How about Monday? I'll leave the file on your desk."

"Sounds good." She leaned back in the rocker. "Did you hear about Lou Sheckter?"

"I saw him in the lunchroom this morning."

"He's back at work?"

"Yeah, he wanted to, and we're short-staffed. By the way, some lady named Simone's been looking for you—insisted on speaking to me personally, like I haven't got enough to do. When I told her I didn't know how to reach you, she hung up."

"I'll call her." Casey gazed at the mess in the room. "Did you ever find out who broke into the lockers?"

"Nah, it's probably a dead issue. How was Europe?"

"Stressful. I'll tell you about it later."

"Good enough. I'll be in on Monday. Take care, kiddo."

Casey looked around her apartment and decided to check out her car too.

She found everything in her glove box on the floor mat. Casey jumped at the sound of a honking horn. She spun around and saw Rhonda coast to a stop. Summer scrambled out of the station wagon and threw her arms around Casey.

"Why didn't you call?" Rhonda shifted the bag of groceries. "I could have picked you up." The half circles under her eyes had grown so dark they looked like two puffy bruises.

"You're busy Saturday mornings." Casey gave her a hug. "I missed you guys."

"Missed you too," Summer replied.

"Have you seen your apartment?" Rhonda asked.

"Yeah, when did it happen?"

"Last night while Summer and I were out. I'd hoped to have everything back in place before you arrived, but I only got the kitchen done."

"Don't worry about it." Casey rubbed tired eyes. "Were the other suites broken into?"

"No." Rhonda turned to Summer. "Would you plug in the kettle for me, honey?"

"Sure." Summer jogged toward the house.

"I phoned the cops," Rhonda said as they started up the steps. "They couldn't find signs of forced entry. Do you know if anything's missing?"

"Haven't checked yet. Where was Darcy when this happened?"

"At the gym."

"Did you know my car's been ransacked too?"

"Hard to tell with all the garbage in there." Rhonda looked at her. "What's going on?"

"I was told that a business deal of Dad's went bad and the people involved want their money back. They think I know where he hid three million dollars."

"Three million?" Rhonda yelped and plunked onto the top step.

"Whoever attacked Lou is probably connected to this deal." Casey sat beside her. "Could be the same jerk who trashed my place, so maybe I should move out for a little while."

"Don't." As Rhonda shifted the grocery bag again, an orange fell out and bounced down the stairs. Casey started to go for it, but Rhonda grabbed her arm. "We'll get police protection, and Darcy's here."

Casey kept her face impassive. "Darcy can't protect all of us at once." Especially when he was part of the damn problem.

"Summer needs you, Casey." Rhonda turned and glanced at the kitchen door. "Something's bothering her but she won't tell me what, just says it's nothing important."

Fear surged through Casey as she thought of Darcy. "Any ideas?"

"Maybe Lillian already told her about her birth, but Summer won't talk because she can't accept it." Rhonda shook her head. "Lillian's calls are more irrational than usual, and I'm convinced she plans to turn you and Summer against me."

"She won't succeed."

"I don't know about that." Rhonda hugged the grocery bag. "She'll accuse me of killing Marcus, and Summer will wonder if it's true 'cause I've kept this huge secret from her." She again glanced at the kitchen. "Lillian's setting me up, you see. She still hates me for getting engaged to Marcus, can't let it go."

"How did Mother react when you first told her?"

"She spewed that crap about him never understanding me as well as she did."

"When Mother called, did she ever talk about her life, what she was up to?"

"She dropped clues now and then." Rhonda gazed at the wayward orange lying on the grass. "Lalonde's been badgering me about the murder, so I got mad and said that if he needed suspects, I'd seen a notebook full of them." She bit her lip. "You're going to give him the book, right?"

"Yeah, I'm done with it."

Darcy's Porsche pulled up. No way did she want to talk to the manipulative bastard.

"Here's my guy," Rhonda said.

Casey stood. "Your guy?"

"Obviously, he's no Marcus, but he's behaved himself and we're having fun. Which reminds me, are you going to see Lou today?"

"Right after I take a nap; couldn't sleep on the plane."

Casey hurried inside and up to her apartment. She dialed Simone's number, but a recorded voice informed her the number was no longer in service. Why would she disconnect her phone and not leave a new number? Casey made her disheveled bed then crawled under the comforter.

→   →   →

A knock on the door woke her. She looked at the clock. A ninety-minute nap was long enough. She stumbled out of bed, opened the door, and smiled at Summer.

"Come on in, sweetie. How are things?"

While Summer described her swim practices and Sports Day events, Casey worked up the courage to raise the next topic. "I heard you had a nice chat with my mother."

"Yeah, she was cool."

Casey manoeuvred her way through the debris to the kitchen. Until now, she'd never discussed Mother with Summer. Too afraid her anger would show through. She didn't want Summer to know how much shame a child could feel toward a parent.

"What did you and Mother talk about?" Casey retrieved a jar of instant coffee from a cupboard.

"Stuff you did when you were little."

To hide her annoyance, Casey looked for milk in the refrigerator.

"I know Mom's still a little mad about it," Summer said. "I tried telling her that your mom was nice to me, but talking's been hard with stupid Darcy always around."

Casey shut the door. "I thought you liked him."

Summer fidgeted as she looked at a collection of postcards taped to the fridge. "He thinks he can go wherever he wants."

"Like where?"

"Like here."

Oh, hell. "When was this?"

"Thursday night. I had to go to the bathroom and when I got back to my room, I heard your door close. I peeked out and saw Darcy coming downstairs."

"Did he see you?"

"I only opened the door a tiny bit. He had his head down and was in a big rush."

Casey gazed at the textbook and papers on the floor under her kitchen table. "You're sure this didn't happen last night?"

"Yep."

"Was Darcy carrying anything?"

"Nope."

"Did you tell your mom?"

Summer shook her head. "She likes him, and besides, Mom asked him to fix your leaking tap." She nodded toward the kitchen sink. "That's why I thought he was here at first, but I didn't see any tools."

They looked at the still leaking tap.

"Your mom knows something's been bothering you. Is it Darcy?"

"Yeah, all he does is talk to her now, especially at night. Sometimes I just want to squish his head and stomp on it."

She probably knew their relationship was sexual. Poor kid. "You should tell your mom when Darcy's out."

"I know, but it's just that she seems, like, happy."

Too happy to notice that her affair bothered Summer? Casey dumped a heaping teaspoon of coffee in her mug.

"Why would Darcy trash your place, anyway?" Summer asked.

"I don't know." But she had a theory. Casey put her arm around Summer. "Tell me, has Darcy done anything else that makes you uncomfortable?"

"No. Mostly, he just ignores me, and he's gotten cranky."

"Thanks for letting me know, but I need to tell your mom about this, okay?"

Summer nodded. "I gotta go. My friend Lisa and her parents are taking me to their cabin at Whistler in an hour, so I won't see ya till Monday night."

"No camping with your mom this weekend?"

"Darcy didn't want to go, so she canceled it. Oh, and she wants to know if you're hungry. She saved you some soup."

Casey smiled. "Thank her for me, but I'm going to see Lou." She hugged Summer. "You sure you're okay?"

Summer smiled, "Totally, now that you're back."

After she left, Casey called work and learned that Lou's shift wouldn't end for two hours. Plenty of time to eat, change clothes, and meet him at Mainland. Boy, would he be surprised.

Casey thumbed through the contents of the file Stan had left on her desk. She'd already read everything once, and had memorized enough new info about the kid to easily recognize the pimply twerp the moment he stepped onto the bus.

She checked her watch. Forty-five more minutes before Lou pulled into the depot. Drumming her fingers on the desk, she looked at the long, rectangular room. Since the administration staff didn't work weekends, the place was quiet. Casey closed the file and stood. Why not meet Lou a couple of stops from here? It'd be fun to see the look on his face when she climbed on board.

As often happened during Victoria Day long weekends in Vancouver, the good weather had left town along with the camping and cottage folks. Cool air and a gloomy sky warned of an approaching rainfall. Casey exited through the front of the building and headed down Lougheed, grateful for the busy mix of retail outlets, car dealerships, restaurants, and light industry along this stretch of highway. Plenty of people around. No reason to feel alone or vulnerable, to look over her shoulder every minute.

She had to admit that recent events haunted her dreams. Separating truth from lies was tough, and the suspect list kept growing: Theo, Gislinde, Mother, Daphne Reid, Vincent Wilkes, and possibly two Mexicans named Joseph and Carlos. Reid was the only one with no clear motive. As for the others, Theo was out three million dollars and a partner. Gislinde might have discovered that Mother was still in the picture and that Dad had been hoarding a lot of cash. Vincent might have worried that Dad wanted his house and architectural firm back. As for Mother, well, their history spoke for itself. Also troubling was the one name Casey hadn't added to her list, yet couldn't forget: Gustaf Osterman.

By the time she reached the last bus stop before the depot, the sky rumbled and a raindrop plopped onto her forehead. As she moved to the covered area, she spotted two men, possibly Mexican, heading for the stop at a quick pace.

They were staring at her. The older man wore a suit while the younger one sported jeans and a T-shirt. She had no idea how long they'd been behind her, but their grim expressions didn't indicate a leisurely stroll. As they drew near, Casey's breathing quickened. She looked for signs of weapons.

The men walked past the covered area. The older man kept his eyes forward and the younger one lowered his gaze. His hair hung to his collar. She watched the men until Lou's bus came into view. Neither of them looked back at her.

The bus pulled to a stop, Casey climbed on board, and wondered if she looked as shocked as Lou did. Bruises surrounded his eyes. Another purple-green bruise discolored his chin. He opened the door and Casey climbed the steps. Cuts and scrapes covered his cheeks. He looked far too battered to be working.

"Casey!"

As Lou stood, she wrapped her arms around him. Two large tears spilled onto his shoulder. "I'm so sorry, Lou. If I'd stayed home this wouldn't have happened."

"Then he would have gone after you." He stroked her cheek and then closed the door. "Have a seat, or passengers will think we've got something hot and heavy going on."

Casey looked around. "Your last passenger just left." She chose the seat closest to him.

"How was Europe?" he asked, merging into traffic.

"Lousy. I'll tell you everything over beer and pizza."

"Could we eat in? I'm kind of tired."

"Sure." She was amazed he'd managed a full shift at all.

"I stayed over three times," he said. "Summer seemed fine, and I never saw Darcy near her."

"Did you meet him?"

"No, the guy was always out; big coincidence, huh?"

"Yep, and he's pretty much ignored Summer since he's become involved with Rhonda."

"I figured that, yeah. So, now that you're home, what's your next move?"

"A talk with Dad's old associate, Vincent. After that I'm pulling the covers over my head and not coming out until the guilty parties are in jail."

"Parties? Meaning more than one?"

"Sure, why not? I've learned that nothing about my family's ever been simple and straightforward."

Her eyes filled again and she wanted to sink through the floor. Where was all this emotion coming from?

Lou pulled into the depot and turned off the ignition. "What has you so upset?"

She wiped her eyes. "The deception went much deeper and for much longer than I thought. Why wasn't Dad straight with me?"

"Lots of parents don't want their kids to know about their dark side, or their failures, or things they're ashamed of. I remember how mad Dad was with Mom for telling us about his mistress."

Lou's parents had been divorced almost as long as Casey's. Every year, he went to see his dad in Winnipeg. Every year, he came back out of sorts, fluctuating between love, anger, and pity. It usually took a couple of days to cheer him up.

"Dad and I went through a lot of crap," she said. "I really believed it was just the two of us sharing secrets and troubles and good times, until he and Rhonda hooked up. Turns out he and Mother had had this whole other life all along."

Lightning flashed. Thunder exploded and the rain that had been sprinkling the windshield became a deluge.

"I talked to the security company," Lou said. "No one's tried to break into the house since the guard was attacked. I don't get why someone had to destroy the floorboards, though."

Probably to look for three million bucks, but why choose that spot?

"The alarm's been installed," Lou added, "and another guard's patrolling the grounds, which must be costing you a fortune."

"I'll be discontinuing that. Did they catch the guy who beat up the first guard?"

"No, but he's the same maniac who ambushed me—tall guy with shaded glasses, wearing a hoodie."

Casey forgot to take a breath. "Were the guy's lenses blue?"

"It was too dark to tell, why?"

"Did you see his hair?"

"The hood covered it." Lou winced as he got to his feet. "What's up?"

"Are you sure you've never seen Darcy? When we left for the airport, he was watching us from the porch."

"I don't remember looking back."

The rain tapped the windows. It was the only sound she could hear.

"Remember me telling you that I hit my attacker with the flashlight and never saw his face?"

"What about it?"

"When I met Darcy the next day, he'd claimed to have had knee surgery, and went down the stairs awkwardly. The knee seemed fine by the time I left for Europe. Darcy Churcott's tall and he wears blue tinted glasses."

"Shit." He shook his head. "I want to see this loser."

"Rhonda said your attacker spoke to you. What did he sound like?"

"Gravelly voice."

Casey shivered. "It's him."

"How does the jerk fit into this?"

"He knows Theo Ziegler and he may want the money."

"What money?"

"I'll fill you in while we eat."

Lou put a comforting arm around her. "We'll need evidence against this freak."

Casey nodded. "I gather you didn't describe your assailant to Rhonda?"

"No, she seems hyper-sensitive these days. I didn't think I should go into detail."

"Good move. She really likes the sick bastard. I'll call Lalonde."

Another bus pulled into the depot. Casey breathed in the familiar smells of diesel fumes. Someone shouted a greeting to a coworker and again her eyes filled with tears. She was home.

Seventeen

CASEY STOOD IN Vincent Wilkes's humid kitchen and sipped a mug of coffee. She'd shown up unannounced to catch him off guard, and the plan had worked, more or less. Vincent was surprised all right, but he was also with a client in the work area upstairs; not something she'd anticipated on a Sunday. When she asked if she could wait, Vincent suggested she pour herself a coffee in the kitchen. He hadn't looked happy to see her, but then Vincent and happiness had always been at odds. Or was there another reason he didn't want her here?

Casey tried to ignore the plate of congealed porridge and ketchup-streaked eggs by the sink. A large bowl of raw vegetables sat on the counter.

The room's pine decor hadn't changed in twenty years. Out of curiosity, she opened drawers in search of loose lining paper, but the drawers had no paper. What about Dad's old desk? Was evidence of illegal imports and exports still in there? Had Vincent given all of TZ Inc.'s files to Detective Lalonde, or had he held something back?

As Casey tiptoed down the hall, she thought about her chat with the great detective yesterday. She'd told Lalonde everything she'd learned about Dad's other life: the missing money, Gislinde Van Akker, Theo, and Darcy. Lalonde responded by lecturing her about taking unnecessary risks.

At the end of the hall, Casey opened the door and entered the stifling heat of lizard-land. Reluctant to look at the creatures, she marched straight to Dad's old desk and sat down. While she listened to the faint sound of voices upstairs, she removed her jacket.

There weren't many files and the labels meant nothing. By the time she'd thumbed through the first half dozen, her focus was drifting to yesterday's unsettling chat with Rhonda. Since Lalonde hadn't yet arrested Darcy on assault charges, Casey felt she had to warn

Rhonda about him. Unfortunately, Rhonda hadn't wanted to hear anything bad about him. In two weeks, she'd gone from searching the man's things to believing she had a real relationship with the scumbag. Casey had tried to reason with her, but Rhonda had told her to stop accusing Darcy without solid proof. Refusing to stay in the house with him, Casey spent last night on Lou's couch. He'd wanted her to take the bed, but she'd declined his offer. And he hadn't suggested sharing it. Just as well.

Her other worry was Simone Archambault. Casey was still waiting to hear from her, and the longer she waited, the more worried she became. She'd pop by her apartment today to see if Simone had left a message there.

Casey finished with the files and closed the bottom drawer. When she sat up she found herself staring at an enormous iguana lumbering toward her. She jumped out of the chair.

"Woah, where did you come from?" She sidestepped to the end of the desk. God, he must have been sleeping or something in front of the easy chairs. "Hi, Sydney, aren't you a big boy."

Nearly six feet long, the beast was a grayish-green color that was dull compared to the vibrant green of the babies she'd seen earlier. Dark bands added a sinister appearance to the tail that swished back and forth. The monster lifted his head higher.

"Nice, Sydney." She glanced at the closed door. "Pretty boy."

His claws looked lethal. The beast lowered his head and raised it again. Oh lord, how fast were these beasts when they attacked? Could she make it to the door? The iguana moved toward the front of the desk. Casey retreated to the chair. The sound of footsteps heading down the stairs allowed her to breathe again.

"Come on, Vincent," she mumbled, "hurry up."

She heard Vincent thank the client for coming by and the client's reply fade. The front door closed.

"Vincent, I'm in here," Casey called out, and tried to appear nonchalant as he opened the door.

"Oh, I see you met Sydney," he said.

"Yes, any other pets wandering around?"

"No."

Sydney lumbered out of the room and down the hall. Mercifully, Vincent shut the door after him, then turned and looked at Casey. His black dress pants and shirt made him look thinner than ever.

"I'm afraid I don't have much time. I have to leave for a family dinner soon."

"Sorry, Vincent, I didn't realize you'd be so busy on a Sunday."

"I'm usually not, but it was my client's only free day."

Casey moved to the visitor's chair while Vincent took his place behind the desk. He seemed shaky. Was it because of his MS or the client, or her visit? The man didn't look strong enough to whack someone fifty or sixty times with a meat cleaver. Besides, Darcy Churcott had soared to top spot on her suspect list.

"I didn't get a chance to see Mother in Europe, but I met Theo Ziegler. What I need to know from you is if Mother's involved in importing illegal or stolen goods for Ziegler."

"I already told you—no, not that I'm aware of."

She stared at him. "Vincent?"

"All right," he sighed, "I think some of their clients were criminals, but neither Marcus nor Lillian ever hinted at moving stolen or illegal merchandise."

"Did Dad ever mention two Mexican clients named Joseph and Carlos?"

"I remember him dealing with a couple of guys from Mexico, but I don't remember the details."

"Then they haven't come here, asking you about some money Dad owed him?"

"No," Vincent frowned. "Why?"

"First, do you know the name Darcy Churcott?"

Vincent sat back in the chair. "He was involved in the import business, but I'm not sure in what capacity. I do know that Marcus thought he was bastard with a real mean streak. I heard him have words on the phone with Churcott a couple of times."

Great, just great. Casey's stomach began to flutter. "Ziegler told me that Osterman was the anti-social mean one."

Vincent shrugged and clasped his hands together. "All I know is that Marcus and Lillian liked him."

"Or Ziegler lied."

"He might be involved in some illegal activity." Vincent gazed at the snake cages beneath the window. "I think Marcus knew it and wanted to break with him, but I'm basing this entirely on bits of overheard conversations. Neither of your parents ever discussed this with me directly."

Or was he trying to protect his own ass? Casey heard a noise at the door. Oh geez, maybe Sydney wanted in again. "Vincent, did you give Detective Lalonde everything you had on TZ Inc., or are there more documents somewhere?"

"I gave him everything, though I'm not sure Lalonde believed me because he hinted about coming back with a search warrant, which he hasn't yet."

Casey stood and picked up her jacket. "The Marine Drive house was robbed and vandalized while I was away. I'm going to check the damage."

Vincent got to his feet. "That's awful."

"Oh, and one more thing," she watched him a few seconds. "Did you know that Dad had access to three million dollars in cash from his import business?"

His eyes bulged as he leaned on the desk. "And he didn't put any of it into our firm?"

"It seems so. There's disagreement about who the money belongs to. Ziegler thinks Dad was murdered for it by these Mexicans, Carlos and Joseph, but I have my doubts."

Vincent ambled to the door. "Where's the money now?"

"No one knows, but I think that's why the house was ransacked. Maybe the thief found it."

"This place was broken into last year."

"Really?"

"I nearly caught the guy once, spotted him bolting out the back when I opened the front door." Vincent leaned against the door. "For a moment, I thought he was Marcus. Guess that doesn't seem so strange now."

"Did you call the police?"

"No, nothing was taken. I drove to Marine Drive, though, to see if he was actually alive."

"And?"

"No one was there and I was too busy to chase ghosts." He gazed at the floor. "Funny thing, though. Twice I've had the feeling someone's been here while I was out. Sydney would be agitated, and the place somehow felt a little different."

"Maybe somebody found a way to deactivate your alarm. Do you keep a consistent routine?"

"Pretty much. Grocery shopping on Saturdays, Sunday dinner with my folks."

As he opened the door Casey stepped back, but Sydney wasn't there. She entered the hallway and spotted the monster heading for the kitchen.

"Thanks for seeing me, Vincent."

Forty minutes later, Casey was showing a security guard her ID and asking to enter the house. The wary guard called his boss. After Casey informed the boss that she no longer needed security personnel, the guard showed her how to operate the new alarm, then left.

Without furniture, the rooms looked larger, the floors and walls dirtier. The living room floor would need replacing. Damaged boards were scattered around a four-foot-wide hole. Stepping up to the hole, she looked down at more debris and a few hand tools. Maybe the vandal wasn't finished.

Casey's footsteps echoed across the hardwood floor and into the dining room. This floor hadn't been touched, or the one in the kitchen.

Upstairs, all that remained were dying plants, silk flowers, and trees. Casey wandered through the atrium and into Dad's now empty bedroom, noting the en suite bathroom and the closet. She strolled to the French doors at the far end of the room and looked at the ocean.

A sailboat bobbed in front of the house, its green and white sails flimsy against all that water. Casey reflected on the violence that had occurred in this house and thought about Darcy. Absorbed in her thoughts, she only heard the footsteps when they were almost at the bedroom door. The clicking heels told her this wasn't a man. Casey's heart pounded, adrenalin surged, and her face grew warm as Mother sauntered into the room.

Eighteen

WHAT IN HELL was Mother doing here? Casey's mouth grew dry as she watched her come closer. It was hard to tell which was more shocking, the tears in Mother's eyes or her youthful appearance. Her hair was the same light gold Casey remembered and, judging from the clingy pink dress, she'd scarcely gained any weight. Pear-shaped diamonds covered her earlobes. She didn't look like anyone's mother. And she sure didn't feel like calling her "mom."

Lillian removed a tissue from her handbag and dabbed her eyes. As she looked Casey up and down, Casey sucked in her stomach. She felt shabby in her navy slacks and jacket, a feeling she wasn't used to and didn't like. A few extra pounds around the middle were nothing to be ashamed of. She let her stomach muscles relax and took a deep yoga breath.

Lillian's glossy lips parted in a tentative smile. "Why did you color your lovely blond hair, Cassandra?"

"I go by Casey now, and I prefer brown to blond." She shoved her hands in her pockets to hide the shaking. "What are you doing here?"

"Vincent phoned. He knows I've been concerned about you."

"He didn't tell me you were back in Vancouver."

"I asked him not to." Lillian swept her hand along the marble mantle above the fireplace. "This is a Marcus house, isn't it? Large rooms, no hallways, plenty of natural light."

Casey's fingernails dug into her palms. "Are you here to look for three million dollars?"

A bold smile this time. "All these years apart and you ask about money? You really are a Holland."

Casey didn't appreciate the insinuation. "Are you here by yourself?"

"Yes." Lillian watched her. "Do you know who trashed the living room floor, and why?"

"I have a theory about the person responsible, and I think it's about the missing three million dollars, right?" She wouldn't be surprised if Darcy's treasure hunt had taken him to her locker at work. "Did Theo talk to you about Rhonda and Summer?"

"Yes."

"Then you'll leave them alone? Rhonda doesn't know anything about the money and there's absolutely no reason to hurt Summer."

"I never had any real intention of telling that poor child the truth about her birth mother. I simply wanted to shake Rhonda up, to let her know that telling the truth is important."

Casey stared. "So, you think that truth is important, huh?"

"I do. You see, I doubt Rhonda's told you that she knows more about Marcus than she wants to you think."

The remark soared at Casey like an arrow made of ice.

"I'm sure she claims to have known nothing about this house or its occupant," Lillian went on. "But ask her to show you a two-month-old snapshot of the man she thought was Marcus. Knowing her as well as I do, I bet she still has it."

Casey couldn't hear this right now, didn't want to discuss Rhonda when more crucial issues were at stake. "Do you know Darcy Churcott?"

Lillian's violet eyes didn't blink. "He works for Theo, why?"

Casey tilted her head back and looked at the ceiling. "I should have guessed." No wonder Theo wouldn't tell her much about him. "He's renting a room in our home. Was that Darcy's or Theo's idea?"

"Darcy's. He believes you've known where the money is all along. I convinced him that you didn't know anything. Marcus wouldn't have dumped that kind of trouble on you."

"So, Darcy decided to go on his own treasure hunt while I was away and tear up the damn house, right?" Not to mention her apartment.

"It appears so."

"Then why did Theo tell me that two Mexican clients killed Dad for the money?"

"Because he figured you wouldn't believe the truth."

"Which is?"

"Your father earned an enormous fee from those clients and put a portion of it back into the partnership, but not as much as Theo thought he should. Theo was furious with Marcus for wanting to end their partnership to start his own company. He believed Marcus stole clients and feels he should be compensated."

"Why did Theo say that Dad left the cash for me to find?"

"To entice you to look for it. If you find the money, he'll take every penny and you'll never see him again."

"Why did Dad want to end the partnership?"

"Theo became involved in controversial transactions that Marcus wanted no part of." Lillian turned and looked at the ocean. "Anyhow, the longer he and Darcy search for the money, the more frustrated they become, and that makes life dangerous for all of us."

"I already experienced Darcy's nasty side when he tried to beat the crap out of me."

The strap of Lillian's handbag slid off her shoulder. "When was this?"

"A few weeks ago, in this house." By the time Casey finished describing the encounter, Lillian's eyes were blazing. Casey couldn't tell if she was angry with Darcy or her. "Why's Darcy going to such extremes to find money for his boss? Is there a finder's fee?"

When Mother didn't respond, Casey said, "I want him out of Rhonda's house today."

"He won't go until he gets what he wants. You and Summer should leave the city until this is resolved."

"Why? Will he tear up Rhonda's house when he's finished with this one? I wonder why he started with the living room?"

"He found a bit of notepaper showing a wall with an insert that he thought was the entertainment center. An arrow pointed to the chair nearest the TV. Darcy searched it and all of the furniture. When he found nothing, he wondered if Marcus had referred to a spot under the floor."

Casey recalled the loose sheet with the squiggly lines she'd removed from Dad's notebook the day she left for Europe. The house address had been written on it, too.

"Darcy took that sheet from my dresser drawer! Summer saw him coming out of my apartment while I was away. He trashed the place, presumably to look for the money."

"Where did you find the paper?"

"In an old address book."

"Where was the book?"

"Doesn't matter," she replied, "and how did you know about the slip of paper? Are you helping Darcy look for the money?"

"No, but I'm kept informed."

Casey crossed her arms. "Obviously."

"Listen to me. Theo suspects you've seen your father's old address book or you wouldn't have visited the places you did in Europe."

How could she tell Mother the truth when she didn't trust her?

"Since the cash hasn't turned up," Lillian added, "Darcy's convinced the real clue is in that book and he wants it badly."

"I gave the book to Detective Lalonde." Or she would soon. "Did Darcy kill Dad?"

"Casey, the murdered man wasn't your father." Lillian's mouth trembled just a little, and suddenly she looked tired. "He was Gustaf Osterman. That's what I wanted to tell you in Paris. I wanted permission to return Gustaf to his family."

"Osterman?" Casey's jaw dropped. "You've got to be bloody joking."

"He and Marcus looked alike. Surgery made it possible for Gus to appear identical. It was like falling in love with Marcus all over again." Lillian's smile didn't match the emptiness in her eyes. "Gustaf loved me, you know, but Theo wanted the new Marcus to continue his relationship with Gislinde. I hear you met her?"

"Uh-huh." This was sounding a little creepy.

"Gustaf didn't really love her or he would have moved to Amsterdam ages ago."

"Surely Gislinde figured out the truth about Dad?"

"Probably, but she's pathetically weak. From what I heard, she couldn't face the fact that Marcus was gone, so she bought into the illusion, as Theo knew she would."

So, Dad hadn't gone underground. He really had died from botulism. Or had she just been given a load of bull?

"Why would Gustaf pose as Dad all that time?"

"To look for the money and find out whom Marcus's clients were. Theo had hoped those clients would contact the new Marcus who would then refer them back to Theo. Gustaf would have received a percentage of any new business generated."

Casey didn't know what to believe. Mother could spin truths with the same finesse that spiders did with webs. "Did Gustaf find the clients?"

"A few, but most of them would have been in the old address book you found."

The guy couldn't have searched the house that thoroughly, Casey thought. She'd easily found the grocery receipt with Simone's name. Maybe Gustaf had wanted the lifestyle more than the finder's fee.

"Unfortunately, Marcus was a bit of a technological dinosaur," Lillian remarked. "He wouldn't keep an electronic address book and only had a few key names in his phone."

As Mother stepped closer, Casey inhaled the scent of lavender and moved away. "Even in the best of circumstances and with the best of intentions, Mother, your credibility is lousy."

"I swear, I'm being completely honest with you."

Revulsion sliced through Casey, as if there was nothing worse than complete honesty coming from this woman. "If Gustaf had surgery just to acquire Dad's clients, why was he given an appendectomy scar?" Mother's perplexed expression was gratifying. For once, Casey knew something she didn't. "I had someone check at the morgue."

"For Gislinde's sake, I suppose. As long as she convinced herself he was the real Marcus then she'd be open to discussing his secrets and plans with the fake one."

"Yeah, right."

"Casey, I swear I'm telling the truth."

"Then why does Theo's story contradict yours?"

Lillian adjusted her purse strap. "Theo wants you to believe Marcus was the victim so you'll stay involved enough to lead him to the money. Financial problems have made him desperate and, like Darcy, he's decided that Marcus hid it someplace only you could find."

"You sound like a jilted lover out for revenge."

"Not jilted, by any means. Trouble is, once you've had Theo, it's hard to get rid of him, don't you think?"

Casey frowned. "That's a bit presumptuous, isn't it?"

"Yes, but I'd like to know how close you two have become."

As if it was any of her business. "Why didn't you tell Theo that Darcy was living at our house?"

"He doesn't need to know everything."

"God, you're not any more honest with your employers than you are with the rest of the world, are you?"

"No man ever deserved my honesty."

"Then I suppose Detective Lalonde doesn't know you work for Theo too?"

Lillian strolled past the fireplace. "Lalonde knows more than he'll tell you. Pay attention to what he's doing, Casey. The man's no fool."

Who the hell was she to reprimand anyone? "Dad would be alive if he hadn't been mixed up with you and Ziegler."

"Have you forgotten the bleak periods your father went through?"

Casey remembered that he'd always seemed so preoccupied, too busy for fun.

"The sad truth is that Marcus was a mediocre architect," Lillian said. "His business suffered and so did his confidence, but Theo helped change all that."

Casey's jaw was so tight she couldn't speak. Dad should have told her.

"The import/export business made your father happier than he'd been in a long time. Marcus was willing to take more risks, and risk was what he was all about. Marcus loved life when it was critical. We both did, which was another reason for starting his own company."

"Dad wasn't like you." Even as she said it, Casey wasn't so sure anymore.

"I understand why you think so. Marcus gave you a stable life, gave up the dangerous sports, the parties, all for you." Lillian moved closer to her. "Your father married me, accepting my past and my values. He grew to understand that my affairs were no reflection on him."

"Oh, come on."

Lillian gave an exasperated sigh. "Rhonda's still fueling your hatred, isn't she? She's been at it since you were a little girl. By the time I realized what she'd done, it was too late. I know she told you about my indiscretions before Marcus ended our marriage."

"I witnessed them, remember? Coming home from school and you were still in bed with some jerk."

Lillian lowered her head. "I knew you were angry long before Marcus kicked me out." Her voice wavered. "That's why you never said goodbye, isn't it?"

What was the use in discussing this? "If you don't get Darcy out of Rhonda's house and her life real fast, I'll have him charged with assaulting me, the security guard, and my friend, Lou, before this day is over, understand?"

Lillian seemed to be appraising her. "You've turned into a tough and resourceful young woman. I'm pleased, but I'm also terribly afraid for you. If you follow through with your threat, Darcy will unleash Armageddon."

"Don't you get it? It's already begun. When I see Theo—"

"Stay away from Theo," she interrupted. "He's mine."

"Excuse me?"

"Theo's no good for you. He belongs to me."

What on god's earth was going on? "I thought you were mad at him."

"One can be angry and still maintain a relationship, dear."

"In other words, I'd better not interfere with your conquests, is that it?" Casey waited for an answer but none came. "Theo said it was over between you, that you'd found someone else. Maybe you didn't get the memo."

"You haven't known Theo nearly long enough to understand that he doesn't mean half of what he says. So, let me tell you this once more, stay away from him."

Casey marched out of the bedroom.

She was halfway across the courtyard when Mother called out, "We had some good times, didn't we? When you were little?"

God, the woman was nuts. Casey walked faster while unwanted memories of good times sprinted through her brain. Periods of harmony during vacations and at Christmas: kisses, hugs, bedtime stories. Memories carved so deeply in her mind that she couldn't pry them free without losing part of herself.

Casey was opening her car door when Mother emerged from the house. She scribbled something on the back of a business card and then handed it to her. "In case you need me."

What was she supposed to need her for? More in-your-face lessons on Holland dysfunction? Casey read, "Holland Personnel, Specialists in All Clerical Needs: Lillian Holland, President." On the back was the number and address she'd seen in Dad's notebook.

"If you're telling the truth about Osterman, you can have his body," Casey said.

"Thank you."

Casey followed Mother's car out of the driveway and down Marine Drive. The more she thought about it, the more she wondered if anything Mother had said was true. She'd seemed bent on discrediting Rhonda. Maybe Rhonda was right: Mother did want to cause trouble, and her possessiveness over Theo and Osterman was definitely bizarre.

By the time Mother had turned off Marine Drive and disappeared, Casey realized she'd have to ask Rhonda if she'd known about Dad and the house after all.

Nineteen

WHEN CASEY GOT home, she found Rhonda's and Darcy's vehicles parked in their usual spots. She hadn't been home in twenty hours and still didn't want to face them. How was she supposed to deal with that violent maniac?

She headed up the steps and into the kitchen, where the scent of garlic and oregano filled the room. Spaghetti sauce simmered on the stove. Surrounded by bags of fruits and veggies, Rhonda was on her knees, wiping a refrigerator shelf.

She glanced at Casey. "How was your night at Lou's?"

"Fine." Judging from the cool tone, Rhonda was still ticked with her for accusing Darcy of any wrongdoing.

"Where's Darcy?"

"Lalonde took him in for a chat. I suppose you're hoping he's gone for good."

Casey didn't want to discuss Darcy. "I just saw Mother," she said, and saw Rhonda stop wiping. "She claimed you knew about the house before the murder. She also said you knew the house was occupied and that you have a two-month-old photograph proving it."

Rhonda stood and closed the fridge door. "I didn't want you to know about Lillian's twisted head games, but since she's forced the issue . . ."

Casey followed her to the living room. Rhonda knelt in front of a secretary desk in the corner. She removed a key taped under the bottom, unlocked the desk, and lifted out a stack of postcards and letters.

She handed the stack to Casey. "Not only was I treated to phone calls, but Lillian started sending letters shortly after Marcus threw her out."

In a thicker envelope, Casey removed a news clipping about "L.H. Personnel" and a half-dozen photographs dated eleven months ago.

Theo was in three shots, Mother sprawled across his lap in one of them. In another, they stood with their arms around each other at the Eiffel Tower. The accompanying note said, "Many thanks for the lovely snapshots of Summer and Cassandra."

Casey looked at Rhonda. "You sent pictures of us?"

"She asked for them, so I thought why not? I'm proud of you two. Lovers and careers mean nothing compared to raising happy children."

But Rhonda hadn't raised her; she'd just been around a lot. A cream-colored card stood out from the pile. Casey picked it up and saw Dad and Gislinde's wedding invitation—real classy of Mother. The last envelope contained a snapshot of the house on Marine Drive. In the photo, Dad, or possibly Gustaf Osterman, was washing the Jaguar. Mother had written the address on the back.

Casey held the snapshot in front of Rhonda. "Did you go to the house?"

She began to shake her head, then stopped and nodded. "I started to drive out there once. Got as far as West Van before I decided the picture was one of Lillian's nastier jokes. She knew I'd try to see him. I figured she'd doctored the photo, hoping I'd freak out."

"So you didn't actually see the property?"

Rhonda's eyes glistened as she took the letters from her, "Seven weeks ago I went back again. That time, I talked to Marcus."

"Are you sure it was him?"

"Totally, it was his voice, everything, though he pretended not to know me." The letters slipped from Rhonda's hand. "Then I realized he really didn't know me. Something had happened to his mind."

"Oh, Rhonda." If the man was Osterman, he wouldn't have known her.

"At first, I thought Lillian had put Marcus up to this, but he didn't even mention you. If he'd been in his right mind, he would have." She picked up the envelopes. "I should have told you about the letters and seeing Marcus, but I didn't want to upset you."

Too late, though she blamed Mother more than Rhonda. Casey put her arms around her.

"I didn't kill him," Rhonda mumbled. "If that's what you were wondering."

"I wasn't, but why keep this stuff?"

"To have proof of how it was between Lillian and me, so no one could accuse me of making it up. I mean, my relationship with her is weird."

Yeah, estranged codependency was definitely weird.

Rhonda wiped her eyes and tried to smile. "You had a right to know about Marcus, but seeing him the way he was wouldn't have brought you much comfort. Let's face it, Marcus was a negligent parent long before he died."

"Good thing he didn't have more kids." She thought of Gislinde Van Akker.

"Don't take this the wrong way, but I don't think Marcus wanted more, which was why he had a vasectomy."

"Really? I didn't know." Was Gustaf Osterman the father of Gislinde's child? Had Mother told the truth about him posing as Dad? But vasectomies could be reversed. On the other hand, Simone Archambault had been adamant about Dad dying three years ago, so maybe Mother had told the truth. It would also explain why Gustaf's ex-wife hadn't been able to locate him.

"You were right about my parents keeping in touch over the years." Casey told her about Theo Ziegler and her parents' role in his import business.

"That explains all his trips to Europe." Rhonda let out a long sigh. "You'd think Lillian would have thrown the news in my face."

"She wouldn't have wanted you asking too many questions," Casey replied. "Mother also said that Darcy works for Ziegler too, and I believe her. Darcy wants the missing three million bucks that he thinks I have. It's what the attacks were about, why my apartment's been trashed, and why he's spent time getting to know us."

Rhonda pulled at her disheveled hair. "Un-friggin'-believable."

"I'm not saying he doesn't like you and that your relationship isn't real," Casey added, "but the money's Darcy's main mission."

"I might believe you if the source wasn't Lillian."

"Rhonda, listen to—"

"No! Don't you get it? This is another way for her to hurt me. Lillian's found out that I have a man and she wants to destroy this relationship too!"

Casey didn't know what to say. Until Theo returned from Europe, she couldn't prove Mother's allegation about Darcy.

"I know you don't want to hear this, but I'd keep Darcy at arm's length until we know the facts." She watched Rhonda lock the secretary desk. "Isn't it better to play this cautiously, for Summer's sake?"

"I guess so. Thank god she's gone to Whistler." Rhonda started out of the room, then stopped. "You might as well have supper with me. The spaghetti will be ready in a half hour, and I'll open some wine. We could both use a drink."

"Good idea." She would have preferred to eat alone, yet she didn't want to leave Rhonda by herself.

Inside her apartment, Casey surveyed the mess. She was placing a teddy bear on the shelf when the phone rang.

"Miss Holland? This is Simone Archambault. I need to see you."

"I'm glad you called. I've been trying to reach you but your number's not in service. Are you all right?" The line was silent. "Simone?"

"You must hear the truth about Marcus's death. I should have told you before but I was afraid."

"What truth?"

"Meet me at the Queen Elizabeth Theater at ten tonight."

"Wouldn't it be easier to tell me now?"

"No. I have things to give you, important things. I wrote down the truth in case we couldn't meet and mailed a copy to your office."

"Simone, where are you staying? Maybe I could come there."

"No, the bus leaves for Vancouver soon. I will meet you outside the theater, by the fountain in the courtyard."

"The bus terminal isn't beside the theater anymore. It moved ages ago."

"I know, but I like the theater. There's a performance tonight so lots of people will be around. See you then."

Simone had sounded nervous. Did she know that Osterman had impersonated Dad, or was she simply a paranoid old lady?

By the time Casey rejoined Rhonda, a third of the bottle of red wine on the table was already gone. For someone who didn't drink much, Rhonda had downed the stuff pretty fast. Rhonda held her half-empty glass while she poured sauce on a plate of spaghetti. She was about to hand Casey the plate when the doorbell rang.

"I'll get it," Casey said.

Detective Lalonde stood on the porch. "May I come in?"

"I'll come out." She didn't want Rhonda to overhear. "I was going to call you."

Although the porch could accommodate a few people, Casey felt claustrophobic next to Lalonde. Ivy enclosed both sides of the porch, making the space feel like a small closet.

"Have you locked up Darcy?"

"No, his lawyer arrived. Mr. Sheckter didn't see enough of his assailant to make a positive ID."

"But Lou heard Darcy's voice and it's really distinctive. And what about the guard?"

"He can't remember anything useful."

"You're giving me a headache." She rubbed her forehead. "Can't you get a warrant to search Darcy's things for traces of blood and hair or something?"

"We're doing what we can."

"So, now what? Darcy has keys to this house."

"I'll have someone watch the place. Mrs. Stubbs should change the locks, and maybe you three can stay elsewhere for a few days, unless Churcott knows your friends."

"I don't think Rhonda'll do anything, seeing as how they're now romantically involved. She doesn't want to hear about Darcy's dark side. Did you know he works for Theo Ziegler?"

"He told us he's between jobs."

"Figures," she shook her head. "I saw Mother this afternoon. She said the murdered man wasn't my father, but a man named Gustaf Osterman, who apparently also worked for Ziegler."

Lalonde pulled out his notebook and glasses. "Anything else?"

As Casey told him about Osterman's quest to locate Dad's clients and the three million dollars, Lalonde scribbled notes.

"There were two good prints on the letters you gave me," he said. "We soon learned that the victim wasn't your father, but it took time to identify Gustaf Osterman. He had no criminal record."

Casey nodded. "According to Osterman's fiancée in Amsterdam, he was planning to leave Ziegler and start his own business. Mother said Dad had planned to do the same thing. Funny how everything about this murder is somehow connected to Ziegler, isn't it? The victim, the suspects, the money."

"It's not your worry, Miss Holland."

"It is when one of the suspects is living in our house. Will you please go and talk to Rhonda?"

Lalonde put his notepad away. "I came to pick up your father's old address book, and I'll need a list of everyone you saw in Europe, including addresses and phone numbers. I'll talk to Mrs. Stubbs while you fetch the book."

"Okay, but don't take it personally if she throws you out."

In her apartment, Casey compiled the list and then straightened more of her living room to give Lalonde time with Rhonda. When she finally brought the notebook and list downstairs, Lalonde was leaving the kitchen.

"Did you get through to her?" she whispered.

"I think so. She said she'd call a locksmith right away."

Casey handed him the items. "Thanks."

When he'd left, Casey hurried back to her apartment and telephoned Lou.

"You sound a little frazzled," he said.

As she gave him the highlights of her chats with Vincent Wilkes, Mother, and Lalonde, the anger poured out. "I can't help wondering what my parents were importing, besides art and tarot cards."

"Information's a hot commodity these days. All you need is a computer and some education, and you've got yourself a cottage industry. It's great for the housewife with a yen for hacking and an aptitude for industrial espionage."

"Oh good," she chuckled, "something to consider when I start a family."

Lou paused. "Are you planning to have kids some day?"

The softness in his tone surprised her. "Haven't thought about it much, but probably."

"Okay then, that's good."

Whoa. Was he really interested in her? But why hadn't he said so?

"You're welcome to hang out here again tonight," Lou added.

"Thanks, but I should stay near Rhonda. And Simone Archambault wants to give me something and talk about Dad. I'm supposed to meet her at the Queen Elizabeth Theater at ten."

"You shouldn't go alone."

"Simone's hardly a threat, and we'll be surrounded by people."

"You sure?"

"She said there's a performance tonight."

"Still, I don't know about this."

"It's okay, Lou, I'll be fine."

"All right, I guess." He cleared his throat. "Stay safe, and call if you need me."

"I will—promise."

In the kitchen, she found Rhonda, eyes red and vacant, sitting at the table and drinking more wine. She hadn't touched her food. Her nose looked as if it had been soaked in beet juice. Rhonda never could handle alcohol well, so she usually avoided it.

Casey tried to eat, but she was too restless. "Rhonda, I have to go out for a little while. Do you want me to call someone over?"

"Going to Lou's again?"

"No."

"You should give that wonderful man a chance, and don't take him for granted." She blinked at Casey. "He's crazy about you."

Lou was also her best friend. Maybe he had doubts about ruining a good thing, too. "Are you okay, Rhonda?"

"I'll survive."

She'd had her share of loneliness and disappointment, and Casey sure in hell hadn't helped. She wished she knew how to make her feel better.

"I should finish putting my apartment back together. If you want to talk, come on up."

Rhonda turned away. "Just go."

Feeling crappy, Casey did as she was told.

Twenty

IT WAS 9:45 PM and spaces near the Queen Elizabeth Theater were impossible to find. Casey finally found a spot in a parkade near the corner of Robson and Seymour, more than four blocks away. She hightailed it back to the theater just before ten.

She strolled around the courtyard's fountain on the theater's south side and waited for Simone. A half hour later, people started leaving the building. By eleven, most people were gone and the courtyard was empty again. There was still no sign of Simone. Worse, the wind had picked up and the temperature had dropped.

To stay warm, Casey took a brisk walk around the courtyard's perimeter. She scrutinized Georgia and Hamilton streets, and the stairwells leading to the parkade below ground. Why hadn't Simone showed up? What had gone wrong?

A misty rain formed pinpricks of moisture over Casey's hair and face, dampening her clothes. She walked back and forth across the courtyard, stopping at the top of the staircase on the southeast corner that separated the theater from a restaurant. As she walked, she began to sense that someone was watching her. She stared at the shrubbery against the restaurant's wall, then turned and headed back to her car.

Two blocks later, she knew she was being followed. The man who'd been trailing her since she'd left the theater kept changing his pace to match hers. When she turned around he lowered his head so all she could see was his hat. Was it Darcy? Adrenalin warmed her body and her pulse soared.

Few pedestrians were still out this rainy Sunday night, but there was a fair amount of traffic. Casey removed her keys from her purse. She gripped the longest key between her fingers, bunching the rest in her fist. Turning left onto Seymour, she began to jog.

The wind grew stronger and the rain fell harder. A bearded man, squatting in a doorway, asked for change, but she was moving too fast to respond. Headlights shimmered off the wet asphalt. Her Tercel was on level two. Casey hurried up the concrete steps, looking over her shoulder as she climbed. No one was there. Only six vehicles were left on this level. Casey raced past each one until she reached her car. Out of breath, she glanced at the back seat to make sure no one was hiding, then unlocked the driver's door and clambered inside.

Peeling out of the parkade, she watched for her stalker, but he'd vanished. She cruised past the theater in hopes of spotting Simone. She parked near the fountain and waited ten more minutes before heading to the bus station.

Forty minutes later, Casey was on her way home, frustrated and worried. She'd walked through the station and had described Simone to anyone who'd listen, but no one had noticed a petite seventy-five-year-old lady.

When she reached Rhonda's house, she parked in her usual spot. Interesting that Darcy's car wasn't here. No lights were on at the back of the house. Casey tiptoed through the kitchen and upstairs. On the second floor, she heard loud snoring from Rhonda's bedroom.

Casey settled into a hot bath to try and relax, but it didn't help. She had a bad feeling about tonight. Something had happened, something involving the man who'd tailed her. Was it Darcy? Theo?

In bed, she tried to relax with deep, calming breaths. The sound of pebbles rattling against her window made her sit up. When more pebbles hit the glass she threw back her comforter and tried to see outside. Occasionally, rowdy kids roamed the lane, but no one was there now. She lifted the wooden windowframe, poked her head out, and looked into the backyard. A man dashed around the corner toward the front of the house. Grabbing her robe, Casey headed downstairs, moving as quietly as possible past Rhonda's bedroom.

She rushed to the front door and then stopped. A shadow floated past the rectangle of thick amber glass next to the door. The shadow reappeared then slowly shifted from view again. Dread took her breath away. It couldn't be, could it? Turning the knob slowly, Casey opened the door just wide enough to see the porch.

She clamped a hand over her mouth and whimpered. A body swung from the rope draped over a beam. She fumbled for the porch's light switch. The dim yellow bulb illuminated Simone Archambault's frozen face. Casey stepped out into the porch and frantically looked for something to cut her down with, even though the logical part of her knew it was too late.

She scanned the yard and saw that the front gate was ajar. Casey hurried down the steps, her shoulder smacking Simone's body and sending it swinging. She opened the gate, darted onto the sidewalk, and stopped. Street lights clearly illuminated Theo Ziegler running toward Commercial Drive.

Twenty-one

CASEY HAD NEW respect for undertakers. There was a huge difference between violent death and a clean, serene-looking corpse stretched out on a bed of satin.

After calling Detective Lalonde, Casey had kept watch over Simone, partly to make sure Rhonda didn't come down or a passerby become too curious. Lalonde had ordered her not to touch Simone or anything on the porch. Still, Casey had wanted to cut the rope and restore a bit of dignity to the poor woman. She looked up at the beam. Rhonda had talked about putting a ceiling under those three big beams when she got the money.

Casey turned off the light and shut the door. Simone's body had begun to smell. In one memorable criminology class, she had learned what happened to a body at the time of death, how bladders and other body parts relaxed. Opening the door again, she switched on the light to see how much cleaning she'd need to do before Rhonda woke up. Not too bad yet.

She switched off the light while she recalled snippets from that course. If the rope didn't break a victim's neck, she would strangle to death. The face would turn blue and the eyes bulge. Simone didn't look like that.

Casey glanced at the street. If Theo was guilty, why pelt her window and hang around long enough to risk being seen?

A Vancouver police cruiser pulled up, followed by an unmarked vehicle and Lalonde's Sebring. Lalonde stepped out of his car and spoke at the gate to some police officers. Krueger also emerged from a vehicle. As he and Lalonde approached the house, Casey switched on the light. Lalonde didn't acknowledge her. His eyes were on Simone.

"Don't step onto the porch, Miss Holland."

"Didn't plan to." She kept her voice low. "I think she was brought here to warn me."

"About what?"

"To hand over three million dollars, or else." Casey shivered.

As more officers arrived, Lalonde said, "Let's go inside."

As they stepped into the hallway, Lalonde murmured something to Krueger, who headed back outside. In the living room, Lalonde and Casey stood at the picture window.

"So, Miss Holland," Lalonde said, "tell me again what went on tonight. You weren't making yourself clear on the phone."

Casey told him about her first meeting with Simone in Victoria and Simone's insistence on secrecy. When she mentioned Simone's request to meet her at the theater, Lalonde's expression became grim. She described the noise at her window and Theo running away. By the time she'd finished talking, Lalonde looked ready to implode.

"You should have told me about the meeting." Anger laced every word. "You know I've been looking for the lady."

"I knew you tried in France, but you never said anything about letting you know if she contacted me. I thought she only wanted to tell me stuff about Dad's last hours and give me a few of his mementoes." Lalonde's don't-play-games-with-me look annoyed her. "Look, she was an eccentric who used to tell fortunes with tarot cards. I really believed she knew nothing about the murder. Simone was adamant that Dad died from botulism, and she seemed totally uninterested in hearing anything about the body in the morgue."

"Yes, well, your belief may have cost the lady her life," Lalonde said.

Casey's face grew warm. God, was he right? Had she misread Simone?

Bright lights suddenly illuminated the front yard.

"Did you find any of those mementoes near the body?" Lalonde asked.

"No."

"Casey?" Rhonda shuffled into the room.

Oh, hell. "It's okay, Rhonda, go back to bed." Casey hurried up to her. "We'll talk in the morning."

Wearing a faded yellow robe that exposed too much cleavage,

Rhonda squinted at Lalonde. The front door opened just enough to admit Krueger who marched past Rhonda, into the living room, and whispered something to Lalonde.

"What's going on?" Rhonda asked on her way to the front door.

Casey rushed past her and stood in front of the entrance. "Some punk's been joking around. Go back to bed."

"Has something happened to my house?"

"It's fine, don't worry."

Rhonda stared at the amber glass. "Why's it so bright outside? What's going on?"

"It's a long story." Casey ushered her to the staircase. "I'll tell you everything in a few minutes, promise."

Rhonda rubbed her temples. "My head's killing me. Too much wine."

"Mrs. Stubbs, have you seen Mr. Churcott tonight?" Lalonde asked, approaching her.

Rhonda blinked at him. "No, why?"

"My colleague just informed me that his car's not here," Lalonde said.

"As far as I know, he hasn't been around. But his suite's at the back of the house and my bedroom's in front, so I might have missed him."

She had started up the steps when Lalonde said, "Where were you on the night of the murder?"

Rhonda's puffy eyes looked at Casey. "We knew this was coming, didn't we?" She turned to Lalonde. "I was watching my daughter's swim practice from seven-thirty to nine-thirty and chatting with the other moms."

"Which club does she belong to?"

"Fathom."

"Does she normally practise Sunday nights?"

"Yeah."

Casey spotted Krueger who was apparently jotting down every word Rhonda spoke.

"All done, Detective?" Rhonda gripped the railing.

"For now."

"Good. So what are you West Van cops doing on Vancouver police turf, anyway?" Both officers looked at her, but said nothing. Casey wasn't ready to explain why she'd called both local police and Lalonde.

"Please, Rhonda. We'll talk soon," she said.

"No, I—"

"Rhonda," Casey's voice rose. She was losing her patience, but didn't care. "I said I'll come see you in a few minutes. I just need you to go right now, okay?"

Rhonda scowled at her. "Fine, whatever, but don't take too long."

While Rhonda stomped upstairs, Lalonde strolled toward the appliquéd "Glamor Ladies" picture. From the window, Krueger watched the action outside.

"Was it necessary to question her now?" Casey joined Lalonde. "And after everything you've learned about Darcy and Theo, why is her alibi even an issue?"

"The evidence only points to one other person, besides Gustaf Osterman, in the house that night. That person was a woman."

"What'd you find?" Ignoring her, Lalonde joined Krueger at the window. "Come on, Detective. I promise this stays between us."

"A blue sequin," he answered, turning to her. "The blood pattern we found on a cupboard door could have come from a dress or formal gown. Not too many men would wear blue-sequined gowns to commit a murder."

"Do you really think Rhonda owns a gown? Look in her drawers and closet some time, and then take a good look at Gislinde Van Akker's wardrobe. By the way, weren't you supposed to have someone watching this place tonight?"

"Arrangements were more complicated than expected." Lalonde checked his watch. "He should be here shortly."

"Too little, too late," Casey murmured.

Lalonde's eyes smoldered in that perpetually grim face. "You claimed you saw Theodore Ziegler running from here. Are you certain it was him?"

"Yes." She turned to watch the activity outside.

"Have you any idea where Darcy Churcott might be?" Lalonde asked.

"Ask my mother. I hear she knows a lot about what's going on."

"Who told you that?"

"Vincent Wilkes, Theo, and Gislinde Van Akker."

A chunky, slightly stooped man entered the room. "Looks like the lady was dead before she got here."

Lalonde turned to Casey. "If this was a message for you, I'd pay attention." He and Krueger followed the man outside.

Casey continued to watch the police work until she noticed that she too was being observed. Beyond the yellow tape now stretched in front of the house, spectators had gathered. One of them pointed at her.

Casey retreated to her apartment and kept the lights off. Part of her wanted to seek the safety and comfort of her bed, but she couldn't sleep. The image of Simone on the porch would probably stay in her head forever. She wished she wasn't here, in this house, but she couldn't leave Rhonda.

Casey heard Rhonda's footsteps below. She was probably peeking out the window, her groggy mind trying to connect the dots. She'd have to see her soon and explain why there was a body hanging on the front porch.

Casey sat on the cushioned seat in the bay window. Was Simone killed because of something she knew, like the money's location? If the killer had found the three million or at least knew where it was, she doubted he would have taken the time to dump Simone's body here. All that cash was still out there somewhere, and it was now becoming clear that no one would be safe until the killer found it and left town. But what if she found the money first and handed it to Lalonde? What if Lalonde used it to bait the bastard? Her thoughts raced with the possibility of ending this thing once and for all.

Twenty-two

WHILE WESLEY MERGED the M8 into Broadway's westbound traffic, Casey stifled another yawn. She sat in an aisle seat, her clutch bag easily visible to passengers. She'd thought about changing to a shoulder bag because the thief was used to taking them, but this bag would make his life easier. In hindsight, though, she realized it might also arouse suspicion.

Casey closed her eyes a moment to ease the burning sensation that sleep deprivation had brought on. Every time she'd dozed off last night, the image of Simone snapped her awake. Letting go of the past wouldn't happen simply because she'd told Lalonde everything, not after Simone's murder, and certainly not now that she'd seen Mother.

She couldn't let tragedy devastate her like it had after Dad's funeral. She was wiser now, more adept at handling loss and disappointment, and lately, the disappointments had been major. Rhonda should have told her about the ongoing communication with Mother; should have admitted she'd tried to confront the man she thought was Marcus.

Casey opened her eyes and glanced at the fitness magazine she'd brought. She hadn't wanted to work today, but Stan doubted the thief planned to stop for a national holiday. The sun was out on this warm Monday and the bus was half full. If the thief appeared, she hoped her speed and reflexes would measure up.

"Why are you frowning at the magazine?" a familiar voice asked.

Casey looked up and saw Theo watching her. Geez, how long had he been following her this time? She glanced at his hands and pockets for signs of weapons. Nothing. She'd love to slap a pair of handcuffs on the bastard, but if he resisted, passengers could be hurt. She scanned faces to see if she'd also missed the arrival of the purse thief.

"I need to talk to you," Theo said.

"I'm working right now. Go away."

Two elderly women, both carrying large handbags, boarded the bus. Rather than use the seats reserved for seniors and the physically challenged at the front, the ladies chose a seat behind the center exit.

Theo sat in front of Casey and turned around. "I saw what Darcy did on your porch last night," he whispered.

Darcy? But he wasn't the one she saw. "I told you, this isn't the time or place."

"Listen to me." Theo leaned closer. "He's on a rampage and you could be next."

A young guy climbed on board. His acne, full lips, ball cap, and a black and yellow backpack matched the perp's description. The kid flashed his pass at Wesley and ambled down the aisle, glancing at every passenger. Wesley looked at Casey and nodded toward the boy.

As the kid strolled past her, she pretended to read her magazine.

"Simone was either unconscious or already dead before he got to your place," Theo whispered.

"I can't deal with this now."

She removed a lipstick tube and mirror from her purse. While applying a layer, she watched the kid settle in an aisle seat three rows behind her.

"Casey—"

"You're the only person I saw near the house, Theo."

"I was chasing Darcy. I saw him throw rocks at a window and followed him to the front, but then I saw the body on the porch. I stopped to see who it was and if she was still alive. By the time I took off again Darcy was too far ahead."

Yeah, sure. Right. "Mother said that Darcy works for you. You're all on the same damn team."

"That's what she wants you to think. Truth is, I fired Darcy six weeks ago. I had no idea he'd decided to keep looking for the money until you mentioned his name. I'm sorry, Casey."

Should she believe him? God knows Mother was more than capable of lying to pursue her own agenda. And Theo had seemed genuinely concerned when he learned about Darcy. Wesley slowed for the Cambie and Broadway stop.

"Why did you fire him?"

"He was becoming too aggressive."

"And violent?"

"Yes." Theo stared at her. "Darcy won't stop the carnage until he gets the money. If you don't find it he'll go after Rhonda and her daughter, too."

"My purse!" a woman behind Casey yelled. "He took my purse!"

A moment later, the kid with the black and yellow backpack was out the door and running.

Casey bolted after him. "Stop! MPT security!"

The file notes had said the suspect was fast. Big understatement. The kid didn't look back. Theo charged past her and went after him. Dodging pedestrians, Casey followed the pair west on Broadway. Both turned a corner. By the time she reached the corner, they'd vanished.

Hands on hips, Casey tilted her head back and took deep breaths. Stan wouldn't be happy. Damn it, she shouldn't have let Theo distract her. Fatigue had weakened her physically and mentally. She re-entered the bus on rubbery legs. Wesley, who wasn't known for his compassion, was looking at the distraught victim and the woman she sat beside. Casey felt a swoosh of heat on her from embarrassment, and knew her cheeks were probably turning a gaudy shade of red.

"Sorry," she said to Wesley and the victim. "I couldn't catch him."

"Yeah, well, the kid's a regular track star. Cops are on their way and I'm behind schedule, so stay with the lady, all right? She and her friend," he nodded to the woman she sat beside, "want to get off."

"I need to call my son," the victim said, dabbing her eyes.

"Would you like my cell phone?" Casey asked.

"You can use mine, Aggie," her friend said.

"Thank you."

Casey escorted the ladies off the bus and to a nearby bench. Holding Aggie's hand, she apologized for what had happened.

"It's all right, dear," Aggie replied. "It was all so fast. What could you have done?"

Her embarrassment deepened. "Can I get you anything?"

"No, thank you."

"Are you with transit security?" her friend asked Casey.

"Yes."

"Well then, you should have caught that delinquent."

"I tried, ma'am. I'm sorry." She removed a notepad and pen from her pocket. "Could you each tell me what you saw? It would also be helpful to know what valuables were in the purse."

The ladies' statements were brief and muddled. After Casey took their names and phone numbers, she handed each lady her business card should they need to contact MPT.

"The police will create a file," Casey said, "and will be your primary source of information. We'll get the officer's name when he or she arrives."

"I should call my son now," Aggie said.

Her friend handed her a cell phone. While the passenger made her call, Casey spotted Theo carrying a straw handbag and hurried up to him.

"Impressive," she said. "So, where's the guy?"

"He got away. Jerk saw me coming and dropped the bag." He handed it to Aggie who disconnected her call and squealed with joy.

"Thank you so much," she said.

"You're welcome." Theo stepped closer to Casey. "Do you have a few moments now?"

"Thanks for doing that, and sure, we can talk." If she kept him here until the police showed up, they could question him about Simone.

"My wallet's gone." Aggie looked at Casey and Theo as if expecting them to produce it.

"Okay, the police will be here any moment." She and Theo stepped away from the women.

"Are Rhonda and her daughter okay?" Theo asked. "Seeing Simone like that . . ."

"Summer's out of town and Rhonda's surviving, secrets and all."

"Secrets?"

"It seems my memories of growing up don't have much to do with reality. The adults in my life, including Rhonda, kept a lot of important things from me, which is rather insulting, to put it mildly."

"What did Rhonda keep from you?"

"That she and Mother have maintained something of a relationship all these years." Casey glanced up and down Broadway. No sign of the police yet. "Maybe I shouldn't be surprised; Rhonda was her childhood friend, after all. She saw Mother as strong, charismatic, and fearless—everything Rhonda wanted to be. She really tried to emulate Mother. Even dressed like her; wouldn't leave the house without makeup and a pair of earrings."

"Lillian's still strong and charismatic," Theo remarked.

Casey nodded. "Just after my parents were married, Rhonda got engaged and then pregnant right after Mother did. She bought a house two doors down from ours."

"Sounds cozy."

"Rhonda once told me that it was fun at first, until she kept having miscarriages and Mother started having affairs. Rhonda babysat me, and I know she provided alibis for some of Mother's trysts."

"Why?"

Casey glanced at the victim who was now on the phone. "I asked her that once. She'd said Mother had such a powerful hold on her there'd been no choice."

Somehow, this explanation didn't quite fit anymore. Secrets seemed as prevalent with Rhonda as they were with Mother. The circumstances surrounding Summer's birth had been hushed up. And she knew Rhonda had eavesdropped on tenants before. Secrets had helped Rhonda stay in control, just like Mother.

"Their friendship ended when Mother slept with Rhonda's husband," Casey said. "After that, Rhonda focused more on me and Dad, and then Summer. Anyway, I just found out that Rhonda and Mother can't seem to leave each other alone."

Casey told him about the letters and Mother's desire to renew their friendship.

"Sounds like they're competing," Theo said. "Lillian thrives on competition."

"Mother thrives on sex, power, and ambition. Rhonda just wants to be needed and loved." She watched Theo survey the intersection. Better keep the man talking before he took off. "Think Darcy killed Gustaf too?"

"I don't know, but Lillian might."

"Why?"

Theo studied pedestrians. "I told you she had someone new in her life. Unfortunately, it's Darcy."

"Oh, just great." Unless Theo was lying. Maybe Darcy was still on the payroll and simply taking orders. "Did he kill Simone for the money?"

"Probably."

"So tell me, are these Mexican clients real or not?"

When Theo didn't respond, Casey pinched the skin on his wrist until he shook her off.

"Have you been eating chocolate?" He rubbed his wrist.

"Answer me."

"They're real, but not dangerous, and there was no money owed to them."

"So, Dad kept the money from you, and when he died you had Gustaf Osterman take his place to find the cash and clients."

Theo's long dark eyes examined her. "That must have been some talk with your mother."

"It was. Tough to figure out whose side she's on."

"Lillian's been trapped in the middle a long time, and believe me, she's feeling it."

"She made her choices."

"As did Marcus." Theo looked around and kept his voice low. "He'd been stealing clients and moonlighting months before I found out. Before we could settle things, Marcus got sick."

"The day of the funeral, his home and car were ransacked. Was that to find the notebook and money?" She watched Theo scan the street. "If you want my cooperation, then tell the truth."

"All right, yes, I sent Darcy over. He couldn't find anything so I sent Gustaf to check out the Marine Drive place. He spent weeks going through files, personal papers, bank statements, cabinets, drawers—anything that might give him a clue. Eventually, he concluded that the information might have been at Marcus's architectural firm. He broke in there once or twice, but again no luck."

"Who stole everything out of the Marine Drive house?"

"Probably Darcy, the greedy bastard."

"Why did Gustaf stay at the house for more than three years? The search couldn't have taken that long."

"Partly to wait for Marcus's clients to come to him, which some did. But mainly because he was in trouble with two ex-wives and some associates. A new face and life in Vancouver solved his problems. Gustaf only planned to move to Amsterdam because of Gislinde's pregnancy."

"You did a good job of creating a double." Casey saw Aggie hand the phone back to her friend, then rummage through her handbag. "I heard he even sounded like Dad."

"Gustaf had a gift for impersonation, and he'd known Marcus for years. Their body type was similar and any differences were sculpted into shape."

"You mean Gustaf gained an appendectomy scar for Gislinde's benefit?"

"Yes. Dental records and fingerprints were left alone," Theo said. "I figured if someone went that far to check him out, the game was over anyway."

Casey recalled Lalonde's comments about a female suspect wearing a sequined gown.

"Could one of the ex-wives have discovered Gustaf's new life and gone after him?"

Theo shook his head. "I verified that they and Gislinde Van Akker have alibis."

"Why does Gislinde have a bodyguard?"

"Darcy interrogated her about a month before Marcus's death, and again before Gustaf died. The second time involved threats."

"Does she know the real identity of her fiancé?"

"We've never discussed it, but I imagine so. Gustaf was supposed to break up with her once he became Marcus but, obviously, that didn't happen."

"From what I've learned, Mother wouldn't have approved of their relationship, since she was quite taken with Gustaf."

He attempted a smile. "Lillian thinks every man she meets falls in love with her and that she's entitled to own them."

"Suppose Mother and Darcy believed Gustaf had finally found the money and they showed up to collect it? When Gustaf didn't cooperate, Darcy killed him," Casey said, "but they still couldn't find the money, so he moved into Rhonda's house to see what I knew. After Darcy failed to get close to me, Mother materialized to take a shot at it."

"Possibly. Did you find Marcus's old address book?"

"Yes, and I gave it to Detective Lalonde."

"What for? There may be a clue to the money in it."

"There isn't. And I'm tired of all the lies and secrets, Theo. Dad wasn't murdered. He ate tainted mayonnaise in a restaurant."

"Casey," Theo said, putting his hands on her shoulders, "Marcus's poisoning was no accident. He was deliberately given contaminated food."

"Bull. Mother said you lied about the timing of Dad's death to get me involved so I'd lead you to the money. This is just another pathetic attempt."

"No." He relaxed his grip. "Haven't you wondered why Marcus was the only one who got sick?"

"He wasn't the only one, there was—"

"Simone Archambault, yes. She was with Marcus and saw him in the hospital. That's why I needed to talk to her. I think she disappeared because she knew something about Marcus's murder. It would explain why Darcy killed her."

"Darcy?" Casey's heartbeat quickened. "Are you saying he killed dad?

"He always denied his involvement. Claimed he'd gone to Paris only to talk to Marcus, but I spoke to the waiter who served Marcus and Simone." Theo paused. "The waiter told me he was paid to give Marcus a special salad dressing, as a joke."

"Who paid him?"

"He wanted more money before he'd give me a name. I agreed, but then the waiter's body showed up in the Seine. He's the suicide victim you mentioned in Paris."

"Oh, god."

"I wouldn't be surprised if the idiot had tried to extort more money from Darcy in exchange for silence."

A police cruiser headed toward them, at last. Theo had his back to the vehicle.

"Did you confront Darcy about Dad?"

"There was no point without proof, which I now have. It's why I had to see you."

"What's the evidence?"

The cruiser pulled to a stop. The ladies rose from the bench and waved Casey over.

"Listen, I won't be long," she said to Theo. "Could you wait?"

"Actually, I think I know where Darcy might be," he checked his watch. "I'll call you soon."

As Casey watched him head down the street, she wondered if Theo had told the truth about Darcy. Either way, both of those guys were bad news.

Twenty-three

FEELING A LITTLE revived after a nap, Casey sat on the yoga mat, legs stretched out, feet flexed, and arms high over her head. She took a deep breath and then bent forward until her hands gripped her calf muscles. The seated forward bend was supposed to help a distracted mind relax. Right now, she'd use any help she could get.

Stan hadn't been happy to hear about the purse thief's escape. The yelling hadn't bothered her—she'd expected that—but his decision to put one of the part-timers on the case sure had. His excuse was that the suspect might recognize her, even though she'd assured Stan that the kid hadn't looked at her as he ran.

She'd studied the suspect's file again to see if she'd missed something, but there was nothing new. Maybe she'd stake out Vancouver Technical Secondary tomorrow and the bus stop nearest the school.

Casey still marveled at the suspect's speed; "a regular track star," Wesley had said. Casey sat upright. Wait a sec, the kid did have a smooth, efficient running style. She recalled how he'd pumped his arms when he ran, how he'd kept his head up and shoulders relaxed. The guy must have had some track and field training. She knew a little about running, thanks to Greg's fifteen-hundred-meter races in high school. This was late May, still track and field season, wasn't it? Greg's track meets had usually been in spring. Tomorrow, she'd check out Van Tech's sports field.

The phone rang. Casey rolled out of her shoulder stand and hurried to answer it.

"This is your mother. Darcy wants to talk to you."

"He can talk to Detective Lalonde." Casey's jaw clenched. "A woman named Simone Archambault was murdered last night and Theo thinks Darcy has something to do with it. Maybe you can persuade Darcy to turn himself in. After all, he is your boyfriend, isn't he?"

A long pause. "Theo told me what happened last night. I'm sorry you had to go through that."

She wasn't denying her relationship with Darcy—god. "Gee, thanks. So what does Darcy have to say about it?"

"He says Theo killed her and he wants to tell you what he knows to clear his name. Darcy says he has proof Theo did it and he wants you to give it to the police."

The tension in Mother's voice made Casey nervous. "I can understand why he doesn't want to see them, so why don't you take the evidence to Lalonde?"

"I suggested that, but he was adamant that you meet him at the house."

"No."

"Casey, listen to me. Darcy said he'd hurt Summer if you didn't show up."

Casey inhaled sharply. "What?"

"I'm sorry, but his search for the money is making him desperate. I'm suggesting you go, but that you have Detective Lalonde meet you there."

"I don't—"

"Please, Casey, for Summer's sake, and Rhonda's and mine, I'm begging you to meet him at six. Call Lalonde."

"Why can't you?" The question was barely out of her mouth before Mother hung up.

Fear coursed through Casey. Had Darcy threatened Mother? Forced her to make the call? Casey checked her watch; almost four now. Lord, she didn't want to go there and especially not alone. She needed to talk this over with someone she could count on. She dialed Lou's number and sighed with relief when he answered.

"How was your meeting with Simone last night?" he asked.

"It didn't happen."

After she described events, Lou groaned. "I don't believe it."

"There's more." Casey hesitated. "Mother just phoned and begged me to meet Darcy at Dad's house in two hours."

"You're not going, are you?"

"I have to. She said Darcy would hurt all of us if I didn't, but she did say I should bring the police, and I was wondering if you'd go with me, kind of as second pair of eyes."

"Have you told Detective Lalonde yet?"

"That's my next call."

"Casey—"

"You wouldn't have to face Darcy. I'm just looking for a little moral support. We'll take off the second Lalonde shows up."

"You know I'd do anything for you," he said, "but—"

"Great, I'll pick you up in an hour."

She hung up before he could finish turning her down. She wouldn't have much time to convince Lou that she needed his help to do this and that she was running out of courage fast.

After wolfing down a mini microwave pizza, Casey hurried downstairs and found Rhonda stirring something garlicky on the stove.

"Summer will be back from Whistler soon," Rhonda said. "Want to have supper with us?"

"Thanks, but I just ate and I'm on my way to see Lou."

"You've been avoiding me all day." Rhonda glanced at her.

"Sorry, but I've been really busy."

"Do you know if the police have arrested anyone for that poor woman's murder?"

"No." Late last night, after she'd told Rhonda about Simone, they'd cried. She hadn't wanted to rehash the whole thing again today. "But I did learn one interesting bit of news." And Rhonda wasn't going to like it. "Darcy and Mother are lovers."

"What a lot of bull crap."

"It's true."

Rhonda's paling face made the blue smudges under her eyes turn dark plum. "Who told you that?"

"Theo Ziegler, and Mother sure didn't deny it when we talked on the phone a few minutes ago."

Her hip bumped against a chair. "They're playing games with you. Isn't Ziegler the man you saw running away from this house last night?"

"Yes, but now I'm not so sure he's the killer. In fact, Darcy's a suspect, too, and last I heard he's avoiding the police. Now that Lalonde has a man watching this place, I doubt Darcy will be back. Please, Rhonda, you've got to believe me. The guy's no good."

Rhonda bit her lower lip. "I suppose Lillian's the one he's been phoning so much. I'm throwing that shithead's junk on the street." She started to pace the room, then stopped. "If Darcy's involved in crime, chances are Lillian is too. God, what if they both killed Marcus?"

"Which is why I need to know how deeply Mother's involved. I'm going to search her place tomorrow, whether she's there or not."

"Not smart, Casey."

"There's not a lot of choice here. Mother is up to her neck in this, and I know she's not telling me everything. Besides, if she catches me, she won't call the police. Despite Lalonde's good opinion of Mother, you and I know that she was raised to hate cops and probably still does."

"True, but what if Darcy's with Lillian?"

"Then I won't go in."

Rhonda stared at her, then turned away and sighed. "I found your lock pick set on the floor while I was trying to put your apartment back together that night. I put them on the top of the fridge because I didn't know if you still kept them in your junk drawer."

"I do, and thanks."

Casey opened the back door and stepped outside, feeling guilty for not revealing Gustaf Osterman's existence. Rhonda should be told, but the news would lead to questions she didn't have time to answer.

When Lou answered her knock ten minutes later, he was buttoning his shirt. Before he could finish, Casey spotted two large bruises on his ribs. Guilt made her want to sink through the floor.

"That looks like it still hurts a lot."

"It's not bad. Come on in." He sat with her on the sofa.

She glanced at his sparse chest hair, the injuries to his face. "Asking you to go was a mistake. Sorry."

"You shouldn't go either."

"Listen to me." She gripped his hand. "Darcy will hurt Rhonda and Summer if I don't."

"The cops can pick him up before that happens."

"What if he makes bail?" She watched Lou cross his arms and frown. "I have to do this."

"For shit sake, Casey."

"Face the fear, act quickly, then move on," she said. "It's what Dad would have done."

"You wouldn't do a lot of things Marcus did, which is good."

Casey glanced at the giant get-well card on Lou's coffee table. She'd read it when she'd stayed over. Seeing Marie's flamboyant signature with the two hearts beneath it still irritated her.

"What about asking Theo Ziegler to go in your place?" Lou said.

"I don't trust him. He showed up on the M8 and said that Darcy paid a waiter to give Dad the botulism."

"Shit." He slumped back against the sofa.

"Supposedly, there's proof, but he left before I could see it. Needless to say, I have a problem with his credibility."

She watched Lou scratch the eczema on his hand. The rash always appeared when he was under stress.

"He left a phone message while I was napping this afternoon, but I haven't returned it." Casey checked her watch. "I should go."

Lou gripped her wrist. "I thought you wanted to move on with your life and let Lalonde handle things."

"That was before Simone died."

"Have you called Lalonde yet?"

"I got his voice mail and left a message."

"What if he doesn't get it in time? He won't want you near the place."

"I'll drive out there but stay in the car, and leave when Lalonde arrives."

"Bad idea, Casey. A million things could go wrong."

"I'll keep the doors locked and let you know how it went."

He wouldn't let go of her. "You're not leaving."

"Lou—"

"Don't try and explain or rationalize your way out of this. I mean it."

She couldn't remember when she last saw Lou this angry. He'd never been much for arguing or physical fights, but even Lou had a breaking point. Slowly, she pried his fingers off her wrists and met his beseeching gray eyes.

"I'll be okay, I promise."

"Call Lalonde again."

She removed her cell phone from her jacket pocket and dialed his number. "Still voice mail."

Lou grabbed the phone from her and stood up. "This is Lou Sheckter. Casey's on her way to the Marine Drive house right now and she's in danger." He paced the room. "Can you go there now, or send help, or at least call us back?" He gave the date and time, then disconnected.

"Lou, I can handle—"

"No, you can't. If this is about facing your fears, then you need to wake up and realize that there are some people you *should* be afraid of."

Casey swallowed back her frustration. Why didn't he understand that saving people she loved from being hurt was worth the risk? She started to head out, but Lou scrambled past her and flattened himself against the door. It would have been funny, if it weren't for the deadly intent on his face.

"Lou, please."

His lips were pinched with determination. Casey brushed brown strands from his forehead and swept her fingertips over the light spray of freckles on his cheeks. Why hadn't she noticed how sexy he was before? When he wrapped his arms around her, she inhaled sharply. She felt his breath in her ear and a soft, heart-melting kiss on her temple. Casey rested her head on his shoulder and turned him around until she was in front of the door.

"You really do care, don't you," she murmured.

"Always have, always will."

The worry darkening his bruised face nearly broke her heart. Kissing his cheek, she reached for the handle and then slipped into the corridor, unable to look at his crestfallen face.

"I'll follow you," he called out.

"You don't have to." She checked her watch. Man, she was going to be late. Casey began to run.

Twenty-four

→

CASEY PULLED ONTO the shoulder of Marine Drive, four houses before Dad's place. Not a great place to park, but the best she could do without announcing her presence to Darcy.

Five minutes to six. She'd hoped to see Lalonde's car and at least one police cruiser at the house, but she'd already driven past the place once and no vehicles were in the driveway. Where in hell was everyone? Had Darcy hidden his vehicle to plan an ambush?

Ten minutes later, the property still looked deserted. Casey turned into the driveway, backed the car out, and parked on the shoulder. Ten more minutes dragged by. Damn it, where was Lalonde? She reached for her cell phone, but it wasn't in her pocket. Oh, crap. Lou hadn't given it back. Part of her wished that he had followed her, but part of her was glad he was out of danger.

Frustrated and edgy, Casey stepped out of the car, noting each passing vehicle on Marine. She needed to call Lalonde, and Rhonda, too. Make sure she and Summer were okay.

Casey studied the property. Where was Darcy hiding? She went up to the front door and checked the alarm. It was undamaged and still on. He couldn't have entered without deactivating the system, could he? She pressed the code, stepped inside, and then reactivated the alarm. Aware of the house's silence, Casey slowly opened the door off the entryway and peered into the garage to see if Darcy had managed to park there. He hadn't.

After a cautious search of every room, she re-entered the living room and looked at the backyard. If Darcy was out there, he was well hidden, or had Lalonde already hauled his ass out of here?

In the den, she knelt by the phone and called Rhonda. The phone rang repeatedly until voice mail kicked in. Why wasn't Rhonda answering? It was nearly six-thirty. Summer should have been back from Whistler by now. Casey left a quick message and hung up. Her palms were sweating. Everything felt wrong. She called Lalonde and got through this time.

"Where are you, Detective? I left a message for you to meet me and Darcy here at the Marine Drive house. Did you get him?"

"No, and I want you to leave the premises right now."

"Fine, whatever. He's not here anyway. And Rhonda's supposed to be home, but she's not answering the phone. Since Darcy threatened to hurt her and Summer, I'm really worried. Can you have the officer watching the place check on her? I'm on my way there now." She hung up to avoid a lecture.

While Casey sped down Marine Drive, scary scenarios tortured her. What if Darcy had set her up so he could assault Rhonda? What if he'd attacked the cop watching the house?

Rounding a curve, Casey thought she saw Theo's Saab coming from the opposite direction. In the rearview mirror, she watched the car disappear from view. If it was him, too bad. No time to talk now.

The horribly slow pace of the Georgia Street traffic frayed her nerves. When she finally reached Venables, things eased up, only to worsen again on Commercial Drive. Casey crossed Commercial and took the side streets to Violet Street, slowing at the intersection's four-way stop. The sight of clothes scattered on the sidewalk in front of Rhonda's house caught her off guard. This had to be Rhonda's doing. Darcy's bicycle had been dumped on top of the clothes.

Casey eased through the intersection, then made a right turn into the back lane. Rhonda's station wagon was gone. No sign of any cop either. Damn. Casey pulled into her spot. Moments later, she was charging across the lawn, up the steps, and into the kitchen.

"Rhonda? Summer?"

No response. Was this good or bad news? Curious about whether Darcy's belongings might have something incriminating tucked away, she headed outside. The police tape had been pulled down and lay abandoned by the fence.

On the sidewalk, Casey looked at Darcy's stuff. The jerk didn't own much: a bicycle helmet, toiletries, clock radio.

A Saab screeched to a halt across the street. Theo opened his door, while Lou jumped out from the passenger side and ran toward her.

"Lou? What are you—"

"Darcy's here! Get inside!"

Darcy emerged from behind the hedge at the corner of Rhonda's lot. He strutted down the sidewalk toward her, carrying a pistol.

"Run, Casey!" Theo yelled as he dived in front of the Saab.

Lou grabbed her hand and pulled her back through the gate, "Inside!"

"No! Darcy has a key!"

They started toward the back of the house when Darcy shouted, "Where's the money, bitch?"

They kept running. Darcy fired and missed.

"Go!" Lou released her hand and spun around to face Darcy. The second shot pierced his chest.

Twenty-five

THERE WAS NO time to let the horror sink in. Lou collapsed and landed on his back. An officer appeared from the side of the house and scanned the premises, gun drawn. Blood ran down his left temple. He called for an ambulance while Casey knelt beside Lou.

"Darcy shot him!" Casey clamped her hand over the wound and turned to the cop. "Where were you?"

"I was knocked out. Which way did he go?"

"Jumped the fence into the neighbor's yard. He could be heading for Commercial Drive." She nodded toward the house to the west "Go get him! I have first aid training."

As the cop took off, Rhonda hurried down the front steps. "What's happened?"

"Get the first aid kit, now!"

Rhonda rushed back inside. Casey lifted her hand for a closer look at Lou's injury. Blood frothed from the wound in his chest. When he inhaled, she heard a sucking sound. Not good.

"Hang in there, Lou. Ambulance'll be here soon."

While she checked his pulse, his fearful eyes watched her. His breathing was rapid and strained, pulse too fast. Casey applied pressure. Blood seeped out from under her hand.

Summer tiptoed toward them, her eyes wide and frightened.

Casey looked up. "I need your help; go get me the plastic wrap and duct tape from the kitchen right away."

Summer dashed inside.

"Please, please stay with me, Lou," she said. "You'll be okay."

Time had stopped. Nothing was moving fast enough. When Rhonda and Summer reappeared, Casey told Rhonda to cut a strip of tape with the scissors in the kit.

"Summer, there's a blanket inside a package in the kit. Could you get it out?"

Both worked on their tasks while tears slid down their cheeks. Casey heard a siren in the distance.

"I called you a couple of times over the past hour," Casey said, glancing at Rhonda. "Where were you?"

"Picking up Summer from her friend's place. The mother wanted to chat, and Summer insisted on playing with their new dog a few more minutes."

Lou opened his mouth and tried to speak.

"No! Don't talk, just lie still." Casey's hands shook as she taped plastic wrap over the wound.

Summer draped the blanket over Lou's legs while he closed his eyes.

"I can hear the ambulance." Rhonda placed her hand on Lou's forehead and looked at Casey. "He's clammy."

"It's shock. We need to prop him up a little so he can breathe easier."

The ambulance arrived. Before Casey could move him, foamy blood oozed from Lou's mouth. His breathing became more labored.

"Lou!" Casey squeezed his hand. Sweat poured out of her and her own shallow breaths sped up. "Don't you dare leave me!" Paramedics rushed to her side. "He has a sucking chest wound and can't breathe!"

As the paramedics worked, Casey told them what she knew about his condition and medical history. She also provided the name of his mother's work place. She'd barely finished when a hand touched her shoulder and Detective Lalonde asked her to step back.

"Darcy did this, and you let him go!? What the hell kind of cop are you?" Casey hadn't realized how hard she was shaking until Rhonda put her arm around her.

"Mrs. Stubbs, did you see the shooting?" Lalonde asked.

"No, I was picking Summer up from a friend's house. We'd just got home when I heard shouting out front and went to see what was going on."

No one spoke while the paramedics worked. When they finally wheeled Lou to the ambulance, Casey followed until Lalonde stepped in front of her. "You can do more for him by talking to me."

"No, I have to be with him. It's my fault!"

Again, she started for the ambulance, and Lalonde gripped her arm. Casey tried to break free, but he was too strong. Collapsing against him, she began to sob.

"He'll be all right," Rhonda said, coming forward to hold Casey in her arms. "You can see him later."

Casey forced herself to calm down. She had to stay strong for Lou. After he was lifted into the ambulance, she glanced at Darcy's belongings on the sidewalk.

"That's Darcy's stuff. Shouldn't you be searching it?"

While Lalonde called to Krueger, Casey felt herself growing light-headed. Black dots blinked in front of her eyes. Lalonde mumbled something she couldn't hear. He was escorting her toward the house when the strength left Casey's legs and she stumbled. He and Rhonda helped her to the stairs. Casey glimpsed Summer in the doorway, wiping tears from her face. Once they'd sat her on the bottom step, Lalonde said, "Thank you, Mrs. Stubbs. Would you wait inside, please?"

She frowned and then sighed. "I'll make some tea."

"I have to call Lou's mom." Casey propped her elbows on her knees and let the tears spill.

"First, tell me what happened."

She took long deep breaths and tried to concentrate. Slowly, she sat upright and described events, including how Lou and Theo had arrived together.

"How is Ziegler connected to Mr. Sheckter?"

"He isn't."

"Then why was Mr. Sheckter in Ziegler's car?"

"I don't know. I didn't have time to ask. I gather Theo took off?"

"Neither he nor the Saab were around when we arrived. I'm waiting for a report from the officer who was posted here."

Rhonda reappeared and handed Casey a mug.

"Thanks." She sipped the tea.

"Thank you, Mrs. Stubbs," Lalonde said. "That'll be all."

"I doubt it." She shut the door.

"Something's been bothering me about Churcott's relationship with Mrs. Stubbs," Lalonde said.

Casey glared at him. "My best friend's been shot and that's what's worrying you?"

"If Churcott thought you were the one with access to three million dollars, why did he spend so much time with her?"

"To see if Rhonda knew about the missing money. He knew I wouldn't tell him much." She sipped the tea. "Or maybe Mother put him up to it for her own amusement."

"Why would she do that?"

Casey explained the relationship between Darcy and Mother, and Mother and Rhonda, and how hurtful Mother could be. She told Lalonde about Mother's numerous affairs, and how Rhonda had covered for her until her own husband became one of Mother's lovers. When Casey told him about Mother's appeals to renew her friendship with Rhonda, Lalonde asked, "Why would your mother pursue a friendship with a woman engaged to her ex-husband?"

Hadn't he been listening? "To intervene, manipulate, and destroy." Casey slowly rose. "I need to call Lou's mom."

As she climbed the steps, Lalonde said, "Do you always run without thinking?"

Casey stopped. "What are you talking about?"

"The first time we met, you ran out of the morgue. The second time, you ran after Ziegler in the cemetery. Next was Europe, then you were running off to see Simone Archambault, and finally pursuing Churcott on your own."

"Better than living with helplessness and self-pity for months on end."

"There is a middle ground, you know."

"When you've been raised by Lillian and Marcus Holland, there is no middle ground, Detective."

"Or maybe you've simply inherited your parents' knack for doing what you want without considering the consequences."

She stepped inside and slammed the door.

In her apartment, Casey googled the name of the dental office where Lou's mom, Barb, worked as a hygienist. A minute later, she learned that Barb had already left for the hospital. Casey was about to follow suit when she noticed Lou's blood on her shirt. She yanked the shirt over her head, grabbed a clean one, and then headed for her car.

At the hospital, Lou's siblings were crowded into a small, private waiting room designated for families. The door was open, a sign marked "Scheckter" and "Occupied" posted beside it. As Casey stood in the doorway, Lou's mother rushed over and embraced her.

"The doctors are working on him," Barb said. "His right lung collapsed."

"I was afraid of that."

"I don't know if they've taken the bullet out yet." Barb's hand fluttered over her silver heart pendant. "I don't understand how this happened."

"I was the target, Barb. Lou was protecting me." Casey tried to tell her why but, judging from the confusion on Barb's face, she wasn't making much sense.

"Go home and rest, Casey. We're here, and Lou's dad is flying in from Winnipeg."

Leaving wasn't an option. Casey walked past more waiting rooms until she came to an alcove containing half a dozen chairs. She plunked into the first one and looked at the dark carpet until her vision blurred. Lalonde might have had a point about running without thinking. Wasn't she just as likely to run from relationships as she was to run into trouble? She'd run from Lou. She saw that now. And he knew it. But he'd waited . . . If he died . . . There was a special kind of hell for her type of cowardice. It consumed spirit the way quicksand consumed bodies. She could almost feel the suffocation starting.

Casey had no idea how long she'd been staring at the floor when she realized she wasn't alone. She looked up and saw Theo. The guy might not be a killer, but Darcy sure in hell was and he might be on Theo's payroll.

"Please tell me Darcy's been caught," she said.

Theo sat beside her. "I can't."

She leaned back in the chair and groaned. No surprise there.

"I followed the cop who went after him until Darcy jumped in his car and took off like a freakin' maniac. I also went to Lillian's place, but he didn't show up."

She opened her eyes. "Will Darcy go back to Rhonda's house? He's still expecting me to hand over that money, right?"

"Yes, but he knows it's too risky to show up right now. How's Lou?"

"His lung collapsed." She shifted in her chair. "I hate hospitals."

"Me, too." Theo glanced at magazines on the round table in front of them. "My wife was in intensive care for two days before she passed away. Hit by a drunk driver with three prior convictions. Guy went to jail briefly. A month after he got out, he died too." Theo met Casey's gaze. "Did you know Lou's in love with you?"

She swallowed back the guilt. "I'd begun to get that feeling."

"How do you feel about him?"

Casey's eyes filled with tears. "More than I can say." More than she wanted to tell this guy. Hadn't Theo played a role in this nightmare? She wiped her eyes with a tissue. "How on god's earth did Lou wind up in your car?"

"You weren't returning my calls, presumably because of trust issues, so I asked for help from the person you trusted. I thought you'd want a witness and good friend close by when I showed you what I had. Lou wasn't hard to track down."

"He wouldn't have cooperated if he thought it would put me in danger."

"Actually, he's the one who told me you were in danger. He was about to rush out the door to follow you to Marcus's place when I showed up, so I offered to help."

Casey blinked back more tears.

"We passed you on Marine Drive and turned around, but couldn't catch up," Theo said. "When we reached Napier, I spotted Darcy's car speeding toward the house."

Casey saw the large clock on a wall outside the alcove. It felt much later than nine-thirty. "You, Mother, and Darcy." She shook her head. "Death and destruction follow you three wherever you go, don't they?"

"They don't follow us. Darcy creates them and I've been trying to stop him."

A nurse hurried by. Other visitors ambled past, glancing furtively at her.

"Maybe Darcy creates chaos with your blessing. Maybe you had him kill Dad, fully expecting to locate the money, only it wasn't where you thought it'd be."

"Darcy acted on his own and here's the proof I told you about." Theo removed a letter, cassette tape, and folded sheet of paper with black smudges from his pockets. He handed the sheet to her. "It was in a locker at the bus terminal. Simone Archambault probably wanted you to drive her there to collect the stuff."

Casey remembered Simone lifting a folded smudged sheet and cassette from her trunk before she handed over the notebook. "How'd you know about her locker?"

"I followed you to the theater, but it didn't take long to realize Darcy was also tailing you."

"Great. Which one of you followed me to my car?"

"I did, to make sure he didn't hurt you. I should have realized the bastard had a reason for hanging back. I'm guessing that he spotted Simone and went after her. Once you were in your car, I headed back to the theater to confront Darcy and that's when I found Simone lying between the building and some bushes." Theo paused as more people walked by. "She told me her name and I called 911. Poor thing was badly beaten."

"I didn't see Simone, and if she was there, why didn't she approach me?"

"Probably because she recognized Darcy when she saw him follow you to the theater. She would have wanted to stay hidden until he left."

"They knew each other?"

"She knew who he was. When I told her my name, she gave me a key to a locker at the bus terminal, and told me to give everything in the locker to you."

"How'd she end up on the porch?"

"That's where I messed up. I'd assumed Darcy took off after the beating, but he must have spotted me coming and hid. I'm guessing he'd planned to get more information out of Simone. Obviously, he didn't know about the key. When I heard the ambulance a couple of blocks away, I took off."

Casey scowled. "If you'd bloody stayed with Simone, she might still be alive."

"Or he would have killed us both. When the ambulance was a block away, I left. I honestly didn't think he'd grab her. I underestimated his need to take his rage out on her and you."

Casey unfolded the sheet of paper and found herself looking at a sketch of Simone and Dad seated at a table. On the left side, a tall man with curly hair and shaded glasses stood in a doorway. Darcy.

"Is that Alvin's All-Canadian Café?"

"Yes. I talked to staff back then and found out that Simone's nephew was eating with them that night. He's an artist. I never did get a chance to talk to the man. All I could find out was that he left for a backpacking trip around Australia the day after that meal."

Casey wasn't sure she bought Theo's story. "I drove back to the theater for a last look, then went to the bus terminal. I didn't see you, Darcy, or Simone anywhere."

"The bushes kept a lot hidden, and anyway, how closely did you look?"

He was right. She hadn't gotten out of her car, but had only driven past.

"You were probably on your way home by the time I found the terminal," Theo added, handing her the letter. "Simone had two keys on the chain she wore. I don't know what the other one was for."

As he showed her the keys, Casey thought she recognized the smaller one. Simone had used one just like it to open the trunk in her home. She held the torn envelope in front of Theo. "Did you read the letter?"

"Yes, and you should too."

She opened the letter and began reading the tiny but legible handwriting.

I should have told you when you came. Darcy phoned after you left. Found out where I lived. I had to hide. Marcus was murdered. He knew there was trouble when Darcy showed up at the café. Marcus asked my nephew to draw Darcy to have a record.

Marcus gave me notebook at the hospital. He wanted to listen to Mozart. He couldn't tolerate light or loud noise. His throat was swollen—could hardly talk or move. I gave him my nephew's old tape player and put it under his blanket so he could reach the buttons. Next day, I heard music playing, then voices. Marcus and Darcy talking. Marcus wanted me to have the tape. I tried to leave the hospital, but Darcy was there, so I hid. Later I learned Marcus was dead.

Simone

Casey looked at the cassette in Theo's hand. *Mozart: The Last Four String Quartets.* "What did Dad and Darcy talk about?"

"What Darcy did to him, and why." Theo paused. "I'm not sure if Marcus was supposed to die, at least not until Darcy found the money. He probably miscalculated the dosage."

Casey turned the tape over in her hands.

"You need to hear it, so I brought this." Theo removed a small cassette player from a pocket inside his coat.

Casey wasn't sure she was ready. How long would it take before she stopped slamming into one crisis after another? She felt like a pinball trapped inside a machine built from her own memories, obstacles, and disasters. The more battles she survived, the more chance she had of winning. But if she rolled between those flippers . . .

Theo popped the cassette in and Casey heard Mozart. Seconds later, the sound of Dad's voice made her tear up. Long pauses separated slurred, barely audible words. When Darcy spoke, her back stiffened.

"Look, Marcus, just tell me where the money is, then you can have the antitoxin."

"There's . . . no . . ."

"Toxin? Sure there is. Didn't I tell you about my brother, the microbiologist? He's spent his stupid life studying botulism. Finally got some use out of him."

"If I . . . die . . . you . . . won't . . ."

"Oh, I'll find the money all right, don't worry. It'd just go faster if you helped. Hell, you could save your useless life if you told me where you stashed it."

A long silence. Casey looked at Theo, who was scowling.

"Think about my offer," Darcy added. "I'll be back for an answer in two hours."

Mozart returned.

"Simone must have visited Marcus after that," Theo said. "Just before Darcy came back."

Casey gripped the arms of the chair. She was so angry she could barely get the words out.

"Darcy worked for you. Was this your idea?"

"I admit I wanted the money and assigned Darcy to help find it, for a commission. But I swear I didn't want Marcus hurt. Darcy was simply supposed to follow Marcus and figure out where he might have hidden the cash."

Why should she believe him?.

"With this evidence, we've got Darcy," Theo continued. "I've been in touch with his brother, who said that some botulism bacterium was stolen from his lab about the time Darcy came to visit him."

"Was there an antitoxin?"

"No."

Casey rubbed her forehead. "How much does my mother know about this?"

"I don't think Lillian ever knew whether the poisoning was accidental or deliberate," Theo replied. "But she wouldn't have confronted Darcy. She knows he has a temper, and if he had any reason to think she might betray him, she knew he'd hurt her."

"I'd burn the money before I let Darcy get a single dime." Casey popped the cassette out of the player. "I should phone Lalonde, see if he's found the bastard."

"If Darcy doesn't want to be found, he won't be."

"Mother will lead them to him and she's not so hard to pin down. All I have to do is tell her I found the cash and she'll come running."

"Have you?"

"No." Interesting how quickly he asked the question. "What's your next move?"

"Find Darcy. Once I tell him about the evidence, he'll come after me for the tape, which is why I should store it in a safe place."

"I'll find the safe place." She dropped the cassette in her purse. "But go ahead and tell Darcy you have it."

"To prove I really am on your side, here." Theo handed her the letter, sketch, and keys. "Be careful, Casey. With or without this evidence, Darcy's not finished with you until he has the money."

"I'm not finished with him either." She opened the door. "What'll you do with Darcy when he comes after you?"

"Turn him over to the police." Theo stood. "I'll let you know when that happens."

Casey watched him leave. She sat there a few minutes, thinking about everything Theo had said and wondering if he really would go after Darcy. Finally, she stood and headed back to the waiting room where she found Barb slumped in a chair and looking haggard.

"I'm still waiting to see him," Barb said. "Maybe you should go home."

"I can't." Casey reached for her hand. "Not yet."

She left the room and started to look for her phone until she remembered that it was probably still with Lou, or in his apartment. She'd have to find a public phone to call Rhonda. She'd need to call Stan, too, to let him know why she might be late for work tomorrow.

Casey didn't know what time she fell asleep in the hospital's alcove, but when she awoke, the clock on the wall showed five-thirty; a new day. With her ears ringing and a migraine forming, Casey shuffled back to the Sheckters' waiting room. Chairs were occupied with sleeping people, many of whom she'd met at barbecues, Christmas parties, and weddings.

Barb smiled wearily at Casey and stepped out of the room. "I've seen him," she murmured. "They took the bullet out and the doctor said he's doing well."

"Will he be okay?"

"They're cautiously optimistic. The next twenty-four hours will tell the story." She hugged Casey. "I have a good feeling about this, so please go home and get some sleep. I'll call when you can visit."

Casey didn't move. How could she crawl into a comfy bed and leave Lou here?

"I'll call, I promise," Barb said.

She gave her another hug and then returned to her family, leaving Casey to wander down a corridor. A sign pointed to ICU straight ahead. Casey walked toward the unit. At the end of the corridor, the wide double doors identified Unit Four. Each door had a narrow pane of glass covered by a burgundy curtain. She tried to peer through the curtains.

"Can I help you?" a woman asked behind her.

Casey turned to find a nurse watching her with curiosity. "I have a friend in ICU, but I'm not sure which room. His name's Lou Sheckter."

"I'm afraid only family can visit patients here."

"I know. His mom said Lou's doing well. Is that still true?"

"He's young and strong, that one." The nurse patted Casey's shoulder. "Hang in there."

The nurse pushed a large button beside the entrance and walked between the opening doors that exposed beds and equipment. Curtains hid patients' faces. She wanted to run inside and look for Lou; even took a step forward, but the doors closed. Reluctantly, Casey left.

At this time of morning, traffic was light and she was home in fifteen minutes. The whole neighborhood seemed at peace, as if nothing awful had happened here. Casey tiptoed through the quiet house, relieved that Rhonda wasn't sitting here, expecting an update. She just didn't have the energy to talk right now. In her apartment, she swallowed a couple of painkillers, shoved the sketch, letter, and cassette under her pillow, and then collapsed into bed.

Three hours later, the rumble of a muffler-less car woke her. Since her head didn't hurt as much, she got up and called the hospital.

All they would say was that Lou was still alive. Casey made herself a coffee, dialed Lalonde's number, and got voice mail yet again. Why didn't that man ever answer his damn phone?

"Detective, it's Casey Holland. I've been given some evidence that proves my father was murdered three years ago, and I was wondering if you could come by to pick it up. The evidence makes it clear that Darcy Churcott killed Dad, so please call me."

The sight of yesterday's bloodstained shirt on the floor made her queasy. She needed to keep busy. Maybe talk to Mother about Dad's murder. She found the business card Mother gave her and then dialed the number. No answer there either. She tried Mother's work number and was informed by a receptionist that Mother wouldn't be in today. Damn it. Was she home or not? One way or the other, she'd find out. Casey retrieved her lock pick set from the top of the fridge. Afraid to leave the evidence here, she shoved it all in her handbag.

Rhonda was sliding a sheet of cookies into the oven when Casey entered the kitchen.

"They're chocolate chip, Lou's favorite," Rhonda said. "How is he?"

"I just called. He's alive, but that's all I know."

"Are you going back to the hospital?"

"After I search Mother's place."

"I'll go with you."

"No, Rhonda, if a neighbor calls the police or Darcy's there, we could be in serious trouble. Summer needs you safe here. How's she doing?"

"Still shaken about Lou. I told her she didn't have to go to school today, but she wanted to." Rhonda paused. "I explained what I could about Darcy to the principal. Staff will keep an eye on her and I'll pick her up after school."

"Does she know he shot Lou?"

Rhonda nodded. "She's handling that part better than I am."

"Summer's a tough kid."

"Glad one of us is."

Casey headed for her car. After a trip to her safe-deposit box, it took twenty minutes to reach Mother's condominium. Three more seconds to spot Krueger in a car opposite the building's entrance, and his head turning as she drove past.

Twenty-six

WHY WAS KRUEGER here? Casey found a parking spot half a block away. She turned off the engine and looked around. It was no surprise that Mother lived in one of Vancouver's trendier areas. The factories and warehouses once dominating Yaletown had been transformed into upscale condos, restaurants, and shops in what were now called heritage buildings.

Casey put on her sunglasses and ambled down the sidewalk. Might as well get this over with. Smiling, she approached Krueger, who was slouched behind the steering wheel.

"Hi, there." Casey leaned down to the open window. "Who are you waiting for?"

"You shouldn't be here," Krueger replied. "Go home."

"Did you find Darcy?"

"No."

"Maybe he'll pop by to see Mother. Is Detective Lalonde watching the back entrance?"

"Go home, Miss Holland."

"If Mother's inside, she'll talk to me, not you. She really hates cops." Krueger's blank expression was getting on her nerves. "I left a message with the detective about some evidence I received this morning."

"He'll call you when he's free," Krueger said. "Better get going."

"Since I came all this way, I'll grab a coffee from the shop around the corner first."

She marched away before Krueger could respond. Maybe Lalonde wasn't here after all. Still, someone else could be watching the underground parking and back entrance.

When she reached the other side of the building, Casey pulled on a hat from her bag, then removed her jacket. Not much of a disguise, but it might be enough. She spotted an entrance right away. Unlocking the door took some time, partly from a lack of practice with the picks, but also because it wasn't easy to look like she was having key trouble when she was trying to manipulate the pick and tension tool. As she'd hoped, some cheapskate had installed a regular pin tumbler lock.

Inside the building, the bank of mailboxes revealed that Mother lived in the penthouse. Figured. Casey stepped off the elevator into a spacious area of slate blue walls, halogen lights, and thick carpeting. She pressed her ear against Mother's door. No sound. She knocked and waited. Still nothing. Casey pulled latex gloves out of her jeans pocket.

Tools ready, she looked at the elevator. The digital message read "lobby." In the privacy of the foyer, it was much easier to feel the vibration of the pins, to keep the pressure on them with the tension tool until she heard the click.

Heart thumping, Casey opened the door. "Anyone here?"

After ensuring the place was empty, Casey began inspecting the large, tidy penthouse. Mother's home was a showpiece devoid of personal items or used coffee mugs. The bathroom contained a soaker tub and a separate shower stall with flowers etched on the glass doors. There were double sinks, light bulbs surrounding the mirror, and what looked like gold-plated faucets. Everything a spoiled woman could want.

In the living room, a computer printer sat next to an answering machine. Mother probably had a laptop with her. The machine's light flashed. Why would she use a machine instead of voice mail? Or did she use both for different numbers? Casey pressed the play button and jumped at the sound of Darcy's voice.

"Some jerk got himself shot at Casey's place and the cops are everywhere. Phone me."

The next three messages were also from Darcy, each increasingly abrupt. The fifth message was from Theo, telling her what had happened, and that he'd lost Darcy. "I'll pop by to see if he shows up," he'd said. "But you'd better disappear a while." The sixth call was Darcy again. He was furious she wasn't home. "Have you turned on me too? Don't do this, Lil."

Darcy's final call was nothing but curses followed by a slamming of the receiver. Casey looked at the machine. So, where was Mother?

In the bathroom, Casey opened the cabinet and drawers. No sign of a toothbrush or toothpaste. She searched bedroom closets for a blue sequined dress and hat. In the living room, she lifted chair and sofa cushions, stopping when she spotted a tiny splotch of dark rust on the pale green and ivory cushion. More traces were visible on the back of the sofa, just above the seat. Why this imperfection in such a perfect place? Casey touched the stain. A fragment crumbled and fell into the crack where the seat met the back of the sofa. She removed the cushion and examined the spot again. Not rust. The stains were too dark.

Staring into the crack, she spotted something shiny. Cautiously, Casey slipped her fingertips into the crevice and touched a hard, cool object. Metal? Slowly, she squeezed her hand into the crevice. Gripping the object, she pulled, but it was wedged in tight. She pulled harder until the end of a cylindrical handle appeared. Casey lifted out a meat cleaver, scattering dried blood on her jeans and the sofa seat. Horrified, she hurried to the kitchen and retrieved a paper bag she'd seen in a cupboard.

After placing the weapon in the bag, she knelt on the carpet to retrieve the cushion that had become partially wedged under the sofa. Peeking underneath, she noticed strips of duct tape running down the lumpy underside.

Casey studied the sofa perched on curving walnut legs. The furniture looked so light that if three people rushed to sit down they'd fall backward. She pulled on the back of the sofa until it thumped onto the floor. The lumps shifted. She stripped off some of the tape, reached inside, and felt sequins. Even before she saw the garment Casey knew the sequins were blue.

She removed the dress and saw splotches of blood. Casey sat on the floor, her stomach roiling. Mother had done a lot of horrible things in her life. But murder?

She placed the dress in another paper bag, then searched the lining again. A sequined hat appeared, also dotted with blood. She re-taped the lining, then set the furniture upright. It was stupid of Mother to have kept these things.

Had she killed Gustaf for the money or had she fallen for the same face she'd married thirty years earlier? One engaged to somebody else? In a sordid twist of fate, Mother would go to jail for killing Marcus Holland's impostor while her lover went to jail for killing the original.

At the elevator, Casey hesitated. She could burn the dress, throw the cleaver off a bridge, and let the crime remain unsolved. After all, Mother was the only family she had; but to help her get away with murder? With a good lawyer using the crime-of-passion tactic, Mother wouldn't stay in prison long. Casey stared at the bags. What to do?

The elevator doors slid open. One glance at the person inside and Casey wanted to sink through the floor.

Twenty-seven

→

CASEY WAS TICKED off with Krueger. He didn't have to be so rude about grabbing the evidence bags from her. Nor did she appreciate the threat to charge her with breaking and entering, among other things. And confiscating her lock picks was totally unnecessary.

From the coffee shop, she'd called Barb Sheckter and learned that Lou was still hanging in there. Barb had seen him again, but Lou had been too out of it to talk. Casey was afraid to ask when she could visit. Barb had sounded so exhausted. Yet sitting around waiting for permission to see him would drive her nuts, so better to focus on work.

She'd called Van Tech Secondary and learned that the school did have an active track and field team, but the woman on the phone said she couldn't give out information about practice times. School security had tightened over the years.

Casey checked her watch. It was nearly noon and a warm sunny day. Lunch break, and lots of students would be outside, and possibly the track team. Van Tech was fifteen minutes from here if traffic moved well. Even if the team wasn't practising, she could still look for a tall kid with a black and yellow backpack. Good running skills didn't mean he was on a team, especially when he was so busy with stealing purses.

A short while later, Casey reached the high school and noticed bus stops out front on either side of East Broadway. She made a right turn onto a side street, then pulled over and studied the layout. From here she could see one of the stops and part of the playing field behind the school.

As expected, students were everywhere. Using a pair of binoculars she kept for surveillance work, Casey scanned the area. One of Mainland's buses arrived, but it didn't stop. She eased the Tercel forward for a better view of the track. The block-long, green space looked more like a small park than a school sports field.

Five guys and two girls were stretching on the track. On the grass inside the track, more boys were playing football. Casey parked near the field's public entrance. The binocs would make her too conspicuous. She put on her hat and sunglasses, stepped out of the car and sauntered across the grass, keeping her distance from the track. A hill led from the track up to the school parking lot. Several girls sat on the grassy slope, watching shirtless boys play football and stretch on the track.

As Casey climbed she heard a girl say, "God, Jason's so flexible; he's awesome."

All of them seemed to be watching a black-haired, broad-shouldered kid who posed with legs apart and hands on hips, like he was used to being admired. The kid had the muscular upper body of a sprinter.

The student who interested Casey, though, stood half a head taller and appeared not to have lifted a weight in his life. His skinny frame was better suited for longer distances. The boy had the same physique as the purse snatcher. Without the backpack and a close look at his face, though, she couldn't tell if this was her guy.

Casey sat near the girls as all five boys, including the tall, skinny kid, prepared themselves at the starting blocks. The whistle blew and the boys took off. The skinny kid stayed in front for half a lap before the others caught up and one guy pulled ahead. Casey watched the skinny kid's relaxed and fluid technique. He sure moved like the perp. At the start of the second lap, he picked up speed and was again in front. The longer he ran, the more distance he put between himself and the competition. He won the race easily.

Afterward, the kid stood apart from teammates and talked to the guy who'd timed the race. The school bell rang and he headed for the gym bags and backpacks near a bench. When he lifted a black and yellow backpack, Casey smiled. Strokes of luck were rare in her business, but not impossible. A familiar backpack and great running skills, though, didn't mean she could confront him. Casey removed a notepad and pen from her shoulder bag and caught up with the girls who'd been ogling the athletes.

"Excuse me," she said, and smiled. "I'm writing an article about promising high school athletes, and I was wondering if you could tell me the name of the tall guy who just won that last race."

"Speed's about all the dork's got going for him," a girl answered.

Her friends laughed.

"That bad, huh?"

"You don't want to know."

"Is he your school's fastest runner?"

"One of them," another girl replied, "but Karl hasn't got what it takes to become a world-class anything."

"Karl who?"

"Karl P. Hawthorne," the girl said. "Or K.P., as he likes to be called. Anyhow, you should talk to Allen and Jason. They're our best sprinters. Karl only does eight and fifteen hundred meters."

"Thanks."

Stan would be happy. She should be, too, but Lou was fighting for his life and it seemed Mother had killed Gustaf Osterman. Worse, Darcy was lurking out there, willing to murder people for three million bucks. Regret, fear, and anger trampled on any good feeling she'd started to have.

Twenty-eight

WHEN CASEY RETURNED from Van Tech at 1:00 PM, Rhonda wasn't home. Just as well. She'd want to know what had happened at Mother's, and Casey wasn't looking forward to answering. Still, she supposed Rhonda should know. But first, Stan needed to hear about Karl P. Hawthorne. She dialed his number.

Stan listened, then said, "I should reprimand you for working on an assignment I transferred to someone else, but I get why you did it. So write up what you saw and I'll call VPD."

"No problem."

Casey glanced at her message machine. Strange that she still hadn't heard from Lalonde about the evidence, unless he'd found Mother and Darcy and was busy interrogating them. She heard Rhonda's station wagon pull up to the house. Casey went downstairs and into the kitchen.

"Damn it!" Rhonda slammed the fridge door. "Forgot the bloody milk!"

She forgot all the time, but usually didn't get this angry. "What's wrong?" Casey asked. "Besides the milk?"

Rhonda let out a puff of air. "I went to see Mom. She's trying to bully me and Summer into staying with her a few days."

"Not a bad idea."

"It damn well is. I'm not living under the same roof with that woman again." She slumped into a chair. "Speaking of mothers, how'd it go at Lillian's?"

"She wasn't there, so I went in."

"God, Casey, are you sure no one saw you?"

"I was seen all right."

As Casey told her about Krueger, the cleaver, and the blue sequined dress, Rhonda's bloodshot eyes didn't blink. When she'd finished her story she waited for Rhonda to say something, but she just sat there staring.

"Poor Lillian," she said finally.

"That's it? That's all you can say?"

"Not much more to say, except that she's finally gone off the deep end."

"I learned something else." Casey hesitated. "It turns out the murdered man wasn't Dad but a guy named Gustaf Osterman. He worked for Theo Ziegler, too, which means he knew Mother and Darcy."

Rhonda frowned. "That can't be. I talked to Marcus, remember? Did Lillian tell you that crap?"

"The pathologist and the police verified her story."

"She probably paid them to."

"I don't think so."

Rhonda stood and leaned on the table. "The resemblance was perfect."

"Thanks to some careful surgery."

"Are you saying Lillian created a twin to upset me?"

"No, Theo arranged it. He wanted Gustaf to find the three million and wait for business contacts to show up, people who could have generated millions more for Theo's company."

Rhonda gripped the table as if to steady herself. She looked kind of dazed.

"You okay?" Casey asked.

"Yeah. Bit much to take in, that's all." She fetched her purse from the counter. "I'm going to get the milk. You need anything?"

"Yeah, I need Darcy caught and Lou to survive."

Back in her apartment, Casey again checked for messages. Neither Barb nor Lalonde had called. She tried some yoga moves to ease the tension that stretched from shoulders to pelvis. But she knew the tension wouldn't go away until questions were answered, arrests made, and the friggin' money found. She couldn't put off the search any further. It was the only way the vultures would leave her and those she loved alone.

Dad had left her the notebook and a key to the house. Was the clue in the book or in the house? She'd already tried every hiding place she knew inside and out. She had to be missing something. Something in the design? She thought of the blueprints. Gislinde said Dad had planned to give them to her when he'd finished the place and supposedly forgot. But he'd died, and Gislinde, probably realizing Gustaf had taken over, was the one who'd forgotten about them. Had Dad inserted a clue in the prints? If Gustaf hadn't told Gislinde about his search for the money, she wouldn't have had a reason to show him the prints; prints she'd stored at her sister's place.

Casey scooped up the blueprints from her bedroom and then spread them over the kitchen table. Dad had loved creating hiding places. When she was little, he designed one in their medicine cabinet to keep drugs out of her reach. Could he have built a spot large enough to store three million bucks? Casey pored over the prints, room by room, until her intercom rang. She hoped it was Lalonde.

"This is your mother. I need to see you."

Oh, crap. Had Mother seen her leave the building? Did she know the bloodstained dress was gone? No way was she ready for a confrontation. Then again, she never would be.

"Are you alone?" Casey asked.

"Yes."

"Be down in a minute."

She hid the prints and hurried downstairs, glad that Rhonda had gone to the store. The last thing she needed was her and Mother under the same roof.

When she opened the front door, Mother made a weak attempt at a smile. They didn't speak as Casey escorted her into her apartment.

"What are you doing here?"

Lillian surveyed the room. "I came to say goodbye. I'm leaving the country."

"Permanently?"

"Do you care?"

"Detective Lalonde will. I imagine he's looking for you."

"Really? I was just approached by a Vancouver police officer who's watching this place. I told him I'm your mother and am here on family business. He didn't seem to care."

Casey sighed. Apparently a rookie on guard duty hadn't yet been informed that Mother was a prime murder suspect.

Lillian strolled toward the bay window. "I'm sure you don't want to discuss us, but I do. Think of it as a last request."

Casey sat in the rocking chair and watched Mother.

"Have I caused you so much pain that you still can't talk about the past, Casey?"

She rocked back and forth. "I've never felt I was important to you." She couldn't quite meet her mother's eyes. "Now, well, you're not someone I'd choose for a friend."

"That's a shame," her voice faltered, "because I'd choose you."

"I'm a hard friend to make. I ask for honesty and trust."

Lillian perched on the arm of the sofa. "I was honest with you the other day, wasn't I? It's the only meaningful gift I have."

Casey wasn't sure she wanted this gift.

"You've gone to a lot of trouble to understand the past," Lillian continued. "You're entitled to the whole truth."

"Speaking of which, have you been in touch with Darcy since late yesterday afternoon?"

"No, and I've dumped that maniac." Anger flashed across her face. "I'm sorry your friend was shot. Theo told me what happened."

Casey stopped rocking. "Did he also tell you that Darcy murdered Dad and that I heard him practically admit it on tape?"

Watching Mother's complexion turn the color of chalk almost made Casey feel sorry for her. After she highlighted what she'd heard, Casey added, "And this is the piece of shit you chose for a lover?"

"Darcy may have acted on Theo's orders."

"Prove it."

Lillian removed a cigarette and lighter from her purse. "Theo had Gustaf take Marcus's place only days after the murder. Doesn't that imply premeditation?"

It did.

"Gustaf was a perfect likeness and too well rehearsed. They'd planned this a long time." Her hand trembled as she lit the cigarette. "He looked and acted so much like Marcus, on the surface anyway. At first it was easy to pretend . . ." The sentence dissolved as she dragged on the cigarette.

"And you went along with the charade." Casey stood. "You've been playing Theo's game for years."

"I didn't know much about Theo's shadier deals for a long time. Remember, I was just the courier, the delivery person. Eventually, I learned more and wanted to leave, but he wouldn't let me walk away."

"Uh-huh. Rhonda thinks you'd do or say anything to protect yourself."

"Rhonda's not fit to judge me!"

Casey wouldn't let the anger faze her. "You've been playing games yourself, and a really cruel one with Rhonda."

Lillian's appraising look lasted a long time. "Rhonda's hung onto you all these years by making you feel sorry for her. When did you decide to compensate her for my mistakes?"

"Compensate?"

"By becoming the daughter she always wanted, until Summer came along, anyway. Rhonda latched onto your kindness, then brainwashed you." As she took another drag on her cigarette, Lillian's hands shook harder. "She's been holding you emotional hostage ever since."

"That's not true."

"The truth," Lillian replied, her voice rising, "is that Rhonda fell in love with Marcus years ago and never stopped trying to drive a wedge between him and me."

"You're the one who had the affairs, Mother."

"And Rhonda couldn't wait to tell Marcus about them, but he knew she was trying to break us up. She was so smug and self-righteous from her perch until I forced her into the muck by seducing her husband."

"That was disgusting."

"And a mistake. It made destroying my marriage so much easier for her."

"You expect me to believe that?"

"Do you think Rhonda wanted you to know that she planned to ruin my life? She's been terrified of the truth for years, Casey. And the truth is she'd been obsessed with Marcus since you were a toddler."

Memories of conversations began to surface: arguments between her mother and Rhonda; Mother warning Rhonda to keep her mouth shut; Rhonda threatening to ruin her.

"Did Rhonda actually tell you she was in love with Dad back then?"

"No, but I could see it in her face."

Casey didn't try to hide her contempt. "Why is it that when the conversation turns to men, you sound like a paranoid nut?" She returned Mother's scowl. "Dad fell in love with her by choice."

"Rhonda didn't hang around me all those years without learning a thing or two about manipulation through emotional blackmail. She worked Marcus well; wore him down until he gave in." Lillian blew a cloud of smoke into the air. "In some ways she was good for him. But once he met Gislinde, how long do you think his interest in Rhonda lasted?"

Casey turned away. She didn't want to go down this road anymore.

"Rhonda did a marvellous job of keeping you ignorant. Offering you shelter when you were most vulnerable was especially effective." Lillian stood. "It's time you saw things for what they are, not for what you want them to be or were conditioned to believe."

"What I see is two middle-aged women stuck on old issues. You can't let go of Rhonda any more than you could Dad."

Casey also saw a woman who'd spent so much time with people like Theo and Darcy that she would stoop to murder to get what she wanted. The woman had become one scary stranger.

"If I have trouble letting go," Lillian said, "it's because Rhonda has you and that is so wrong."

"I live my own life, Mother."

"How's that possible when you live under her roof?"

"Staying here is only temporary."

"You call two years temporary?"

"I call it none of your business."

"You play the victim role too well, Casey. Marcus's death and your husband's infidelity made you weak. You wound up relying on anti-depressants and shrinks and Rhonda. That is not what I wanted for you. You should have lived more selfishly, my darling."

"Like you?"

"Listen to me." Lillian stepped closer. "I don't want you to be con-troled or influenced by anyone, and I don't want you to break down every time you suffer a major loss. Since we might not meet again, this is really what I wanted to tell you."

Casey smelled her mother's lavender scent and moved away. "Was your desire to say it here based on a need to hurt Rhonda again?"

"She's already hurt herself more than I ever could. It's over. There's no point in staying to watch the end. The idea has no appeal."

"What end?"

The door opened.

"The end of me and Lillian," Rhonda said, entering the room.

The hatred on Rhonda's face shocked Casey. She retreated to the window seat.

Ashes fell from Lillian's cigarette as she glowered at Rhonda. "Still haven't squashed those eavesdropping tendencies, I see."

Rhonda sauntered up to her. "Coming here was stupid, Lillian, which is why I'm happy you did, but if you were hoping to turn my daughter against me—"

"Why is *my* daughter living in your house?"

"Because she wants to."

No, Casey thought, not anymore.

"It's only fair," Rhonda added, "since you took my husband from me."

"Do you think you'll ever outgrow your jealousy?" Lillian asked.

"What was I supposed to be jealous of? You whoring around at fourteen? Cheating on your husband repeatedly and intentionally destroying other people's happiness? Leaving Casey alone downstairs while you screwed someone's husband upstairs?"

"You hated that I had Marcus. Admit it."

"Marcus only became appealing once he stopped martyring him-self over a tramp like you. As for your pathetic attempts to be friends again, I always knew what you really wanted." Rhonda's eyes blazed. "I know your soul, Lillian. We were inseparable for years, right? All you wanted was to get Casey back in your life and make sure Marcus stayed out of mine."

Casey drew her knees up to her chest and wrapped her arms around her legs. She'd never heard so much venom coming from Rhonda. Had her forgiving attitude been an act? Or had the news about the dress set her off?

"Luckily, we won't have to put up with your garbage much longer," Rhonda went on. "Casey found the clothes and weapon in your place and handed everything to the cops."

Casey inhaled sharply. Oh god, why was she saying this?

The cigarette nearly dropped from Lillian's hand as she turned to Casey. "What clothes?"

Casey tried to speak, but the words wouldn't come.

"The shimmery little number you wore to kill Marcus," Rhonda blurted. "Or Gustaf, I should say."

Casey shook her head. Why wouldn't she keep her mouth shut? "Rhonda, let the police handle—"

"Is that what you and Darcy do for fun now? Shoot and hack people to death?" Rhonda asked. "You need to find a better hobby, hon, 'cause that one really sucks."

Lillian's puzzled expression vanished. "I didn't kill anyone, *hon*. You did."

Rhonda glanced at Casey. "I told you she was devious." Her hands curled into fists. "You began setting me up the day you sent me the picture of Marcus."

"Why did you send the picture?" Casey asked.

Lillian removed what looked like a compact from her purse. When she opened the lid Casey saw a mini-ashtray. "It was just part of the game. I had no idea Rhonda would completely unhinge." Lillian mashed the cigarette butt in the tray, closed the lid, and dropped it in her purse.

Rhonda laughed. "Smooth, Lillian, but let's not forget darling Darcy. You planted him in my house, probably to fabricate evidence against me." She began circling Lillian. "You sent the photo and wedding invitation, which you knew would make me confront Marcus. After all, his betrayal would make a great motive for murder. Now you want to plant suspicion in Casey's head."

Lillian looked at Casey. "She's lying. As I said before, coming here was Darcy's idea. He thinks you have the money. Since he was here, though, I suggested he look around and see if he could find evidence against Rhonda."

"He didn't find anything because there was nothing to find!" Rhonda shouted.

"The tragic part," Lillian said, "is that you butchered the wrong—"

"When I heard your voice, I went downstairs and called Lalonde before I came in," Rhonda interrupted. "He's on his way."

"I'll wait for him outside." Lillian walked to the door.

"If she's so innocent," Rhonda said, turning to Casey, "why's she taking off the moment I mention cops?"

As Lillian started to leave, Rhonda grabbed her arm and hauled her backward. "You're not getting away that easy!"

In an effort to break free, Lillian dropped her handbag. Rhonda held her arm with both hands.

"Stop it!" Casey jumped up from the window seat. "Both of you!"

Lillian kicked Rhonda in the shin and jerked her arm free. She grabbed Rhonda's hair and pulled her head back. Rhonda collapsed onto her knees, wrapped her arms around Lillian's legs and attempted to take her feet out from under her. Lillian hit Rhonda on the side of her head, knocking her over. Grabbing her bag, Lillian ran out of the apartment. Rhonda stumbled to the door, her eyes wild, hair twisted in all directions.

"Don't worry, she won't get away." Rhonda wiped her face with her sleeve. "The bitch will finally get what she deserves."

Casey's stomach churned so fast she thought she'd be sick.

Twenty-nine

CASEY DIDN'T TRY to follow Mother. Rhonda did, and probably had her in a headlock by now. Curled up in the window seat, Casey tried to understand what Rhonda had said, to make sense of the intensity of her rage. Mother had been right about one thing. Rhonda wasn't herself these days. But Mother had been totally off base to accuse her of murder. Did she really think Rhonda could afford a sequined gown? If she'd done her homework, Mother would have known that Rhonda was at Summer's swim practice when Gustaf was killed.

Police sirens grew louder. Casey didn't want to hear Rhonda's version of events. Besides, three million dollars needed to be found before more people died. She fetched the blueprints and hurried to her car.

Eager to avoid Rhonda and the police, Casey started the engine and cruised down the back lane. Five seconds later, cold metal pressed against her neck and she gasped.

"Oh!" She hit the brakes.

The metal pressed harder. "Drive," a familiar voice ordered.

In the rearview mirror she saw Darcy's grim face.

"You should clean your car more often." He tossed her sleeping bag and pillow to the side.

Her heart tried to leap up her throat. "How'd you get in with a cop here?"

"He's having a little nap. Now drive."

Sweat beaded along her lower back. "Where to?"

"The Marine Drive house." He lifted the blueprints off the passenger's seat. "Where'd you get these?"

"Gislinde Van Akker."

"I was right. Money's in the house." Darcy reached over and dumped her purse's contents on the seat. "Where's the tape?"

"Tape?"

Once again, he pressed the weapon against the back of her neck.

"You like Mozart, Casey?"

"Theo has it."

Darcy thumped the side of her head with the pistol. "Wrong answer."

Wincing, she struggled to stay calm. What in hell had Theo told him? "It's in my safe-deposit box, I swear." She eased the vehicle forward. "I was on my way to the house to try and find the money."

"Well, sweet thing, if I don't get the cash and tape today, I'll kill Summer and make Rhonda watch. Or maybe I'll kill Rhonda and make Summer watch."

Casey gripped the steering wheel so hard her fingers ached. She turned right onto Commercial Drive. "The police think you killed Simone Archambault."

"I didn't kill the old broad, Theo did. He came to Lillian's place after it happened and told her while I was listening in the bedroom."

"Why would Theo murder Simone, then drop by to tell Mother?"

"He needed Lil to give him an alibi. Anyway, if I wanted the old girl dead, I would have shot her. Think about that."

How long had he been carrying the pistol? "Mother came by a few minutes ago. Did you see her?"

"I was focusing on that cop in your yard." Darcy paused. "What'd she want?"

"To apologize for things that happened in the past." Casey turned left onto Venables.

"She did, did she?" He leaned a little closer. "Does Lil know about the tape?"

"We didn't discuss it," Casey lied, "only talked about her and me." She prayed Darcy believed her. If he found out she'd told her . . .

"What about you, Casey? Did you have a nice long listen to the tape?"

"For a few seconds. Dad mumbled so much I couldn't understand what he was saying."

She tried to ignore Darcy's stare and focus on her driving. Five minutes later she reached Georgia Street. By the time they were crossing the Lions Gate Bridge into West Vancouver, his silence was frightening her more than his words.

"Mother also came to say goodbye," Casey said. "She's leaving the country today."

Once more, she felt the gun against her neck. "Lil wouldn't leave without me. She knows how much I love her."

Casey swallowed back her revulsion. "She wants to get away from Theo. I think she feels betrayed by him."

"For good reason. Anyhow, we're gettin' married as soon as we get the money. Guess that'll make me your stepdad."

Oh, that was good news. "I'm glad you love her. She needs someone in her corner." Casey glanced at the rearview mirror, hoping she sounded sincere. "See, the cops are about to arrest her for Gustaf Osterman's murder."

"What are you talking about? Lillian didn't kill Gustaf."

"Evidence was found under her sofa."

"What evidence?"

"A bloodstained, sequined dress and the murder weapon."

Darcy's brows scrunched into a long, ugly line. "She didn't do it. I was with her the night it happened, at a restaurant."

Sure, right. Again, they drove in silence until Casey pulled up to the house. When she saw Theo's car parked in the driveway, she began to relax.

"Theo's been waiting for you," Darcy remarked.

"I see." Leeches on her legs couldn't have been more repulsive than his amused expression.

"Park on the street," he ordered.

She did so and stepped out of the car. Grabbing her wrist, Darcy pulled her past Theo's vehicle. Casey scanned the windows and yard for signs of him. The alarm's cover was missing and cut wires were exposed. Darcy opened the unlocked door and hauled her inside.

"I want to show you what will happen if you try to cross me," he said.

Oh no, was Theo dead? Darcy pulled her into the living room, toward the hole in the floor.

He gaped at the hole. "What the hell?"

Darcy started to turn as Theo shoved him into the hole.

Darcy landed hard, dropping his pistol. Cuts crisscrossed Theo's forehead and his left eye was nearly swollen shut. His split lip had dripped blood onto his chin and shirt.

"So, you two caught up with each other," Casey said, shaking with relief and fear.

"I told Darcy I had the tape and he insisted on meeting me here." He pointed a pistol at Darcy.

"And when he realized you didn't have it, he came to me. Or did you send him?"

"He guessed."

Darcy looked incensed. When she saw he was within arm's reach of his gun, she stepped back. "I'm amazed you didn't shoot each other."

"Didn't have a weapon—I took this one from him." Theo kept the pistol leveled at Darcy's chest. "Who knew he had two?"

"I'll call the police."

"No cops," Theo replied.

"Why?"

"Because he knows that if I'm charged with murder or killed," Darcy answered, "a certain piece of incriminating evidence will be sent to the cops on my behalf."

"Evidence of what?" Casey asked.

"Something that proves Theo killed the guy who crashed into his wife."

"I've told you a hundred times," Theo said. "The guy was drunk, couldn't swim, and was stupid enough to fish alone. He fell in the water. I had nothing to do with it."

"So why do I have pictures of you at the lake the same weekend he drowned?"

"Circumstantial, that's all."

"Why have you kept me around when you hate me so much?"

"Because you did your job until you started losing control."

Darcy lunged for his gun.

"Casey, run!" Theo fired a shot.

On her way outside, Casey heard a second shot. She raced to Gil's place next door and rang the bell. Gil took a few seconds to answer.

"Can I use your phone? It's urgent!"

He opened the door wider.

Seconds later, she contacted Lalonde who ordered her to stay put. "I'll be there shortly."

"Where have you been all morning? Did you get my message?"

"Yes, and I've been busy. This case isn't just about answering your phone calls, Miss Holland. There are meetings, new witnesses to interview, and more evidence to analyze."

"Like the dress and the meat clever?"

"Among other things. As I said, stay put and we'll talk when I get there."

Staying put wasn't easy. She desperately wanted to know what was happening next door.

"Man, I didn't hear or see anything," Gil said as he shut the drapes. "Are we safe?"

"I think so." She tried to sound reassuring. "I'm betting Darcy wants to get far from here."

Casey paced the room, partially aware of the scent of lemon oil. Tabletops shone and magazines were attractively displayed. The plush carpet looked like it had just been vacuumed.

Judging from the way Gil fidgeted, she was making him nervous, but she couldn't help it.

"Are you parents back from Arizona?"

"Yeah, they're at work."

Casey headed for the doors that led to the balcony overlooking the backyard. Through the drapes, she peeked outside. From what she could see of Dad's yard, no one was around. Whether Theo and Darcy were still inside or down on the beach was anyone's guess. Casey wished she heard sirens or even shouting. Anything was better than this silence.

Thirty

$\longrightarrow$

TO CASEY'S RELIEF, vehicles screeched to a halt outside. "It must be the police." She ran to the door.

"Think you should go out there?" Gil asked.

"Probably not." She turned to him. "The other day, you said you could see my dad's driveway from your bedroom window, right?"

"Yeah."

"Maybe we can see what's going on from there."

Gil looked worried. "I don't know."

"Just a quick peek, that's all." He still looked uncertain. "I promise to ignore any mess and posters of naked people. Is it up here?"

"Uh . . ."

She started up the stairs. "Which door, Gil?"

"Last one on the left," he answered, lagging behind.

When she stepped over the threshold, Casey stopped. She hadn't expected this. The room was spotless. "You must have a really good housekeeper."

"No housekeeper." He blushed, "Just me."

Looking at his hands, Casey saw the red cracked skin of someone who spent far too much time with chemicals and hot, soapy water. No wonder the living room was spotless.

"It's kind of an obsession thing." He shoved his hands in his pockets.

Poor kid. Casey looked out the window. Theo's car had been replaced with a police cruiser and Lalonde's Sebring. How was it that he always managed to stay one step ahead of them? Years of practice maybe? Two uniformed officers were in the front yard while two more were heading toward the back. Lalonde and Krueger emerged from the house.

Casey ran downstairs and bolted straight for Lalonde. "You didn't find them?"

"We're checking the beach," he answered. "Tell me exactly what happened."

A gust of wind swept over them and slate gray clouds sailed across the sky. After Casey finished her story she waited for a response, but none came.

"Have you managed to track Ziegler down since he's been back in Vancouver?"

"Yes, we spoke briefly, but there was nothing to hold him on at that time."

Meaning what? That there might be later? Was he still investigating TZ Inc.'s activities?

"I saw my mother this afternoon," she said. "Did your people pick her up?"

A pained look deepened Lalonde's wrinkles. "Mrs. Stubbs said a murderer was in her house, then hung up before we could learn more. I thought she meant Churcott."

"Since we're dealing with three, maybe four, separate murders, there could be at least two killers."

"Four murders?"

"Gustaf Osterman, Simone Archambault, my father, and possibly a waiter at Alvin's All-Canadian Café, which the French police think was a suicide. You really need to see the evidence Theo gave me. It proves that Darcy arranged to give Dad contaminated food."

She told him what she'd heard on the tape and Theo's conversation with the waiter. While Lalonde scribbled notes, raindrops began to fall.

"If you can get the evidence out of your safe-deposit box by the end of the day, I'll have it picked up."

"Fine. Meanwhile you'll probably want to pick up Mother too, because she's leaving the country today. She should be at the airport by now."

"Then why is she speeding along the Sea-to-Sky Highway toward Whistler?" Lalonde asked. "Her movements have been monitored since she left your apartment."

Why in hell was Mother heading north when the airport was south? Had she changed her mind, or had she lied about leaving?

"Go home, Miss Holland," Lalonde said.

"Can I check something out in the house first?"

"Like what?"

"A hiding place for three million dollars."

Lalonde tried not to smile. "Think you'll find it, do you?"

"Darcy's convinced it's there or he wouldn't have put a big hole in the floor."

"He could come back."

"You'll have officers around for a bit, right?" She nodded toward the handful of men and women standing about, looking like they needed something to do. "I won't be long."

Lalonde nodded. "Fine, but when they leave I suggest you do, too."

"Sure."

Casey grabbed the blueprints from her Tercel and dashed inside the house. Starting with the den, she walked through each room, comparing written measurements with the actual size of rooms and examining every cupboard and closet. Upstairs in the master bedroom, she found a discrepancy. The closet looked slightly smaller than the prints indicated it should be.

She stepped into the closet to look at the wall separating Dad's bedroom from the courtyard. On close examination, the wall seemed a bit too near, as if it didn't quite extend far enough to be level with the doorway and the rest of the wall. Was there an empty space on the other side of this closet? Casey looked for latches, buttons, and loose boards. Nothing.

She left the bedroom and took a close look at the wood-paneled wall. It was a bit odd that the paneling covered only the lower half of the wall, but then oddity had been somewhat of a trademark for Dad, and he'd loved wood. She felt around for latches, switches, depressions or other weaknesses. Still nothing.

Stepping back, she studied the area. The trees had started to lose leaves and the live plants looked thirsty. The whole place was becoming a jumbled mess.

Casey gazed at the six trees. Three on one side of the courtyard, three on the other. And then she remembered . . . two vertical rows of x's and o's, plus squiggly lines on the slip of paper Dad had left in the notebook. A jumbled mess.

Darcy had assumed the insert drawn on the note referred to the entertainment center on the first floor, and that the x's and o's represented the furniture. There'd been a sofa and two end tables on one side of the room, and two chairs separated by a table on the other. If he'd taken the chairs apart and come up empty, this could explain why he tore into the floor below the furniture.

But what if the insert referred to a hidden space in the closet on this floor? The x's and o's could have meant the two rows of trees. Casey recalled seeing an arrow pointing to the left. Closing her eyes, she visualized the diagram and recalled that the arrow had pointed to an "x" at the top of the row.

She opened her eyes. It was the first tree on her right, the one Lou had said was a Japanese maple. The tree was only a little taller than herself. Casey gazed at the gracefully arched branches and leaves. Its clay pot looked heavy. The floor tiles were about the size of the palm of her hand. The tiles around this pot weren't as stained as the ones surrounding the other five pots: apparently, Gustaf hadn't been a great gardener.

It took repeated pulls before Casey managed to move the pot enough to see the tiles beneath. She ran her hands over the floor and grinned when a tile moved. Using the tip of her car key, she pried up the loose tile to find a rusty keyhole corroded by water. So, where was the key?

Casey thought of the extra house key Dad used to keep buried in the potted plant at their old place, and how she'd occasionally asked him to use a fake plant with sand. She studied three silk flower arrangements displayed on a narrow table. Fake flowers sitting in sand.

She yanked the flowers out of the nearest pot, dumped it upside down, and raked her fingers through the sand. No key. Dumping sand out of the second pot, she spotted a piece of plastic. Inside the plastic was a small silver key. Casey smiled.

No wonder the money hadn't been found; she was the only one who knew that Dad had kept a spare key in dirt and that he liked secret compartments. After some jiggling, the key turned forty-five degrees and a two-foot wide panel next to the bedroom door slowly swung open. Casey shook her head and again smiled. The narrow, vertical rivets in the wood paneling hid the fact that the panel wasn't completely sealed.

Casey saw a cardboard box sitting on six black briefcases. She lifted the lid and saw her old, one-eyed teddy bear. Beneath the bear was a baby sweater and several crayon drawings. Her heart sank. She'd had no idea he'd been so sentimental.

Casey lifted the first briefcase out. She opened the case and gaped at American bills bundled with elastic bands. Each bundle looked the same size and each appeared to contain hundred dollar bills. She counted fifty bundles, which amounted to half a million bucks. If every case contained the same thing, then all of the missing money was accounted for.

"Casey!" Rhonda shouted from downstairs. "Are you here?"

Casey shoved the briefcase in the closet and pushed the wall back into place. "Upstairs!"

She removed the key and closed the tile as Rhonda ran into the courtyard, her expression frantic.

"Darcy's got Summer! He says if you don't give him a cassette tape and the missing three million, he'll kill her!"

Thirty-one

CASEY GRIPPED RHONDA'S shoulders. "When did this happen?"

"Forty minutes ago. We went straight from school to the pool for practice and Darcy approached us in the parking lot and—oh god—he had a gun!" She choked back a sob. "He told S-Summer to come with him or he'd kill me."

As Rhonda cried, dread prickled down Casey's spine. Darcy must have stolen a car. She took deep breaths. "Did you call the police?"

"You didn't hear what Darcy said he'd do to her if I told them anything."

"When and where does he want the money?"

"I'm to meet him at B-Britannia's, parking lot at six."

Casey pictured the parking lot at the Britannia, community center. The skating arena was next to the indoor swimming pool and fitness rooms. Plenty of places to hide. She checked her watch. Four-fifteen.

As Rhonda collapsed against her, guilt overwhelmed Casey. "I should have done more to stop him."

"How could you? He's out of control."

"I know." Casey told her about this afternoon's encounter with Darcy and Theo.

Rhonda stood up straight. "That explains the blood on his shirt and the cop cars out front. The shithead didn't act like he was hurt, though." She brushed away the tears. "He even told me where I might find you."

"Lalonde needs to be told, Rhonda."

"No!"

"It's all right, I found the money. We'll get her back."

"Thank god!" She embraced Casey. "What tape was Darcy talking about?"

"A chat between Dad and Darcy that made it clear Darcy arranged the botulism poisoning. He'd promised Dad an antidote if Dad told him where the money was."

"If Marcus had told him none of this would have happened!"

"He still would have died. Darcy didn't have an antidote. Casey started to ease away from Rhonda, but her friend wouldn't let go.

"I wish I'd known about the impostor," Rhonda mumbled. "Thought Marcus pretended to forget the past to get rid of me. And when I saw Lillian's picture on his night table, I . . . I couldn't handle that."

Casey pushed herself away from Rhonda. "You were in his bedroom?"

"Once, briefly," Rhonda's eyes flashed with anger. "No way in hell would I let Lillian have him again."

"What do you mean?"

"I fought back." Rhonda reached for Casey's hands. "Summer's Sunday practices are two hours long, so I had time to change into something nice and go see him." Her lips quivered and her eyes couldn't quite meet Casey's. "I always returned in time."

Casey didn't want to hear this. She tried to step back, but Rhonda's grip was firm. "Rhonda, we need to focus on Summer."

"You have to hear! That man died because of me." She squeezed Casey's hands. "The harder I tried to be close to Marcus, the further he pushed me away. So I had a dress made in his favorite color. Wore it that night so he'd see how sophisticated I could be."

"Stop it!"

"He tried to convince me he wasn't Marcus. Said he was engaged to some European woman. Then I remembered the invitation Lillian sent." Anguish twisted Rhonda's features as she released Casey. "She'd thrown his betrayal in my face. Only it wasn't betrayal, was it? He really wasn't Marcus. Marcus loved me. I know that now."

Sweat trickled down Casey's sides. Her cheeks burned. "Rhonda, please don't say anything else. We've got to think about Summer."

Rhonda gazed across the courtyard. "I honestly believed he was Marcus, and when I thought of all the pain he'd caused you, me, and Summer . . ."

"Not now!" The strength drained from Casey's legs and she grabbed the table. Sand clung to her damp palms. A fake geranium fell on the floor.

"Yes, now! You're like me. You always need to know why. That's what Europe was about, right?" Tears dropped from Rhonda's chin. "Marcus was making supper when I arrived and didn't want to talk, but I shoved my way in."

"Shut up!" Casey covered her ears.

"We went into the den," she murmured. "He said he'd be leaving the country for good."

Casey lowered her hands. "Rhonda—"

"I asked to use the bathroom and snuck into his bedroom for the second time that month." Rhonda's tears trickled down her face. "I saw photos of a woman and Lillian, of course, and wondered how many other women he'd had, and . . ." She dragged her hands down her face. "I don't know."

Casey's heart was trying to pound its way out of her chest. Bile burned her throat.

"I don't remember going into the kitchen . . . picking up the cleaver. I don't remember anything until I was in my car, hands on the steering wheel, and then I saw the blood." Rhonda wiped her hands on her jeans, as if it was still there.

Tears welled up in Casey's eyes. This was all wrong.

"I went back inside to wash and change clothes," Rhonda went on. "I was going to clean the cleaver and leave it, but Summer's practice was almost over, so I brought it home." She looked nervously at Casey, as if aware of her own irrationality and her helplessness against it.

"How . . . how often did you come here?"

"Three times. I wanted so much to be with Marcus again. To be his glamor lady."

Glamor lady? She thought of the appliquéd picture in Rhonda's living room. Oh god, the blue sequined dress was an exact replica of the one in the photo. How could Rhonda have lost it like that? How could she have let rage and jealousy drive her to murder? Something else occurred to Casey, a thought that horrified her almost as much as Rhonda's confession. By finding the dress and hat, she'd probably provided the last bit of evidence needed to convict Rhonda.

"Where'd you get the money for the outfit?"

"Bank loan." Her quivering smile unnerved Casey. "Told them I needed to renovate."

"But the dress was at Mother's place."

"I took your lock picks while you were at the hospital."

"You remembered how to use them?"

"Pretty much, though Lillian's lock gave me problems." She wrung her hands together. "I followed three young guys into the building. They never gave me a second glance."

"When exactly were you there?"

"After eleven, while Summer was asleep. I called ahead to see if Lillian and Darcy were there, but no one answered. If they had, I would have told her that you needed to see her urgently. Lillian would have bought it."

"You took a huge risk."

"I've always taken risks where Lillian's concerned."

Casey swiped at the tears trickling down her cheek.

"Before I wore it that night, I kept the dress in a locked trunk under boxes in the basement." Rhonda wiped her face with the back of her hand. "I was going to burn everything when I could, but when Lillian threatened me, when she said she'd tell Summer the truth about her birth, well, she deserved to be blamed. Your plan to search her place gave me the idea. After you went there, I tried to get hold of Lalonde to let him know you were searching for the dress there, but he wasn't available so I talked to his assistant."

Krueger. "Oh, Rhonda." This was insane.

"My alibi the night of the murder is shaky. I did talk to people at the pool, but then I left. Most of the parents do because the practices are so long."

"Oh, god." Casey tried to take deep calming breaths, but it wasn't working.

"Don't worry, hon, you won't have to lie for me. I told you all this because I think Lalonde's interviewed all of the team's parents now.

One of the moms I'm friendly with called yesterday to let me know he'd contacted her. He probably suspected me all along." Frightened eyes blinked at her. "He'll prove I was the killer, won't he? I mean, there's no way around this."

Casey didn't have the courage to confirm it.

"I'm sorry I killed Gustaf Osterman," Rhonda mumbled. "For his family's sake, I truly am sorry."

Casey knelt down, lifted the tile, and looked up. "You knew Mother was innocent, yet you called the police and tried to keep her from leaving."

Rhonda's expression grew harsh. "If there was anything I could do to make Lillian's life more difficult, I would. It's only fair since she tried to ruin mine. Besides, I'm sure she has crimes to hide, given the losers she associates with."

Mother had said Rhonda would hurt herself more than anyone else could. She must have figured out the truth. Casey turned the key.

"Holy crap," Rhonda said, watching the panel open.

Casey removed the first briefcase and slid it to her. "We need to make a plan. Once Darcy takes the money, he won't let you and Summer walk away."

"I can't involve you more than I already have." Rhonda opened the case.

Casey was frightened for Summer, not only for the danger she was in, but also for subsequent events that would destroy her happiness once Rhonda was arrested, with one awful truth after another exposed. The truth that would eat at her. Whether Rhonda realized it or not, she was going to cause Summer more pain than any enemy ever could.

"You'll look after Summer, won't you?" Rhonda's voice shook. "Buy her a puppy. God knows she's earned it."

"Rhonda, you've got to let me help you! Darcy's killed more than once."

Her fearful eyes met Casey's. "What can you do?"

It took five minutes to come up with a plan that could work if no glitches cropped up, but the potential for glitches was great. Still, what the hell choice did she have? After ensuring that each briefcase contained the money, Casey and Rhonda carried them outside. Casey scanned the yard. No officers were around and the police cruisers were gone.

After they placed the cases in Rhonda's station wagon, Casey said, "Remember to back the car into the parking space."

"What about the tape?"

"It's in my safe-deposit box, but the bank's now closed. Use one of your old Mozart tapes from home."

"And if he wants to play it?"

"Hopefully, he won't get a chance to see it, let alone listen. But you have to stay calm for Summer's sake, okay?"

Rhonda trembled. "Whatever it takes."

Watching her drive away, Casey stood there, thinking and worrying. They needed help. She headed back inside and called Detective Lalonde.

Before she could explain what was going on, he said, "Are you still at the house, Casey?"

"Yeah." Lalonde had never used her first name before. "Where are you?"

"Outside Mrs. Stubbs's home."

"Did you find Theo and Darcy?"

"No. Do you know where Mrs. Stubbs is?"

"That's why I called. She's on her way to rescue her daughter." Casey's legs started shaking again, so she sat on the floor. "Darcy kidnapped Summer and Rhonda was determined to get her back on her own. I talked her out of it by coming up with an alternate plan." Casey told him their plan.

"I can think of a dozen reasons why something could go wrong," Lalonde said. "You should have called me sooner."

"I just learned about this, Detective. What was I supposed to do?"

"Can you call her back and tell her we'll deal with him?"

"She doesn't have a cell phone, and she'll panic if you guys show up in my place. But if you're there without either of them seeing you, then we have a chance."

As Lalonde swore and started lecturing her, Casey cut in. "There's something else you should know." She swept a tear away. "Rhonda just confessed to killing Gustaf Osterman."

"I see."

He didn't sound surprised. "You already knew, didn't you?"

"We confirmed it this afternoon. One of the people I interviewed this morning was a neighbor who'd been out of town when the murder happened that Sunday night. We'd talked to her when she returned, and she told me her children had been house-sitting. The daughter had been out that evening and the son had returned to the University of Victoria Saturday morning, or so she thought."

Casey feared what was coming, but she had to know, "Meaning?"

"Yesterday, the mother phoned her son and at some point in their conversation, she mentioned my chat with her. That's when her son confessed that he'd held a huge party in his parents' home Saturday night and spent most of Sunday recovering. He wound up catching the last ferry to Swartz Bay that night."

Casey fought back the tears. "Did he see Rhonda?"

"No, but he saw her station wagon pull into your father's driveway. The boy was on his way back from walking the family dog just after seven-thirty. The kid knows cars and he was able to describe Mrs. Stubbs's vehicle in detail."

Casey closed her eyes. God, it really was over. "Rhonda originally hid the clothes in a trunk under some boxes in her basement. Her voice caught. "You might find more sequins there."

"Thank you." Lalonde cleared his throat. "I have more bad news, I'm afraid."

She wasn't sure she could take much more. "What is it?"

"It seems that your mother lost control of her car on the Sea-to-Sky Highway between Squamish and Whistler. According to witnesses, she was speeding when she missed a curve and hit an oncoming truck. The impact sent her over an embankment. By the time anyone could reach her she was gone."

"What?"

"She died. I'm sorry."

The floor blurred around Casey.

"Are you there?" he asked.

"Yeah." Anguish burned her throat. "Darcy and Theo are responsible, I know it."

"They're responsible for many things."

"Both my parents are dead because of their relationship with those two," she said, struggling to stay in control.

"Charges will be laid, I promise you."

But it wasn't nearly enough. Casey hung up and started to cry.

Thirty-two

CASEY PARKED ON McLean, just west of the community center's tennis courts. She stepped out of the car and scanned the area for Lalonde. No sign of him, but then, he and his team wouldn't be obvious.

She removed the tire iron from her trunk and hid it under the jacket she was carrying. Casey walked down a lane toward Britannia's parking lot. She felt shaky especially with the news about Mother and Rhonda's confession, but getting Summer back was too important to let emotion overwhelm her again.

To Casey's right, a concrete wall prevented her from seeing the tennis courts on top of a small hill. Buildings on her left partially blocked her view of Venables Street.

Darcy would either have to drive along this lane to enter the parking lot or turn off Venables onto Cotton Drive, a short road leading directly into the center's lot. Either entrance would be easy to watch from several vantage points, which was why she and Rhonda had agreed to arrive early.

The tennis courts were vacant. The rain had stopped, but the gray damp air chilled her. Casey stayed close to the wall and peered around the corner. The parking lot served Britannia Secondary on the south side, the ice arena and indoor pool on the east. No sign of cops yet. Between rows of parking stalls, a variety of bushes and small trees had been planted. Several bushes were large enough to hide behind if she crouched.

The lot was two-thirds full. Sports weren't the only events held at this complex. The center also offered activities for families, teens, and seniors, as well as a day care. If Darcy pulled a gun here, someone could get hurt.

Rhonda's station wagon was plainly visible. As arranged, she'd backed into a parking space fairly close to Cotton Drive. For now, the stalls on either side of her were empty. Behind the steering wheel, Rhonda didn't move. She was probably staring at Cotton Drive, waiting for the first glimpse of Summer. All of the other vehicles in the lot were unoccupied, yet this could change any moment.

Casey walked toward the bushes separating the station wagon from the vehicle behind it. She didn't try to make eye contact with Rhonda. Rhonda wasn't supposed to acknowledge her at all.

The largest bush was behind Rhonda's car and a little to the side. Casey knelt down and through a gap in the foliage, spotted the Cotton Drive entrance. If she scooted to the other side of the bush, she'd be able to see the lane entrance. Darcy wouldn't be driving his Porsche and he wasn't likely to approach Rhonda on foot. On the other hand, anything was possible with that freak. If he refused to get out of his car, their plan would collapse.

A green Jeep Cherokee entered the lot from Cotton Drive. The vehicle stopped a moment before cruising toward the station wagon. Blue eyeglasses and tight blond curls made Darcy easy to identify. Summer sat beside him. Darcy backed into the stall on Rhonda's right. It looked like he wanted a quick getaway too.

Casey ducked down and heard a car door open. Peeking through the gap, she watched Darcy step out. The left shoulder of his shirt was covered in blood. Judging by the scowl on his face, pain wasn't helping his mood. Leaving the driver's door open, he kept his gun lowered. From this angle, Casey couldn't see Summer's face.

Rhonda was supposed to keep Darcy busy examining the contents of each briefcase while Casey crept up from behind and struck him with the tire iron hard enough to knock him out. Casey started to move when a moist salty hand clamped over her mouth. She gagged and tried to suck in air. Someone began massaging her neck.

"Did you find the money?" Theo whispered.

As his hand slid away, Casey turned her head. She hoped Lalonde was watching this. "How'd you find me?"

"How do I always find you?"

Casey shook her head. God, she must have been too preoccupied to notice the tail.

"Where's the money?" he asked.

"Rhonda's about to give it to him." Her voice was hushed as she watched Rhonda open the back of the station wagon. "She killed Gustaf Osterman—thought he was Dad."

As Theo raised an eyebrow, Darcy began speaking again.

"You must have been shocked to learn of Casey's new-found wealth," he said to Rhonda.

"There isn't a secret on this planet that could shock me right now." Casey spotted the pistol in Theo's hand.

"Open the case," Darcy ordered, pointing to the one nearest him.

"I want Summer in my car first."

"Do it!"

She opened the briefcase and Darcy examined the money. "Good, now pull all of them out and open each one," he said. "I've worked too hard and waited too long to be cheated."

As Rhonda did so, Theo whispered, "If they end up in his car, we're lost."

Summer stepped out of the Cherokee. Darcy looked up at her.

"Darcy!" Theo jumped up.

Casey followed suit. "Summer, get down!"

Darcy spun around and aimed his weapon at Casey. "Try anything, Theo, and I'll kill her right here."

Rhonda shoved Darcy, knocking him off balance. The gun fired. Rhonda screamed, but no one was hit. Darcy tried to regain his balance as Theo tackled him. The gun flew out of Darcy's hands, landing between the two vehicles. Summer scrambled into the station wagon while Rhonda grabbed the gun, then slid behind the wheel.

"I'll get help!" she shouted and sped away.

As Darcy and Theo fought, a woman and two toddlers approached a car on the lot's east side. The woman saw the brawl, then picked up her kids and ran toward the ice rink.

Theo wasn't holding his weapon. After a quick search, Casey found the gun on the ground, two stalls over. Why hadn't he used it? And where the hell was Lalonde?

She left the tire iron by the bush, picked up the pistol, and watched the men cling to each other as they fell into the bushes and rolled onto the asphalt. Darcy's glasses went flying. Theo knelt on his chest and struck his face while Darcy punched him in the abdomen. Theo gasped and recoiled. Darcy pushed him backward and started to stand, but Theo hauled him down again. Darcy swung at Theo who returned random punches.

Casey raised the gun. "For crying out loud, knock it off!"

The men slowed and finally collapsed. Darcy wheezed and coughed while Theo struggled to his feet. Sweat slid down his face. He stumbled toward the briefcases Rhonda had left behind while Darcy retrieved his glasses.

"Mother's dead," she announced.

Both men said nothing until she'd finished repeating Lalonde's news.

"She wouldn't have died," Darcy said, "if she hadn't wanted to protect you, bitch!"

Casey aimed the gun at his head. "Shut up!"

"You didn't deserve her. You treated her like shit!"

Theo picked up a briefcase.

"Put it down!" Darcy reached for the tire iron Casey had left by the bush.

He flung the tire iron at her. Before she could move, the bar struck her arm and she dropped the pistol. Darcy lunged for it, but Casey kicked the weapon out of reach. Darcy grabbed the tire iron instead.

"Lil thought you were special." He held the weapon like a raised bat. "Said you were the last decent person on earth, but she didn't know the real you, did she, Casey?"

Casey stepped backward. Darcy moved closer. She turned to run, but the tire iron hit her back and she fell. As she tried to stand, Darcy tackled her to the ground. He climbed onto her back, wrapped his hands around her neck, and began to squeeze. She tried to pry his fingers loose but couldn't, and then the pressure stopped. Casey's forehead smacked the asphalt as she gulped down air. A moment later,

Darcy was sliding off her back and slumping to the ground. Blood soaked the front of his shirt.

Casey looked up. Theo stood before her, holding the pistol. She nudged Darcy. No movement. She nudged him again. When there was still no response, she checked for a pulse on his wrist and neck.

"He's dead."

A man darted coming from the pool building toward his Toyota. A senior stood by the ice rink and talked on his cell phone while he watched them.

"Why didn't you shoot when you had the chance?" Theo asked.

"Couldn't." Casey wiped the sweat off her face with the back of her hand. "Glad you did, though."

"It was either your life or his."

"Thank you." She looked around. Where were the damn cops? They had to nab Theo. "I need to know something, Theo, and I want the truth. After Darcy killed Dad, how long was it before Gustaf moved in?"

He looked everywhere but at her.

"I heard it wasn't long. A month maybe?" Casey went on. "You said you didn't condone what Darcy did, yet you were planning to get rid of Dad, weren't you? Let's face it, a month isn't long enough to undergo plastic surgery and perfect someone else's voice and mannerisms."

He shrugged, "Doesn't matter now. It's over."

"The truth is important to me. Anyway, your key witnesses are dead, and it'd only be my word against yours."

"Marcus was going to destroy me, but I didn't want him to die. The plan was to let him change his identity and go underground, only Darcy grew impatient."

Maybe he wasn't the only one. Casey fought the urge to hit him. "You needed to know if I really had the address book, so you either ransacked my hotel room or paid someone to do it. Did you pay the American kid to steal my purse?" She didn't bother waiting for a response. "I suppose I'm lucky you didn't steal the book in Paris."

"I wanted you to feel you could trust me."

"All because you needed my help finding the money." She glared at him. "I wish my parents had never met you."

"That night in Paris, you said the more truths you learned, the darker things became," Theo replied. "You must feel completely blind now."

Police cruisers raced into the parking lot. Theo grabbed two briefcases and started running. Casey doubted he'd make it out of the complex.

Thirty-three

CASEY FOUND RHONDA'S station wagon parked in its usual spot at the house. There were no police vehicles anywhere, no hint of the day's death and destruction. Sitting in her Tercel, Casey gently pressed the back of her hand against her face. Her skin felt hot, her body still weak from everything that had happened.

Thank god Theo had been caught only five minutes after he'd bolted. While she'd been giving the cops a detailed account of events, Lalonde showed up and apologized for having been delayed over a search warrant. Apparently, he'd arrived at the scene just as Rhonda was speeding out of the lot and decided to intercept her rather than stop Darcy because he'd been assured backup was there. It seemed there'd been a communication breakdown, however, and VPD officers actually had been sent to two serious traffic accidents, one of them fatal. An angry Lalonde had made it clear to the VPD officers that he'd expected better. After he told Casey that Summer was now at her grandmother's, she headed for home. Poor Summer. She could well imagine how deep that child's grief, confusion, and sense of helplessness must be.

Casey slogged up the back steps. Pressure encased her skull as if someone had placed a snug metal cap on her head and was tightening a clamp at each temple. Lalonde had said that bail for Rhonda was a possibility and that since she didn't have an attorney, one would be provided for her. Given the backlog in Vancouver's courts, her trial wouldn't take place for months.

Casey stepped into a silent kitchen. Emptiness clawed her insides. When would Summer be back? If Rhonda went to prison, she wouldn't want Summer living with Winifred's strict rules. Tears blurred her vision and Casey felt thirteen years old again, sitting in the dining room as her mother left, unable to fix her family or even gather the courage to say goodbye.

Wiping her eyes, Casey headed upstairs and entered her apartment.

Her message machine's light was blinking. Had Summer called? Was there news about Lou? Casey pressed the button and listened to Stan tell her that purse snatcher Karl Hawthorne had been arrested. "When the cops came to see his parents, the kid freaked out and confessed." Stan gave her the names of the officers who wanted to speak with her.

Casey looked up the list of numbers by her landline phone. Rhonda had given her Winifred's number in case of emergency. Winifred picked up on the second ring.

"This is Casey Holland. May I speak to Summer?"

"One moment," Winifred replied, sounding none too pleased. On the occasions Casey had met Winifred, the woman was usually unhappy about something. This time she had good reason.

"Casey?" Summer's quiet voice sounded weak and uncertain. "Grandma says I have to spend the night, but I want to come home tomorrow. Can you pick me up early? I'm not going to school."

"Sure. Is there anything else I can do?"

"Get Mom out of jail."

"I'll do my best." But then what? How would she deal with Rhonda, knowing that she'd killed the man she thought was Dad? At this moment, she couldn't begin to process the conflicting emotions swirling around her head.

"Grandma says I have to go now. She needs to make some calls." Summer started to cry. So did Casey.

Once she'd hung up, Casey retreated to her window seat. Like an evergreen covered with snow, she felt weighted down, cold and dormant. Tears slid down her face as she thought about her mother. The way Mother had talked this afternoon, it was as if she knew something might happen. Had she planned to drive off the road? Darcy's anger could have prompted her to do something drastic. The Sea-to-Sky Highway was treacherous at high speeds. If a car had gone over an embankment, everyone would assume it was an accident. Mother must have known the police were closing in on Theo and her, too, perhaps. What sins had she committed for him and Darcy?

If she hadn't been so cold to Mother, if she'd been able to let go of the past, things might have been different. But there was the blue sequined dress. And the sinking realization that even if Krueger hadn't grabbed the bags from her, she would still have handed them in, no matter who'd worn the outfit.

Casey wrapped her arms around her legs and rested her chin on her knees. Had Lalonde told Rhonda about Mother's accident? Would she rejoice? She wished she'd paid more attention to the signs . . . Rhonda's eavesdropping on tenants' conversations, how she'd searched Darcy's belongings, and the hidden correspondence with Mother. No wonder Dad had distanced himself from her. He must have learned about her secretive, manipulative side that was so similar to Mother's.

She'd missed other signs too. Greg's adultery for one, and Lou's feelings for her. Had denial, fear, and cowardice been that much easier to bear than the truth?

When the phone rang, Casey leapt up to answer it.

"Casey, it's Barb. Good news—Lou's doing much better. Doctors say he'll make it."

"Thank god." She brushed away more tears.

"He wants to see you."

"Really? Can I go now?"

"Absolutely."

"Be right there." Casey grabbed her purse.

Second chances didn't happen every day. This time, she'd gather the courage to tell Lou how much she cared about him. Maybe even ask him out. If he wanted to go, she'd take him some place special, see what developed. There was hope, wasn't there? Casey hurried out of her apartment.

Acknowledgements

WRITING MIGHT BE a solitary endeavor, but preparation for publishing and the publishing process are something else altogether. I'd like to thank those who read earlier drafts of this novel, especially Ellen Godfrey who saw the possibilities in protagonist Casey Holland ages ago. Also, a big thanks to editor Joyce Gram for her valuable input in a later draft, not to mention her encyclopedic knowledge of grammar and syntax. Where would I be without the incredibly helpful comments of the Kyle Center Writers' group on all my writing projects, including future Casey novels?

Gratitude and a huge thank you go to Ruth Linka for taking a chance on this book, and for matching me with editor Frances Thorsen. Frances's skill, enthusiasm, and insights were amazing. Last, but never least, love and special thanks to Bark, Elida, and Alex for putting up with my many retreats downstairs to slog through draft after draft. Without your support I wouldn't have come this far.

To avoid confusion, please note that Violet Street in East Vancouver, Cedar Ridge Cemetery, Mainland Public Transport, and Alvin's All-Canadian Café in Paris are fictitious. The hotel in Goathland is also my own creation.

DEBRA PURDY KONG has a diploma in criminology and has worked in security as a patrol and communications officer. She is the author of two other novels: *Taxed to Death* (1995) and *Fatal Encryption* (2008). Debra has also published over one hundred short stories, essays, and articles in publications that include *Chicken Soup for the Bride's Soul*, *Dandelion*, *NeWest Review*, *The Vancouver Sun*, BC *Parent Magazine*, and several anthologies. She lives in Port Moody, British Columbia. Find Debra on Twitter at @DebraPurdyKong.